Aberdeen's Haunted Heritage

By
Graeme Milne

Published by Landon publishing

First Edition

Copyright © Graeme Milne 2021

Cover Design: CruzzCreation.

All rights reserved.

No part of this publication may be reproduced, stored in a retrieval system or transmitted, in any form or by any means electronic, mechanical, photocopying, recording or otherwise without prior written consent of the publisher. Nay person who does any unauthorised act in relation to the publication may be liable to criminal prosecution and civil claims for damages.

This book is sold subject to the condition that it shall not, by way of trade or otherwise be lent out, re-sold, hired out or otherwise circulated without the publisher's prior consent in any form of binding or cover other than which it is published and without a similar condition including this condition being imposed on the subsequent purchaser.

Dedication

To Stanley Robertson and Norman Adams two great authors sadly no longer with us. To Wilma Mackland, a good quine, sadly missed. To my Mum and Dad, Geraldine and Alan, daughters, Tabitha and Geri, grandson Liam and especially to Carol whose support and love has been invaluable.

Also respectfully dedicated to Arthur Conan Doyle and Daevid Allen whose spirit in life is a continuing source of inspiration.

Table of Contents

Acknowledgements ix
Introduction xi
The Seven Gates: Sheddocksley 1
Aberdeen New Market 6

SPIRITS GALORE

Krakatoa/Formerly the Moorings Bar: Regent Quay 13
The Old King's Highway 18
Ma Cameron's Inn 20

DREADING THE BOARDS: ABERDEEN'S HAUNTED THEATRES.

His Majesty's Theatre 26
Tivoli Theatre 35
The Lemon Tree 39
The Palace Theatre 41

THE CASTLEGATE

Former Royal Bank of Scotland, Castle Street 46
Victoria Court 50

Commerce Street 53
Castlehill Barracks 58
Marischal Court 61
Peacocks Close 68
Bosies Charity Shop: Justice Street 70
Religious Figures 73

SCHOOLS OUT

Kaimhill Primary School 88
Beechwood School 91
Hazlehead Academy 95
Victoria Road School 99
North Silver Street 105
First Bus King Street 109
The Tolbooth 121
Provost Skene's House 125

COMMUNITY SPIRIT

Powis House 134
Rosemount Community Centre 142
Sunnybank Community Centre 146
The Ghosts That Never Were 149
View Terrace 153
Kincorth Tales 157
Nazareth House 164

Union Street 167
Old Aberdeen 183
St. Katherine's Centre: Shoe Lane 191
The Gordon Barracks 196
Ouija Boards: Just Harmless Fun? 202
Strange but True 212
Marischal College 225
Torry Tales 230
Miscellaneous Ghosts 243
The Aberdeen Sack Murder 257

COUNTRY STRIFE: ABERDEENSHIRE HAUNTINGS

Crathie 262
Braemar 264
The Gelder Bothy 267
Aden Country Park: Mintlaw 270
Fraserburgh: Kinnaird Head 275
Port Elphinstone Inverurie 279
Cove 281
Oldmeldrum 285
Conclusion 290
Index 292
Further Reading 295

Acknowledgements

A huge thank you to everyone who assisted with this book, particularly to Aberdeen City Council and its employees for allowing access to various locations, providing archival material and for sharing their experiences. Also, a big thank you to all the many contributors, you know who you are, and without whom this book would not have been possible.

Introduction

Using the word 'haunted' in the title implies permanence and is a term often bandied about in traditional ghost story fiction to describe a location. Perhaps then it is a bit of a misnomer, however I think you would agree that calling the book 'sporadic phenomena' would have lacked the gravitas it deserves. The activity of 'ghosts,' in fiction at least, traditionally caused discomfort and terror, sometimes even death, but during my research this is something thankfully I have not come across otherwise it would have been a very short book indeed. The incidents recounted in the following pages have still caused fear and alarm however and many have felt aggrieved they have been singled out for 'treatment'. Some 'ghosts' it would seem still enjoy keeping close company with the living, whether they like it or not, while others less obtrusive are mere shadows from the past.

It is hard to believe that my first 'Haunted North' book appeared all of twelve years ago, and so once again I find myself in the unenviable position of trying to sum up this 'new' volume. Since we last met, I am now residing in Edinburgh regarded as one of Europe's most haunted cities, where I lead ghost walks of an evening, so no surprises there! I have to say though, and with my hand on my heart that although Aberdeen has a quieter voice when promoting its spookiness, we should be very proud of our haunted heritage, as we are right up there with the best. There are schools, civic buildings, shops, houses all with a story to tell and within these pages lies the evidence. It is, I have to say, still very gratifying to me after all these years to be frequently asked about my books, will there be more? Would you like to hear of my experience? Happily, this ongoing interest has been the main catalyst for my latest venture. And so, as only a limited run of the second volume was ever printed and as I had the beginnings of a third lurking in my files, I came to the decision to create an omnibus of all my findings thus far. I must admit it was quite refreshing to revisit these stories after so many years. In this new collection I have taken the liberty of omitting a few, expanding on others and adding some real gems, which I am glad to say will see the light of day for the first time. For those who are already acquainted with my previous offerings I hope you will find something new to your liking to make re-taking the journey worth your while, and for those who have yet to read about one of Scotland's most haunted cities, welcome!

The Seven Gates: Sheddocksley

The 'Seven Gates' is a story of two halves. The first part I came across some years back and had all the elements of a classic fictional ghost story, the second part I know is true. The 'Seven Gates' in the report was described as an area (whose exact location they were unwilling to disclose) in the west of the city. According to the report it lay on the outskirts of a housing estate, near an old burial ground, the last resting place of those who had fallen under the anatomists' knife. The story then went on to give a lengthy description of what befell the protagonists while looking for some midnight thrills, witnessing the manifestation of ghostly children before being threatened by a large ominous shadowy figure. Whether the following is true you will have to decide.

I first read the account in a report posted on the internet around ten years ago. The publisher of the report was a student who having heard rumours of the area being haunted, had planned an overnight investigation. The area which he later admitted to having no prior knowledge of at the time, was remote and so the group felt very isolated on arrival. Nothing much happened according to his account, until a group of ghostly children appeared. The 'ghosts,' or whatever they were then surrounded the group. They were described as looking like skeletal children, who danced round the group, taunting them. The witnesses by now cowering in fear, then ran for their lives at the sudden appearance of a tall dark figure. No doubt leading to a sleepless night. Strangely, in the cold light of day, some of the group decided to return the following evening, which begs the question, why? As before, similar manifestations occurred causing the group to flee yet again. You might assume this would be the end of it, but incredibly they decide a third visit was needed, which again ended in their flight. Sometime later, the now traumatised student, went on to describe finding an old book on the history of Aberdeen in the library, where a shocking discovery was made. The area was allegedly a secret burial ground for anatomists. His account ended with him vowing never to return, which under the circumstances I thought sensible.

Afterwards, despite the authors assurance that it was a legitimate paranormal experience, I questioned its authenticity. It somehow sounded too fantastical. My cynicism however was dealt a blow some year later when I received news suggesting there may have been some truth in it after all. The news which will be revealed soon prompted a quick visit to the library, where I discovered, like the student a book called, 'The March Stones of Aberdeen.' This pointed me in the right direction. And so, with this new information I arranged to see the place for myself.

It was claimed to be an old anatomists' burial ground which according to the book was situated on Gilahill. Never having visited before I spoke to Mike Middleton an authority on Aberdeen history, who knew the area well and who invited me to join him for a dander. On the day of our visit the sky was bright and clear, as we headed up a nearby path, situated off the Lang Stracht. In the distance we could make out the distinctive landmark thought to be the burial ground, now surrounded by a large consumption dyke. Crossing a nearby field we reached a substantial 'island' of trees and on entering the cooling shade of the outcrop it proved to be boulder strewn. The ground, a tangle of knotted roots, compacted soil, and rocks would not have been conducive to burying a mouse we concluded, though perhaps in the past it may have been otherwise. We then retraced our steps, scrutinizing an old map as we went, attempting to ascertain where the legendary seven gates sat. We reached the beginning of a straggling tree-lined path which according to the map ran through both Sheddocksley and Springhill. It was then we knew we had found our location.

Springhill, as many will know is infamous as being the site of a mass cattle grave. Over a thousand carcasses were buried due to an outbreak of foot and mouth in 1963, the escaping gases creating 'Will o' the Wisps,' which were often mistaken for ghosts. I remained convinced that the story was a fabrication at worst or a misinterpretation at best until a fortuitous meeting with a former colleague cast new light on the situation. Long- time resident Averil, well placed to provide further evidence met with me soon after to discuss an experience which has bothered her for over thirty years. It was wintertime and her daughter Leanne who at the time was a young teenager had been out playing by a strip of woodland near her home. Her mother takes up the story:

'We lived at the time in Sheddocksley and I remember that particular evening well as she came home in a terrible state. They had apparently been playing on the path near the woods when a man on a horse wearing a huge black cloak came out from the trees. The kids were terrified at the sight of him and ran. When Leanne got home, she was in a terrible state and begged me to go look. I thought it was a load of nonsense, but as she was so upset, I took our dog and went back to prove there was nothing there. When we got to the location, there appeared to be footprints in the snow but no sign of anything else. I was then surprised to see an old woman suddenly walk out from the trees at the exact same spot. I was going to speak to her, but my daughter got upset and begged me to leave. Just at that moment, the woman put out her hand and pointed at us saying "there's nothing here for you," and we just turned and walked away. I still don't know to this day, why we left. It was as if I had been hypnotised. She was quite scary looking, with red cheeks a head square and odd-looking clothing. She had sacking which was tied with string halfway up her leg. I turned back towards her to say something, but she had disappeared. There was not a soul to be seen. I have never forgotten it and I still cannot explain it. In the area there had always been talk of seven gates, and supposedly those gate posts were made from some old standing stones, but that may be a myth. I know local kids have always maintained that they have seen strange things near the trees and get bad feelings in that area but whether that's imagination or not I cannot say. There have been incidents where people have taken their lives in the woods, but other than that I am not sure. My dog used to go mad when taken there for a walk and would become very upset, barking, and whining at nothing, so we stopped going. I know others have experienced the same. Perhaps they had sensed something.'

My research uncovered little else, but I did recently manage to speak to Leanne, now an adult, regarding the incident and she recalled the story in her words. She told me: 'I saw a couple of strange things as a teenager. Kids used to see guards, at the seven gates, or spirits who wanted to stop people from going. One time myself and a friend were there when it was white with snow. We could see the silhouette of someone wearing a cape who was on horseback riding very fast along the path. We whistled at it, and it seemed to grow huge in stature before vanishing behind a tree.'

She continued: 'Another time I was with my mum, and we were walking the dog who was agitated and refusing to walk. As we approached the seven gates' we saw an old woman standing there who had yellow looking skin. She wore what I can only describe as a sack or something similar, tied around one foot and leg, with string. She just kept saying "there's nothing for you here" to us. We walked away and when looking back noticed she had totally vanished. There was nowhere she could have gone that quickly. The dog then refused to walk to the end of the field, so we had to turn back. I recall other children mentioning seeing the same figure.' When speaking to the witnesses both stated, that after what happened they stopped going there. Was the figure on horseback a replay from the past? Was he connected in some way to the old woman? Do dogs become upset because of what is buried there? I cannot at present offer any further explanation, but I can assure the reader both witnesses were adamant that, that is what they had seen.

Aberdeen New Market

Aberdeen New Market built 1840-42 was considered a masterpiece of neo-classicism and was one of the largest indoor markets at the time. Designed by renowned architect Archibald Simpson, it was subsequently destroyed in a massive blaze in 1882. Two years later however, it rose like the veritable phoenix and was rebuilt retaining the grand façade and surviving walls. One of the largest covered markets in Britain the 300ft long structure, was 100ft wide by 50ft high an impressive temple to commerce, beloved by generations of Aberdonians. Its' ignominious end came in 1971 not by something as cataclysmic as the fire that destroyed its predecessor, but by the decision to have it replaced by British Home Stores planned extension. The city wept. Its namesake and replacement also 'The New Market,' came to occupy the lower reaches of the extension, being regarded as a shadow of its former self. Still popular in its own way, it too has now fallen by the wayside with its recent closure. Recently I spoke to the former manager, John Dow, who provided the following detailed accounts of the various incidents he bore witness to while working there. Suffice to say there had been rumours of ghosts being seen in the building for many years and it is known that at least one porter died in the conflagration of 1882. John sent me the following accounts which I have presented in his own words.

'Around 1995 a female stall holder was closing up at the end of the day when out of the corner of her eye she saw a man in old-fashioned clothing walk past her shop. It was around 5.50 and as the market was closed, she assumed he had sneaked in and so went to get security, but on searching he was nowhere to be found. She described him as being around 5ft 5 inches in height, wearing a Tricorn hat, a long coat and in her own words, 'like Dick Turpin would wear.' This became a bit of a joke and people would ask, has Dick Turpin been in today? One day while shopping an elderly lady in her 70s overheard the banter and said, that it wasn't funny as she had worked there in the 1950s and 1960s and the same figure had been seen many times.' I asked him to go on.

'In 2004 I was working in the Union Street passageway, pulling down old plasterboard, the area was always cold, and I had often got the sense of being watched, before the hairs on my neck would rise. It was very dusty work and when I returned to the office for a cup of tea, I asked one of the security guards to get our drinks as I wanted to keep an eye on the CCTV. This was in case customers went into the area. When he returned, we sat down in front of the camera and to our astonishment we both began to see footprints forming in the dust on the stairs. They were in the middle of each step and appeared right before our eyes. I said to the guard, did you see that? We were both lost for words. It took us about an hour to find the courage to go back down by which point the prints had become very faint. I was never a believer in ghosts but that changed my mind. After several days passed, I again felt a severe chill in the area and so called another guard,

Philip. When he arrived, I asked if he would give me a hand. He was a young lad about twenty and having heard the stories before just joked about them. When we began to work, he felt the same chill and left, refusing to go back.'

John told me that he kept the tape, afterwards showing it to a few select people including both mediums and spiritualists to get their thoughts. Apparently, they all said the same thing. that spirits were around in the building and were particularly active in the East and West Green area. One medium, Gabriel, described one spirit as being a man in his 40s who wore a long dark coat and cloak, a white shirt and black hat. She said he was a friendly and that people, should not be scared.

Moving on to 2008 John informed me that his colleague Robert Radford had an interesting experience early one morning. Being the only two people in the building at the time, Robin was surprised to see the figure of a man in the distance and followed him assuming of course, someone had broken in. The figure just as before, was described as wearing a big black hat and dark cloak and was around medium height. It then dawned on him, what he had seen. Suffice to say the figure suddenly vanished. I was informed that sightings of this nature became quite frequent as did late night call outs because of the alarm being triggered. Described as being a frustrating aspect of the job, John had on occasion been dragged from his bed because of this, though on arrival found the building empty. Being motion sensitive, one can only wonder what had set them off.

Speaking of alarms our next incident occurred when a group of children took it upon themselves to break the glass at an emergency point. Prior to discovering vandalism was to blame, everyone was obliged to evacuate the building. John and assistant manager Angela had then to call the fire brigade and explain the situation before ushering everyone back inside. They then had to replace the damaged box however it was nowhere to be found, despite it always being kept in the exact same spot in the office. Perhaps someone had moved it? so they began searching at opposite sides of the room, until Angela's scream halted proceedings. He explained: 'She shouted out that's not funny, there was no need to throw it at me, I didn't have a clue what she was on about but when I looked, I noticed that her neck had a red mark on it where the box had struck.' Helpful or mischievous? They could not decide but it was an unpleasant experience.

Like most buildings where there is alleged activity, some people seem to be on the receiving end of the phenomena more than others and the market was no different. Take for example one trader who approached John to complain that someone had gotten into his store during the night, throwing his stock on the floor. Of course, they could have fallen by accident, but as nothing was amiss before lock-up, it seemed unlikely. A few days later he was again called to the stall and witnessed the same scenario as before. He then made a flippant remark about it being the ghost, which he conceded in hindsight had not gone down well. And so, the routine of having to placate traders continued, coming to a head soon after when called again to the same spot. The traders, Stevie and Hal, were now at their wits end which was obvious by their demeanour. Another trader, Robin, had joined them and they appeared very animated on his arrival. As the story unfolded the younger of the three, Robin claimed that as he was walking towards the unit when he had been struck on the chest by a pack of socks which had appeared out of nowhere.

He then claimed that other packs began flying at him. John attempting to calm the situation was then taken by surprise by a loud bang, finding the bookstand which stood in the unit now lying on the floor. Afterwards it was duly chalked up as just another unexplained incident.

But, before we leave the New Market, I was told of one more incident, again forwarded by John, this time involving his assistant manager, Colin. John stated: 'In January 2020 I had an early meeting but was going to be back by 11am. At around 9.30am Colin phoned sounding agitated and said that he was going to go home but would not say why. I asked him to keep calm as he was ranting and suggested he go get himself a coffee and have a walk. He just laughed. When I arrived, a co-worker Sandy, told me that he was in a right state but would not tell me why, so I went to find him. When we spoke, he told me that at 9.05am he came into the office, finding the kettle boiling which then switched off. He assumed whoever had switched it on had just left the room and thought nothing of it. While sitting at my desk he said it began to boil again and so he switched it off at the socket thinking it was faulty. A few seconds later he heard a click, and again it began to boil. The lights then began to flicker and reaching for his fags, which he kept on the desk, he was surprised to find they had gone. Goosebumps then went down his arms. When he explained all of this to me, he was shaking like a leaf, but I assured him that as far as I was concerned there was nothing to worry about. It was harmless in my opinion.'

Whether Colin was convinced of this is another matter. John then went on to explain that the phenomena, longstanding and varied, had even included sightings of a ghostly black cat often seen wandering around the units before vanishing. The market now earmarked for development is likely to be turned into offices and though its' too late to investigate personally, I am curious to see whether the phenomena will continue in its new guise. Only time will tell.

SPIRITS GALORE

Krakatoa/Formerly the Moorings Bar: Regent Quay

Pubs are full of spirits so they say, and not just the liquid variety it would seem. Living in Edinburgh I have noticed that many pubs claim to be haunted. Whether they are or not is debateable. There is an embarrassment of riches to be found, so much so, they even have an annual, most haunted pub competition. Aberdeen on the other hand, is a little shy on entering into the spirit of things, if you pardon the pun, and drags its heels a little. Perhaps many of our ghosts faded away with the introduction of such modern trappings as Sky Sports, I know a lot of the punters did. Traditional pubs in Aberdeen, like ghosts it would seem, are thin on the ground these days. There are a few though that have done their best to keep the tradition of the haunted pub going whether they liked it or not, which the following prove.

We start our journey at Trinity quay, where twelve years ago the Moorings bar had earned a reputation as being very haunted. Witnesses included both staff and regulars and the phenomena ranged from sightings of full-body apparitions to unaccountable mists and poltergeist activity. But what was the cause? Well, I am afraid to say there are still no definitive answers though on hearing the reports one may makes ones' own conclusions.

An old building, the earliest records date from 1841 although in earlier maps other buildings are clearly shown. The first owner of note, Simon McLeod, was born on the 28th of August 1857 at James Street in Aberdeen and the bar was named after him. It retained his name for many years, even though Simon either sold or leased it out from 1911 onwards. Simon himself died in 1949 at the ripe old age of 91, then residing at 7 Queens Road. In 1965 it became the 'Moorings' a title it held for around fifty years until its re-christening as 'Krakatoa' in more recent times. I first contacted owner Craig 'Flash' Adams around 2007 after hearing intriguing rumours about unquiet entities. Of course, from small acorns do mighty oaks grow, and so with some half-whispered truths I approached in the hope of finding out more and was pleasantly surprised to find that he was more than willing to share his experiences. Ironically, and in keeping with the traditional clichés of the ghost story, I picked a night of hellish weather to visit and on arrival was taken down to the cellar, an alleged haunted hotspot. Ghosts of course interfering with beer kegs appear to be a common problem in many hostelries and suffice to say here was no exception. The cellar of course was claustrophobic as all cellars are and had an off-kilter atmosphere which I suspect might not have been too appealing for those making the daily exodus to turn the taps back on (at this point, and to emphasise the strength needed to turn a tap off, I was given a brief demonstration). As our conversation continued, the phenomena I was told appeared to follow no obvious pattern which raised the following questions in my mind. Was there more than one spirit present? and if so, what did they want?

One of the alleged ghosts, for example was thought to be that of Ted, a former Canadian airman who had worked for the previous owner in the bar. It was mentioned he had a fondness for playing jokes and so on passing over was much missed. But had he left completely? It would appear not, as he has reportedly been seen in both the cellar and bizarrely, in the space between the inner and outer toilet doors. This is possibly significant due to the many reports of people being tripped in that area. I was then told he had also been seen 'appearing to work' in the cellar, near to an old wooden staircase leading up to street level. One witness even claimed to have seen him pushing a barrel, the task being undertook in complete silence This I reasoned might not be as unusual as it seems, for it is believed that people in spirit like to engage in the tasks they did in the physical life and return to familiar surroundings. It is not without substance either to suggest that the witness may have been picking up on residual energy, a recording of Ted and his activities rather than an interactive visitation.

The next stop on our tour was the landlords' office where I noticed an old 1970's price list hanging on the wall. Craig informed me it had been destined for the bin until a little spiritual intervention made him change his mind. The incident occurred when he decided to conduct an EVP (electronic voice phenomena) experiment in the hope of capturing some hard evidence. The theory behind EVP is simple, just leave a recording device playing in a sealed room and if in luck spirit noises or voices can sometimes be captured. The downside of course is having to listen to hours of white noise but sometimes the results can be startling as Craig soon found out. On the chosen night and after moving the recording equipment and speakers into the cellar, they were switched on and left running. Returning next day, the tape was retrieved and the onerous task of sifting through the recordings began. All was normal until suddenly a booming voice shouted: 'put the price list back.' Craig surmised that the male voice could potentially have belonged to the previous owner, upset over the changes taking place. The price list was duly returned. This event later backed up by barman Frank, stated that the equipment used that night was top-notch, and unlikely to cause sound abnormalities. Frank himself, soon became the recipient of some unexplained phenomena himself and when interviewed stated:

'A door was pushed against me, when there was no one else in the building and I saw what seemed like smoke or steam appearing in a mass for no apparent reason and then dissipating quickly.' He pointed out that although some people get freaked out by these incidents, he felt relaxed about it all which I found very admirable.

A more sinister incident however, occurred in the late spring of 2005 when Craig was approached by the police who were attempting to ascertain the whereabouts of a regular named Anne. Craig however was as much in the dark as they were, not having seen her for some time, and so put it to the back of his mind. A few days later he was in his office having locked up for the night and was absorbed in his paperwork when something fluttered down from the ceiling above him landing onto his desk. On examination it was an old black and white passport photograph; he recognised the youthful face as that of the missing regular and written on the reverse side in biro was her name. It was dated 1972. A surge of fear sent him racing outside where he stood for some considerable time before he plucked up the nerve to re-enter the building to set the alarm. He showed me exactly where the photograph had come from which was a crack in the ceiling and to this day has no idea how it got there or who put it there.

Knowing of the phenomena of apports (objects relating to someone who has passed, which suddenly appear) I was convinced that someone in spirit had been trying to pass on a message to Craig. Soon after I made an appointment at the council register office where armed with some basic facts, I made a startling discovery. Anne it appeared had died at the beginning of May in hospital around the time Craig had his experience.

In conclusion it has been noted that near the sight of the current building lay a natural pool known as the 'Pottie,' which was used as a means of executions. It is known that around eight people lost their lives there being drowned for the crime of infanticide. Were they responsible for the phenomena, or was it someone connected to the pub? We may yet find an answer.

The Old King's Highway

This ancient hostelry nestling in the 'Green' is a perfect encapsulation of a traditional pub, cosy and compact. To spend a few hours idling inside is a lovely thing indeed, made even better by its alleged haunting. The 'Green' of course features in numerous reports and is regarded as one of the most haunted areas in the city. The New Market, Shirlaws (RnB music), BHS, Littlewoods, The Tunnels can all stake a claim to being haunted as can many private properties nearby. Ghostly sightings have included figures in 18th century costume, music from phantom pipes and numerous monks and as this was the site of an ancient monastery the latter comes as no surprise. Many of these stories we will look at later, but for now let us step inside the Old King's Highway.

Within the pub, three areas are known to have witnessed phenomena. These are the main bar itself, the cellar (compulsory in a haunted pub) and the upstairs. function room. Upstairs, staff have been noted as seeing ghostly reflections in the mirror lined walls, and not their own. There have also been reports of both male and female figures, seen throughout the premises, but who they are remains a mystery. Perhaps an old owner? Or maybe a former patron drawn by earthly desires? The question will no doubt remain unanswered. There have of course been investigations that have taken place over the years though the evidence proved inconclusive. For instance, the basement area, noted as having a chill in the atmosphere could arguably just be cold, however if you add the following a different picture emerges. Take for example a pot of paperclips suddenly thrown from a desk in the staff office by invisible hands or the staff member who walked into a cold spot and on retreating had his name shouted after him. It comes as no surprise that many workers preferred to remain upstairs while on duty. Also noted has been the formation of puddles of water from no discernible source despite the surrounding area being checked regularly.

In the bar itself phenomena has also been reported for years, again figures have been seen and now and then a little poltergeist activity has been thrown into the mix. One patron witnessed a fork literally jump from the glass in which it rested, landing next to him on the seat. My favourite though concerns one of the night staff who was chatting with her friends at the bar. According to the report the mobile phone belonging to one of her friends started ringing and on being checked indicated the call was coming from the 'Old King's Highway.' It was stated that the pub phone was still on the receiver so whoever made the call was working miracles. Eventually it rang off before someone then humorously remarked that it must have been the 'ghost,' only to have the lights at the end of the pub start to flicker.

Ma Cameron's Inn

After a long climb up 'Boots' staircase we cross Union Street onto Back Wynd where we come upon Cameron's Inn. This is one of Aberdeen's oldest and most beloved pubs and was built on the site of a much older establishment known as The Sow Croft Inn. As the name suggests it is assumed that they kept pigs there. Being a common practice at the time, many families owned livestock and nearby St. Nicholas Kirk was known to be a magnet for such foraging creatures. Known to disinter corpses, a bylaw was passed banning people from letting their animals root in the grounds under pain of a heavy penalty. One can imagine that the owner of the Sow Croft Inn must have had his work cut out, keeping a wary eye on his wandering swine.

Sow Croft was eventually replaced by a coaching inn under the management of then owner John Ross and in the late 1800s the family most associated with the inn took over, the Cameron's. It was John Cameron's wife Amelia who earned the homely soubriquet of 'Ma' who continued to run the pub till 1933. During the Cameron family's tenure, it should be noted that 'Mas' was an elite howff which catered for the well- heeled class of citizen. This was due to their policy at that point of not selling draught beer which was considered a lower-class drink. The pub we know today of course has undergone many changes. Initially a lot smaller, with stables at the rear it traded solely at number six Little Belmont Street before incorporating its neighbour, number eight. It is regarded as being haunted and the stories well documented including those of a decorator working alone, forced to flee the building, which is why I wanted to know more.

Soon after I approached the current manager Jason for his comments and had the opportunity to meet with him one afternoon in the snug, the oldest and most atmospheric part of the pub. In conversation it came to light that there had been numerous incidents during his time there though he had not been directly involved himself until recently. He explained what happened when joining other staff for a drink in the snug:

'We were sitting having a quiet chat when suddenly a few of us noticed a dark figure out of the corner of our eyes moving past the serving hatch towards the door that leads to the toilet. Thinking a customer had been locked in I went to search for them and discovered no one in the corridor, I then checked the toilets in case someone was hiding in them, again no one. I went through the entire bar and returned to the snug, we deliberated whether it was our imagination or not.'

After further investigation it was found that the activity was prevalent in three locations. Firstly, the area near where the stables once stood, the front lounge of what was originally number eight and lastly, the top floor of number six, once used as accommodation for staff. It was noted that the atmosphere in those areas was best described as uneasy, as testified by one of the bar staff who stated: 'It's not funny when you are on your own and the lights keep getting switched on and off.' She went on to describe that when changing a barrel in the tap room she was suddenly aware of someone standing directly behind her and was too scared to turn round, saying 'I just stood still till whatever it was left and when it felt safe to turn round, I got out quick.' Despite her account being doubted she has remained adamant that there was someone observing her.

After a few weeks I returned to Cameron's to try and meet those I had missed first time round, and again I met up with Jason. He immediately mentioned that a regular Alistair, had been sitting having a lone pint in the snug, sitting near the serving hatch looking ahead. Noticing movement from the corner of his eye he glanced through the hatch and was surprised to see a beer tap turn itself on and proceed to pour a drink. The staff member on duty at the time had briefly left the bar and was unaware of the incident until Alistair called out and on returning promptly switched the tap off. Both were shocked and left speechless as the tap turned itself on, twice more in quick succession. To emphasise the point, I was shown that it takes a certain amount of strength to turn the tap on and was unlikely to have been caused by a fault in the mechanism. I was told that on all other occasions it had worked perfectly well.

As luck would have it, I had the good fortune to mention my visit to a work colleague Mike who had been a regular for years. He did not seem in the slightest bit surprised when told of my findings. It turned out that in a strange quirk of fate the witness to the beer pouring incident in question was a good friend of his and I was assured that he was not prone to flights of fancy. Mike then informed me that he was on friendly terms with previous owners, the Bruce family. They had owned the bar since the 1970's and had only recently moved on. He suggested I contact Alison Bruce for further information, who appeared extremely interested in contributing and provided me with some great stories.

She stated: 'The most reliable incident was an account by Mr. Masson who was locked in and painting the ceiling of number eight. He had heard three knocks from above and returned three knocks with his paintbrush. Three knocks from above were then returned. He was so spooked he left the building. The flat above number eight was empty and had not been used for years and the only access was through a window in the lane, the incident occurred in the early hours of the morning.'

She went on to say the other incident of note happened to employee Elaine who was sent to get crisps. The crisp boxes were on the top floor of number No.6, and on entering the room thought someone had followed her and was standing behind. She then began chatting to them but receiving no reply, turned round and found she was alone. She then ran down the stairs and, described by those who saw her as being very white and shaking. Alison went on to say that when she saw Elaine's expression, she had shivers up her spine. She was later quoted as saying. 'I have felt a presence on many occasions while I was working in the pub. It is not an evil presence but nevertheless I have been spooked on dark nights or in the early morning. Charlene, our cleaner, also thought she saw a figure while working in the old stable area, early in the morning. It was just standing, watching.'

On a final note, I remembered an incident which I had forgotten about until recently, when I had visited Cameron's. One Friday evening as my partner and I sat in the snug I became acutely aware of someone wanting to make his presence felt, who impressed the name John onto my mind as well as a visual description of himself. He appeared to be dressed in clothes from the late 18th century with waistcoat, breeches and tailcoat and had a strong connection to the building. His presence remained with me for some minutes. It was only much later when I realised that one of the original owners was called John Ross that I entertained the possibility that perhaps he might be responsible for the activity.

DREADING THE BOARDS: ABERDEEN'S HAUNTED THEATRES.

His Majesty's Theatre

Like any self- respecting theatre, it has had its fair share of supernatural occurrences over the years including sightings of its most celebrated spirit, 'Jake the ghost' or John Murray to give him his real name. The building designed by Frank Matcham has undergone various refurbishments in its lifetime including those in the 1930s and the 1980s, when much of the stage area was modernised. Since the theatre's opening night performance 'Red Riding Hood' in 1906 it has been a bastion of culture for the people of the city, playing host to innumerable stars from the golden age of theatre and cinema. Even during the hard times of the Second World War, when performances could stop mid flow due to bombing raids it has entertained and enthralled, and it is during this period that our story begins. During the Christmas period it was and still is customary to play host to a pantomime or similar family show as was the case in December 1942 when hosting a circus. A circus in those days was an event guaranteed to generate excitement and during the war years it was not unusual for one to be held within the confines of a theatre rather than a traditional big top due to the blackout. The Royal Britannic Circus was well publicised in the local paper for weeks in advance proclaiming it as a 'colossal Christmas and New Year attraction.' Highlights included 'forest bred lions' an equestrian act, a Russian troupe described as 'our allies' and performing pigeons, an eclectic mix if ever there was one. I find it difficult to imagine how they could have carried out these acts on stage but nevertheless they did much to the appreciation of the crowds, it was by all accounts a roaring success. Unfortunately, it did not end well, for the 'Press and Journal' of Monday the 27th of December contained a story stating: 'Tragedy in H.M. Theatre,' in which readers were horrified to note the death of a long-term employee.

The man in question was John Murray, 69 years of age and head 'flyman' for nearly twenty years. On that fateful night, the ponies, an integral part of the show, were being lowered in an aged lift from the stage to the basement. We will of course never know who made the fateful decision to lower all of them together. Perhaps the men had wanted to finish up quickly, it was Christmas after all and their families would be waiting, but whatever the reason, all were crammed into the lift. The men then began turning the winch to lower the cage, but the combined weight of the cargo sent the lift plummeting sending the wheel spinning uncontrollably. John was alleged to have leant forward to apply the break and was struck by the handle revolving at such speed that according to an eyewitness at the time, it decapitated him. The death certificate tells a slightly different story citing the cause of death as a 'compound fracture of the skull and destruction of the brain.' Either way it must have been a terrible scene. Dougie Monaghan who started work at the theatre in 1938 as a page boy was there and witnessed the events as was colleague Dougie White, who attempting to stop the wheel, was struck on the arm and badly injured. His compensation at the time for his injury was 'two free tickets for life.' John, as stated, had been with the theatre for many years and took a keen interest in all the productions which visited Aberdeen. From a notebook he kept, and carried with him, Mr Murray was able to recall details of every show which had appeared at His Majesty's during his tenure. It also stated that he left a widow, two sons and two daughters behind, his third son was tragically killed in action earlier in the year. In a strange quirk of fate, former theatre archivist Edi Swan told me that he was giving a talk to the Women's Guild in the early 1980s, mentioning the ghost. He was surprised at the end of the talk to be approached by one of the women who said: 'that's my father you were telling us about.'

Edi Swan, a gold mine of information on both the theatre and the haunting has also had strange experiences himself, which he was happy to share with me. They began in the late 1950s, when as a young man he was employed along with other art school graduates as scenic painters before becoming a long serving artistic director. His experiences have already found homes in such books as 'Theatre Ghosts' by Roy Harley Lewis and Norman Adams 'Haunted Neuk' and gives credence to 'Jakes,' benign nature. With this haunting, there have been distinct periods of activity some triggered by revamps within the building. During the 1980s for example much of the original equipment was replaced by a more efficient system and during this period there were frequent sightings. It would appear ghosts like people, do not like change!

Jakes earliest appearances, well certainly those recorded, are from the 1950s and it was then Edi had his first encounter which he described during our interview in 2007. He was, he explained, grateful for 'Jake's' intervention on two occasions, the first after a bad fall. The resultant injury, a possible break, left him in the unenviable position of having to crawl to the rear exit outside of which lay the accident and emergency unit at nearby Woolmanhill. After a painful journey to the basement the doors which were normally locked were found to have been mysteriously opened allowing him to exit, even though the manager Bert Ewen swore they had been padlocked. Why was he so certain? Because he had locked them personally as he had done so every night for years. The second incident and potentially more dangerous, also involved Edi and occurred as the result of a malfunctioning spray can which temporarily blinded him. Alone on the stage and in agony, his only hope of salvation was the prop room sink which he reached after being 'guided' by a presence. Both incidents he claimed, had happy endings due to Jakes spiritual intervention.

Speaking of paint, I was told recently by a former employee, Neil Newcombe, that it was quite common for the mischievous spirit to play tricks on staff.

He takes up the story: 'I was given the task of painting the basement with masonry paint, while painting I shifted the pot to allow me to paint another area. When I went to dip my brush into the tin, it had disappeared, and I never found it again. I had locked myself in the bottom of the stage lift/access area so that no one could walk over my Bonnie floor, that was a very strange one. The theatre director (Edi) told me that the same thing happened to him all the time, he was the technical director and was a fine artist. He would touch up or paint scenes for shows. He said to me things like paint pots would vanish never to be found. He would also be working and then try to dip his brush into a pot and find that it had been switched to one with a lid still on it. Nowadays we would just put it down to absent-mindedness, but he was a young man at the time and not affected by that.'

Another infamous area, the 'Lambeth Walk,' is a long gloomy passageway running down to the exit doors below. Known to suffer from dramatic temperature drops it is considered by many to be one of most haunted areas in the theatre. Stories include the perennial tale of a night watchman, whose dog was apparently stopped in his tracks refusing to go into the area. Dogs are very clever after all. Neil Newcombe again provides the following account, having been the 'night watchman,' in question.

He takes up the story: 'I took the guard dog, called Savage on my rounds, checking that the emergency light systems were working on all the exit signs. An old exit, which runs to the lane situated at the side of the theatre (the Lambeth Walk) was quite creepy and old looking. I did not like going down there myself so that's why I took the dog. It was a huge German Shepherd belonging to my colleague Pat, the stage doorman. As we patrolled, I threw his ball down the corridor for him but instead of chasing it, he lay on his belly and crawled backwards whining and crying. He was terrified! I can't think if I ever went there alone again after that.' Having been in the area described myself I can well imagine how it must feel to be alone there. A case of rather you than me.

The fly floor bridge, a walkway above the stage where much of the old equipment was once situated is another area favoured by 'Jake' who has been spotted standing on the walkway on occasion. It was in this area that Peter Thorpe, a former stage manager was apparently very surprised to meet an apparition. Described as wearing a 'brown dust coat or apron,' the figure proceeded to walk towards him before disappearing. Another sighting of 'Jake,' this time attired in blue, came later and from another location, the props room. Neil Newcombe whose experience of the Lambeth Walk we have already noted was witness to this full figure manifestation as were others. Neil explains:

'One time we were all in the props room, at the back of the stage, having our morning cup of tea. An old man in bib and brace strolled passed the open doorway. We all saw him, and someone said, who on earth was that! We jumped up and all looked to see where he had gone as he had vanished. There is a door either side he could have theoretically exited from, but these were at least forty feet away!'

Not long after I was put in touch with an ex-employee Kenny Luke who had worked at the theatre for many years but in 1983 was still quite new to the building. One evening while working on a show, a sudden call of nature had him heading to the toilet at the back of the stairs. The old hands in the theatre used to talk about the areas reputation but of course many believed this to be just a wind-up, a way of keeping the newer recruits in line. Unfortunately, there was good reason for this as Kenny was about to discover.

Kenny takes up the story: 'I went into the corridor, from a very hot backstage, and walked into what I can only describe as a sensation of freezing cold water! I felt uncomfortable. Then I heard the door which connects to the basement open followed by the sound of someone approaching. I waited and waited to see who was coming up the stair, but no-one appeared so I hot footed it back to the stage pronto. When I got there, it was around interval time and I was spied by

Dougie Monaghan who with a knowing smile enquired, I take it you've just experienced Jake.'

Around ten years later 'Jake' made a more startling appearance, again which Kenny was on hand to witness. 'I was working on the stage show 'Scotland the What' and as the stage manager Graeme Shepherd who was running the corner (this is an area downstage left where all technical aspects of the show are controlled), turned to speak to me, he looked upstage right, smiled, and beckoned me over saying we have a visitor. I looked to where he was pointing and distinctly saw a dark shape move from the door to the upstage area. Concerned that it might be someone who should not have been there I went upstage to see if someone was heading towards the break room, but again no one. Graeme and I both agreed on what we saw and put it down as unexplained.' Kenny who very rarely works there now, finished off by saying, he was told by Graeme Shepherd that since he left there had been many more incidents in both the basement and cellar. Unexplained noises, figures, caught out of the corner of the eye, and equipment being mysteriously moved have all been mentioned. There is of course an abundance of stories to pick from, but I have a few favourites including one provided, again by Neil. It took place on his birthday, the ensuing prank, making it an unforgettable experience as he explains.

'My friends, both stage- hands, tied me up and bundled me downstairs into the dark creepy storerooms under the theatre for a joke where they left me in the pitch black for an hour. Now, they knew I was quite afraid of the dark and was frightened, and would also be annoyed, but the game went on anyway. I did however think that my friends were there with me because I kept seeing someone moving about in the shadows. I also heard what I thought sounded like someone sliding on the floor. I then kept hearing someone going Shhhhhhh! Eventually they came and got me, and I found out they had both been upstairs getting showered and dressed the whole time, ready to take me to the fair, so they could not have been crawling about in front of me. I didn't appreciate that prank!' There has, of course been many other incidents over the years witnessed by multiple people and there is a veritable abundance of stories, and I for one am glad as who doesn't love a haunted theatre?

To conclude I was given two further accounts, one of which was told to me by a friend, whose sister was once employed as a front-of house worker. On the evening of the incident, she had arrived at work and was standing alone in the main auditorium waiting for the doors to opened when she became aware of a sudden cold sensation surrounding her. She then felt herself nudged as if pushed slightly and turning quickly, noticed the drapes behind her had moved apart as if someone had walked through them. She panicked and left the area joining her colleagues who were at the front of the building. It came to light that others had also experienced the feeling of a 'barrier' put in their way which had prevented them from moving forward. It must be said though that they did not find the experience negative.

And finally in the spring of 2007 when 'Cats' began its run at the theatre, I was told that actors were becoming increasingly annoyed to find their costumes scattered on the floor each morning on their arrival, despite everyone maintaining their innocence. Was this the work of 'Jake' or a prank played by a work colleague? The answer remains unclear, though it would appear that the theatres longest serving employee has no plans to retire yet.

Tivoli Theatre

Some of the most enduring tales of 'hauntings' are attached to theatres and in Aberdeen this is no exception. His Majesty's Theatre as we have seen has many documented tales, but what of the others? Take for example, the Arts Centre on King Street. This former church has been home to reports of the paranormal including those of a supposedly haunted caretakers' flat and the slightly more alarming floating head that has allegedly been seen in one of the ground-floor rooms. Also included in this list is the residual haunting of the old Palace Theatre on Bath Street (now Liquid), where the sound of a frenzied stampede was heard by an unfortunate electrician undertaking some maintenance work. Unsurprisingly he left the building immediately after he came to his senses, but more on that later.

My favourite theatre however is the once derelict but now reborn Tivoli. Though the story I was told is not the most dramatic, it is however possible proof that on stage even death cannot stop entertainers from performing in some capacity at least. The Tivoli Theatre situated on Guild Street, was first opened in 1872 by the Aberdeen Theatre and Opera House Company Ltd built by architects James Mathews, a local man, and C. B. Phipps of London and on opening was named Her Majesty's Theatre. The auditorium was rebuilt some 25 years later by legendary theatre architect Frank Matcham and it is his design that can be seen today. However, despite its new-found grandiosity it closed temporarily in 1906 with the opening of the larger and more dominant, His Majesty's Theatre. It did not remain dormant for long however, and in 1909 was reconstructed by Frank Matcham and renamed the Tivoli.

Despite various changes throughout the century the Tivoli remained active until 1966 when due to the falling number of theatre goers, it closed. This was due in part to the impact of television and to changes in public taste. It did not remain closed for long though as in no time at all it received a new lease of life, this time as a bingo hall and survived as such until the 1980s when it eventually closed seemingly for good. And there it remained unloved and uncared for except by a handful of dedicated enthusiasts who devoted many hours, attempting to keep its name in the public consciousness. Events such as 'Doors open' days proved how captivating the building could still be despite its faded grandeur. Suffice to say, with the changes in public taste the concept of music hall entertainment became somewhat old fashioned. Many mourned its passing and the lack of interest in such a venerable building was sad to witness. In recent times various ideas were proposed in an attempt, to have it re-opened but for reasons which remain unclear they never happened. One such proposal, for a museum of variety unfortunately never reached fruition, and although it is great to now see it open again, one cannot help but wonder what that might have meant for the city.

Going back around fifteen years ago I approached the Tivoli Trust to arrange a visit and was kindly granted access by Alan. My colleague Duncan and I were given a free run of the building, photographing the interior. It was an immensely enjoyable experience and one that allowed me the opportunity to explore the building at length. Of course, during the visit, the subject of ghosts cropped up, but I was told by Alan that he had personally never heard of any stories associated with the building.

It was two years later and just prior to the building's imminent sale when we revisited it. Again, allowed to roam free, we noticed in the intervening years that the elements had been somewhat unkind, so certain areas were out of bounds. It was on this visit while we were exploring the ground floor area that I captured a strange anomaly in one of my photographs. The dressing room in which it appeared was without lighting and being the professional that I am, I pointed my camera into the darkened room pressing the flash twice. On checking the image, I was surprised to see an unidentifiable blue shape which appeared to be hanging from the ceiling. It roughly had the appearance of a head and a pair of shoulders hanging upside down. It did not appear on the second image which I took a few seconds later. In that image all that could be seen was a hole in the ceiling and from it some dangling stray wires. Perplexed, I filed the image away and thought nothing more of it until a chance meeting with a former cleaner Lorna brought fresh information. This is what she said:

'The sighting took place took in the old Tivoli Theatre in Guild Street where I was working as a cleaner in and around the old dressing room area of the building. I was told that

Florrie Forde a variety actress and singer was coming up from the dressing room onto the upper stage when she became ill and collapsed and died on stage. The only way to describe this sighting was that when I was on the stairs leading up to the stage, I was passed by a blue coloured, tall, elegant figure in the corridor. At the time I thought I was seeing things, maybe a trick of the light and because of this I mentioned the incident to my colleagues. I was surprised to hear that other people had seen the same thing but had never said anything. They all described the same figure. I believe it was of paranormal origin especially after what I described was backed up by others. At the time I noticed the air to be chillier than normal and the sighting though not frightening did leave me feeling a little shaken. My colleagues also reported seeing a similar figure at different times in the vicinity of the stage.'

I later found out that Florrie Forde, a popular Australian singer, was one of the biggest stars of her day. She was noted as having made over 700 recordings of popular music hall numbers such as 'Down at the Old Bull and Bush' and 'Only a Bird in a Gilded Cage,' between the years 1903 and 1936. In her later years she toured extensively and was in the city at the time of her death where she was entertaining troops. I had previously read that she had fallen ill whilst returning from a show in the back of a taxi, while others have claimed she died in the Tivoli itself.

The Lemon Tree

The Lemon Tree or St. Katherines as it was known, was built in the late 1930s and is now a popular concert venue. Around fifteen years ago I met up with a former colleague Dave Cook, who unbeknownst to me had worked as manager at the afore-mentioned venue. In our meeting he described having seen a ghost on several occasions. As keyholder he was usually first in and last out which he did not enjoy due to 'intense feelings of being watched.' This was especially true of the theatre production box, an area that others had felt uncomfortable in. Typically, whatever was around appeared elusive however after closing one evening staff enjoying a late drink saw what was described as 'a pair of legs which walked across the stage.' When Dave went to investigate it had of course vanished. He described the incident as 'unnerving.'

A further example of its insidious nature, occurred soon after when a visiting photographer, spooked by feelings of utter malevolence was forced to flee. The circumstances around the incident of course became common knowledge as was the reputation of its location, dressing room one. Regarded as a haunted hotspot, it is an area to be avoided at least from what I was told, however this was where he was based on graduation day. He was of course unaware at the time that the room had a 'reputation.'

Dave takes up the story: 'He was there for about three hours at the computer and after that time left and refused to go back into the room. When confronted, his explanation was that a horrible feeling of dread had overcame him. He became uncomfortable and as the atmosphere intensified it became unbearable. He just packed up and refused to go back.' Wanting to find out if there had been any further incidents, I took it upon myself to contact some of the current staff. Unfortunately for me, but fortunately for them the current crop had heard the rumours but had not personally experienced anything themselves. I was a little disappointed.

The Palace Theatre

As we draw the curtain on our theatre visit as it were, we make a brief stop at one of Aberdeen's lesser-known venues, the New Pallas Theatre or Palace of Varieties. Situated on Bath Street, The Palace Theatre became a cinema house and for later generations a music venue, Fusion, Ritzys and Liquid, being just some of its names. It is also quite possibly haunted as the following suggests. Around 15 years ago I was investigating another haunting, but disappointingly it turned out to be nothing more than a case of the jitters. There was however a silver lining when one of the interviewees told me about what had happened to his old gaffer. It had happened during his apprenticeship when his boss, a local electrician had been tasked with repairing a socket on the main stairway of the building. I might add it was during the day a time not usually associated with ghost sightings.

Once inside he set to work, it was an easy repair which would literally take minutes, but he had no idea of what was to follow. According to his former apprentice, he suddenly became aware of an approaching cacophony of noise and was pinned against the wall by a rush of energy hurtling by him. Afterwards he described it as sounding like many people moving at high-speed with the accompanying screams being deafening. The babbling of the voices then receded down the staircase and faded as quickly as they had begun. He was so shaken by the incident he ran from the building without finishing the job. His friend said he had been genuinely terrified by the experience.

Curious to find out more I researched the buildings history and soon found the answer. On, the 30th of September 1896 the theatre then known as the People's Palace was the scene of a terrible fire in which seven people perished. It transpired that during a performance, part of the stage set had brushed against a naked gas jet, the blaze taking hold instantly. Despite the best efforts of the staff, it spread rapidly and before half the audience had the opportunity to flee, the flames had rushed along the wooden ceiling and reached one of the exits. Reports at the time stated that in the ensuing panic many were injured. This terrible fire, one of many to hit British Theatres at that time, prompted architects to use non-flammable materials in their constructions, paving the way for greater emphasis on public safety. These included the introduction of adequate escape routes. From his description I was convinced that the electrician had been unfortunate to have been caught up in some terrible replay from the past, witnessing the sounds and sensations from the trapped residual energy. He may even have unwittingly been in the building on the anniversary of the tragedy though this is pure speculation. I was intrigued but my investigations drew a blank until recently in an unexpected way. On researching the afore-mentioned fire I discovered that Scotland's worst poet William McGonagall had penned a response to the events. Known as a tragedian he was constantly inspired by gloomy and morose incidents, of which there were an abundance in Scotland. The poem as expected, was unintentionally amusing despite his obvious sincerity when penning the words. Next to the poem were a few comments one of which dating from 2012 caught my eye. It was from an employee of the nightclub called Sean and his comments were startling. This is what he had written:

'I work in the building and have done for only eight weeks. It's the largest nightclub in Aberdeen and I can tell you it is haunted. I am a cleaning supervisor and go in four days a week, having to open in total darkness. It is only when you are upstairs that things start to happen, even more so when the lights are on. Shadows, smoky shadows, and apparitions have been seen and just today another cleaner saw a man standing on the stairs. I am not a big believer in ghosts, or I wasn't, but I am now. I found this page as I was investigating to see if anyone had died there. I never knew there was a fire until now, that explains a lot!'

Again, quite recently, I noticed a Facebook post on the former theatre and in it the author described it as being one of the most haunted buildings in Aberdeen. He went on to say:

'I never saw it myself, but I know lots of other people who worked there, who saw, 'the boy'…. a kid in the early 20th century clothing sitting on the stairs crying. Apparently when the circus caught fire, there was a wee lad crushed as people ran out.' It remains an intriguing story and I hope one day to interview the people who bore witness to this and find out more. As I have mentioned on numerous occasions, cleaners seem to bear the brunt of paranormal experiences, as my files prove. Perhaps then, ghost hunters should consider this as a possible career move as by all accounts if you work unsociable hours, you are almost guaranteed to see something. Joking apart, there is something intrinsically creepy about working alone in a building out of hours, particularly one so large and with such a tragic history and it's a job that many do not envy.

THE CASTLEGATE

Former Royal Bank of Scotland, Castle Street

P itfodels Lodging was erected about 1530 as the townhouse of the Menzies of Pitfodels and by its description stood three storeys high and was turreted. It has been thought that the courtyard of the house was used to store one of Aberdeen's first means of public execution, the Maiden. The Scottish Maiden essentially a precursor to the guillotine was allegedly wheeled from there on execution days to nearby Heading Hill where justice was swiftly meted out to the delight of blood thirsty crowds. The town council employed someone with this task whose other duties included 'soaping the rope' which allowed the blade to fall swiftly and presumably clean the machine afterwards. It has been recorded that it was used frequently on murderers and those who committed lesser crimes and although cited as being more humane than hanging, it still induces an involuntary shudder when thought about. Records of the area are scarce though prior to the construction of Marischal Street in 1782, the Aberdeen residence of the Earl Marischal also stood nearby. It was from the window of this house that Mary Queen of Scots allegedly watched the execution of Sir John Gordon. Son of the earl of Huntly, beheaded after the battle of Corrichie in 1562. With all this history in the area, much of it violent, it is surprising that there has not been more 'stories' connected to the Castlegate area but as you will see, it still has its share.

The first story on our tour of the area took place in the former bank building (now the courthouse) which was described as having a cobbled area in the cellar and which, by all accounts housed the remains of an old road apparently complete with pavements. But what were these remnants of an earlier age? Unfortunately, this remains a mystery as the area in question was recently converted into holding cells for the court. Notwithstanding there have been rumours circulating about the area having secret tunnels and vaults beneath it for years. Shades of Edinburgh's South Vaults springing to mind.

The following story was related to me by a former colleague Duncan Haig and concerned a close friends' daughter, Adele. Her employment at the Royal Bank of Scotland on Castle Street provided a frisson not often associated with the banking profession. As a junior, her duties included frequent trips to the storeroom to retrieve documents, a task she didn't enjoy due to the 'atmosphere' in the basement. Staff used to describe the location of the filing cabinets in the basement as being 'across the road'. The road being the partial remains of a street, which ran through one half of the basement. Despite her trepidation nothing out of the ordinary took place until one day, when she described being unable to move after held by an unseen force. It was by all accounts a terrifying experience and only ended when the caretaker, who lived in the upper part of the building, coincidentally descended the stairs only to find her frozen to the spot. She recalled saying, 'I can't cross' and stood while the caretaker retrieved the file. Only then the entity relinquished its grasp and she was at last able to move. Later she could offer no rational explanation as to what had just occurred. The caretaker as a means of response stated that his wife, did not like going down there. When she returned home that evening her father, Bill, was aware of her upset and both he and his wife clearly recalled that, 'she was very shaken' and initially reluctant to talk about her experience in case 'they laughed.' She was told later that the road had originally led from the harbour to the gallows, historically situated in front of the Tolbooth. Whether this has any bearing on the incident who can say. Sometime after Adele got in touch and provided her own first-hand account, and this is what she said:

'There was a concreted section to the floor, however if you turned to the right the concrete ended, replaced by dirty cobbles. There was a large, heavy wooden door in front of you. The door had a small window in it with bars like a prison cell and there were several more doors like this.' Adele described the area as being like an alley that had been built over and was told that originally it had led all the way to the harbour and possibly used as a route for prisoners who were to be transported. Whether this is historically accurate is open to debate however the area was obviously older than the building above and behind each door lay a cell.

She had only ever been in the first two and described them as being rough-hewn rock, black with age, dirt or smoke, and intriguingly containing locked wooden chests. The temperature changes between the two basement areas were also described as being noticeably different and though there might be no overt supernatural explanation for this, it was enough to make the hair on her neck rise. The caretakers' cats were also prone to act strangely in this area, avoiding the cobbles, preferring to pace the new concrete floor. I was also told it was also common to hear creaking doors, shuffling noises and a distinct feeling that someone else was there.

Victoria Court

Around eight months later while photographing the 'Shiprow,' I found myself overlooking a curious old building. Hidden from view by a monstrous car park, it was a nice surprise to find this hidden gem tucked away at the end of a lane. The building albeit in a state of dilapidation was still the epitome of Georgian elegance though now only home, to a flock of pigeons. With my interest piqued I decided to approach the council to establish who owned the property and in quirk of fate was told that there was a visit planned by the factor the next day.

I was given permission to have a look round, though I was made aware that the building had been derelict for some years and therefore likely to be unpleasant. This turned out to be something of an understatement. I must point out also that the idea of ghosts and the paranormal had not entered my radar as I was just excited to be taking pictures. I arrived the next day and the first indication that there might have been something unpleasant within became apparent as the factor (Nick) was only able to partially open the front door due to a build-up of pigeon excrement. This excrement sat directly behind the door and proved to be the ultimate draft excluder with the door creaking in protest before becoming entrenched in the crust. Squeezing in we found ourselves in what is best described as a lunar landscape of dried manure. Strange amorphous shapes peppered the hall and preceding rooms, with some sporting ancient nest like hats. As we crunched through decades of filth not daring to look too closely in the gloom or indeed at our feet, the factor commented that this was probably the worst infestation he had ever seen, a sentiment which I could not disagree with. The decades of accumulated filth proved vile, but worse still was the constant shrieking of the baby birds that crawled among the debris. The floors themselves were littered with hundreds of pigeon corpses in various states of decay while all around others flapped furiously away on our approach, battering against glass in a frenzied attempt to escape. This was far the worst surroundings I had ever been in, and my skin crawled at every turn. I then noticed that the rooms despite their condition still retained a modicum of elegance and were vast in scale, products of a by gone age.

Being asked if I would like to see the basement, we retraced our steps which proved even more hazardous. We now headed towards the foreboding basement whose open doorway lay dark and uninviting. We crept gingerly down the stairs while the constant crunching of dirt or worse caused all manner of horrible images to come flooding into my head. On reaching the basement I was surprised to find something akin to Adele's description of the adjoining bank including rough-hewn cellars, cobbled floors, and discarded boxes, looking for all the world like small treasure chests. Birds shrieked as we crept ahead, the flash of my camera sending wild eyed flurries rushing noisily into the air and most alarmingly round our heads.

As I looked ahead Nick explained that there had been an extension added much later and he was about to take me to what was originally the outside of the building when I became aware of a shadow detaching itself from the dark below the staircase. Nick who had his back to it remained unaware as the figure now rushed towards us. A quick glance showed it to be man-shaped, possessing both arms and legs and it was upon us in seconds. It was too late to react, and I felt myself cringe in anticipation as an icy blast went right through me. A second later we were alone. It was apparent that Nick had felt nothing, so I remained silent, leaving him to the unenviable task ahead.

On leaving I noticed that opposite sat another building and on investigation discovered it was a bus drivers' canteen. I decided to pop in on the off chance of getting some new leads and got into conversation with employee, Susan. She was quite amused when I told her of my recent adventures in the building opposite, stating: 'Oh that place, it's meant to be haunted.' She went on to add that many people had also seen the spirit of a male figure in the canteen.

Commerce Street

The following story was related to me by a work colleague and took place when she first moved to Aberdeen. The paranormal activity was mainly aural rather than visual but none the less terrifying for her and other family members. Diane had been on the lookout for a flat to buy and was soon lucky enough to find one that suited her needs, in Commerce Street. Situated near the harbour and much like any other, it consisted of a long row of undistinguished tenements with shops below, once belonging to the Northern Co-operative. Built around a hundred years ago they now sat alongside more contemporary premises. At first glance the area seems nondescript, however one has only to look at the city's past to realise that this was not always the case. The immediate area has a very dark history possibly more so, than most and may go some way to explaining the phenomena that Diane witnessed.

If one looks at city plans of Aberdeen from the eighteenth and early nineteenth century, they show a natural valley running towards the harbour. With Castlehill on one side and Heading Hill on the other, the area is synonymous with the barbaric practice of public executions. Commerce Street today, practically sits on the site of witch burnings where in the year 1597 twenty-three women and one man were burned at the stake. It has a gloomy air to it, and I have on occasion suffered an involuntary shiver at the thought of what went on there.

It was in this location that Diane and her cousin moved into a first floor flat. At first though all was quiet, but in the late Autumn a series of curious events began to unfold. In conversation, Diane recalled that it was on a Wednesday evening around seven when the first signs of paranormal activity began to manifest.

Diane takes up the story: 'I was sitting in the living room at the front of the building watching television. I was feeling relaxed when the temperature dropped rapidly and I heard what I can only describe as voices talking and chanting, but not in English.' She went on to explain: 'It sounded like it was in Latin and the voices seemed to move across the top of the room going round the ceiling before stopping. My hair stood on end or so it felt, my heart was racing, instinctively I knew these sounds were not from a normal source. I ran to the kitchen and paced the floor knowing that I would have to return to the room and tried to rationalise it. I made tea and plucking up the courage to return, did so only to find everything, including the temperature was back to normal.'

Things remained normal and the incident was all but forgotten, until one evening when friends were over. Again, as before, the temperature dropped while the archaic language was heard in the room. Her visitors, alarmed, were placated by her explanation, suggesting a passing taxi was causing interference, though she knew this was a lie. She continued the ruse until they left, afterwards reluctantly checking the stereo, knowing full well it was unplugged. Other seemingly unconnected phenomena now occurred, which included the appearance of Kirby grips. There was no discernible reason why, however they were described as having been constantly found around the flat despite no one using them.

Attempting to discover the areas' history she began casually asking people and was told from various sources that there had been a murder committed there and even further back a witches' coven. In more enlightened times however, it is generally acknowledged that witches of old were no more than poor unfortunates accused of the black arts after falling out with neighbours and executed due to ignorance. There was never any coven and though there was a murder nearby in the 1960s, the two incidents appear unrelated. Soon after she sold the flat and moved on.

An interesting coda to the story occurred soon after, when Diane volunteered to show myself and two others the location of the flat. When we got there, she recounted the story and was surprised to find that one of her students had often visited next door. After a brief explanation it transpired his friend, James had once rented in the next block, and like Diane had left in similar circumstances. We asked why, and he said that an accumulation of events had built up over time, convincing him it was haunted. He went on to say that it got so bad that most of his friends refused to visit. Below are some of the details he provided.

The first event of note occurred when James had been busy ironing. Leaving the room briefly to answer the phone, he returned to find that the shirt he had been ironing had vanished. He searched the room, puzzled at its disappearance but concluded that perhaps he had ironed it already, having several others like it. He put his absent-mindedness down to being tired, put them away and forgot about it. When changing a fuse some weeks later he discovered to his astonishment the missing shirt, now crumpled inside the box. There was, as you can imagine no reasonable explanation and his mounting dread slowly grew.

The second event, which finally convinced him of a supernatural presence occurred soon after when having spent the evening watching television, he decided to call it a night. He soon fell asleep, the night passing uneventfully. In the morning he went through to the living room to have a cup of tea and a cigarette, where he made a shocking discovery. At first glance it appeared that during the night someone had opened his cigarettes and scattered them about the living room floor, though on inspection he realised that they had been arranged into a pattern. This time he was convinced, remembering clearly, he had left them unopened on top of the television. He quit his tenancy soon after.

The events in Commerce Street remain unexplained. Diane and Rob, both reliable witnesses, were very measured in their descriptions and I have no reason to doubt their testimony. I have omitted the house numbers, but I will give you a clue, they are situated next door to what was once the 'Crows, Nest' pub.

In conclusion one possible explanation for the apport (a term for the seemingly random appearance of objects) could be a family member trying to let their presence be known. This could explain the appearance of the Kirby grips, though Diane did not understand why this was relevant. The Latin chanting is far more intriguing, and possibly a recording in the fabric of the area, most likely associated with the witch burnings. It has been noted that during executions a priest would be given the task of performing the last rites, a prayer in Latin for those about to meet their end.

Castlehill Barracks

This story happened just after World War Two and though the building in question has long since vanished, I felt it was so intriguing that I had to include it. The story was related to me by the late Stanley Robertson a fine musician and storyteller who kindly allowed me to use it for this book. It was related to him many years ago by his school friend's mother and took place in the Castlehill barracks. The barracks were built in 1794 for the Gordon Highlanders and used by the regiment until 1935 when they moved to their new headquarters at the Bridge of Don. After the war and prior to its demolition it was used as a temporary measure to alleviate a housing shortage offering cheap but inadequate housing, eventually being classed as slum dwellings. The barracks a sprawling Georgian construction was a prominent feature of the Castlegate until the arrival of the Salvation Army Citadel in 1896 which in its grandeur promptly overshadowed its more elderly neighbour. In 1965, the area was developed, and the barracks left to near ruin before being demolished and replaced soon after by Marischal and Virginia Court, respectively. They may have offered all 'mod cons' but no one could argue which was the most aesthetically pleasing.

The young mother's husband on returning from the war had become a 'hawker.' An itinerant lifestyle, he spent more and more time away from home, leaving his young wife to fend for herself. An acquaintance of the family (and key holder for the Castlehill Barracks) had promised to help find accommodation because of impending homelessness, no doubt influenced by her likeness to Hedy Lamarr. The offer when it came though not ideal, was better than being destitute so was gladly accepted. The room was situated across the bridge spanning Commerce Street was in the former hospital wing. There she was offered a basement room for the knockdown price of literally pence, which she promptly took. Stanley described the room as being down three flights of stairs in the 'sunks' and there being no working light. Once at the bottom a solitary door stood and behind it a huge, long room with no windows. The room was described, as being painted a nondescript greenish murky colour, and with the antiquated gas lights provided very little illumination. There was no natural light which did not elevate the grim surroundings. A room no matter how desolate was still better than the unthinkable and so they were grateful for having a roof over their heads. Not long after her youngest child Shirley fell ill, her raging fever prompting her mum to seek help from her upstairs neighbours. Having no medicine to give, one neighbour suggested she should try the nearby district nurses' headquarters at Ingleborough House. It was used by both District and Queen Anne nurses and seemed a good option under the circumstances. The frightened mother, certain she would find help there, took the neighbour's advice and hurried off.

On arriving she was disappointed to be told that there wasn't anyone available to make a house call, and that the nurse on duty was unable to leave the building unattended. She assured her that if anyone came back, she would ask them to drop by. With no other option, she returned home to wait anxiously by her daughter's bed. The fever showing no signs of abating raged on and she had all but given up hope when she heard a noise outside the door. Rushing to open it she found the welcome sight of a nurse standing in the gloom. She was ushered in and immediately sat by the patients' bed. She remained silent while tending the young patient and indicated that the mother should sit down and rest. After some time, the nurse rose and left, leaving the grateful mother to doze next to her sleeping daughter. By the morning, her daughter's condition had improved greatly. Leaving her briefly she ran down to the nurses' home to pass on her thanks only to be met with a blank stare. They had sent no one. Insisting they had, she went on to describe her attire, so it came as quite a shock to find the description was that of a nurse from the Great War. A short time later a startling piece of information came to light, their home at Castlehill Barracks, the room with no windows and ghastly green walls, had been used as a mortuary during that period.

Marischal Court

Could it get any stranger? Well, yes, it could as you will soon see. The buildings themselves are not historic or architecturally pleasing but the area itself is rich with bloody historical incident and, to quote from the film Ghostbusters, could well be a candidate for 'spook central.' I was unable to personally visit any of the properties within the blocks and have had to accept the stories at face value, but I must state that I have known most of the witnesses for a considerable time and can vouch for their integrity.

The first building of note on the site which can be backed up by historical records is Aberdeen's castle, an early fortification which was destroyed along with its English garrison in the dim and distant past. Details of these events are sparse to say the least, the castle being so completely dismantled that researchers have never found any physical evidence of its existence other than in a few written records. In later years, the area became an Observatory and then a grand Georgian military barracks which after being built in 1796, remained home to various regiments including the Gordon Highlanders. In 1935 the regiment marched out for the last time to take up residence at the Bridge of Don. By this time, the barracks were becoming somewhat dilapidated, however they survived until the 1960s providing temporary housing. As the former residents began to move into new purpose-built municipal housing around the city, the fate of the building was sealed. Soon afterwards the bulldozers moved in and it was raised to the ground in preparation for the construction of both Marischal and Virginia court (multi-story flats) and it is here that our stories take place.

I first became aware of the area's dark history whilst undertaking research for a walking tour and during this time a chance encounter with a former resident provided me with some startling and unique stories. I met Lynn Fallon through my work, and she described to me, how as a child she had stayed with her parents in Virginia Court, the smaller of the two buildings. It transpired that despite the modernity of the building the family had been subjected to a prolonged series of inexplicable incidents which had started in Lynn's early adulthood and continued after she had left home. She explained.

'My bedroom was the back one. I painted it and moved in and at some point, I started waking in the middle of the night. I remember the room used to feel icy and I had the distinct feeling I was not wanted there. I took my quilt and moved downstairs. This happened on several occasions over a period of weeks. Sometimes when I woke it felt as if there was a heavy weight pressing on my chest and a couple of times I felt as if I was being pulled from the bed by my feet. After two weeks of disturbed sleep, I rearranged the furniture to claim the bedroom, told the room that I lived there now and 'it' or 'they' were not supposed to be there anymore and for a time that was the end of it. However, when I moved out my parents began to use the room and it started again.'

She went on to state that on occasion when passing the open door of the darkened bedroom a strange bluish glow appeared to emanate from her parent's bed which was witnessed by different people. Her father seemed to be particularly plagued by vivid nightmares in this room and would awake abruptly with a feeling of dread and so I asked for permission to contact her father to clarify this. They had of course moved away many years ago, but he remembered the following incidents with great clarity and was happy to recall them.

He explained: 'I woke up in the middle of the night and on the left side of the bed I clearly saw a three-legged stool on the floor, I suppose much like a milking stool. It began to rise slowly in the air vertically and disappeared through the ceiling. A minute later a woman wearing an old - fashioned crinoline bonnet came through the wall next to the headboard. She was like a silhouette and moved straight past me to the opposite side of the room where she disappeared through the wall. I woke up my wife in a panic but when she had awoken it was gone. It was the kind of thing you never forget.'

He went on to say that there were other incidents which made their stay uncomfortable, like hearing disembodied voices and the feeling of being watched became common. He concluded by saying that when his wife was in the house alone, she became convinced that the living room was full of people, though she was at a loss as to explain this. She just felt it to be.

Following our conversation, I started to ask around if anyone from the area had heard of anything unusual connected to the flat, there was the usual hearsay though nothing concrete until I bumped into an old family friend, Dave Hardy. As it turned out he had at one time lived in the adjoining Marischal Court during the early 1990s. Having a lifelong interest in the occult and the paranormal and having had premonitions as a child he was the perfect candidate to experience the supernatural. Dave had moved into Marischal Court in 1990. The house was a maisonette which had an unusual layout, bedrooms on the bottom floor while the living room, kitchen and bathroom on the top. Dave generally lived alone but his three children would visit regularly sleeping over in one of the downstairs rooms. At first the only sign of anything untoward happening was the sound of whispering when there was no one about followed by icy temperatures. His eldest son David would later verify this and explained that at first, they suspected the noise of whispering was travelling up the walls from neighbouring properties, however he noted that when they listened at the walls the sound would cease abruptly. Dave was keen to point out that this was a regular feature of living there but to put things in perspective the more unusual experiences took place over a prolonged period and were never constant. And so, one would recover from any given experience and have peace for considerable lengths of time.

On the day of our meeting, his eldest son David joined us for the interview. There were three major incidents of note during their tenancy, and I have tied to describe them as accurately as possible.

The first began when the children were visiting. Christopher and Fay being the youngest were fast asleep downstairs while Dave and his eldest were watching a film. Dave then went through to the kitchen and began doing the dishes while his son chatted to him. They both then heard footsteps coming along the corridor towards the kitchen door. Dave, still at the sink, turned and asked them to get back to bed suspecting the kids were playing up. He then described how his jaw dropped as he saw what was standing in the corridor. David, standing behind the open glass door could see the silhouette of a small figure in a long white gown and was equally transfixed. The figure then turned silently and walked back down the corridor. Putting down the dishcloth and grabbing his son he followed thinking the children had manufactured a prank, but they were found to be sound asleep. He described the figure to me as being that of a small child with short blond hair and pale complexion who looked ill. It was not till years later that he discovered that the now demolished Sick Kids Hospital stood nearby which could account for the 'ill looking girl.'

Some considerable time passed before the second incident of note. It was in the early evening and Dave was in the bathroom while his son was making tea. Both were startled by the sound of loud thumping coming from the stairs. They immediately went to investigate and witnessed an entire shelf of books flying off a nearby case. He stated: 'The bookcase was around four feet from the banister of the staircase which led to the bedrooms and the books were shooting over the top of this rapidly one by one and falling down the stairs. We stood in terror, and I remember thinking, what is going on with this house? We then crept downstairs to the jumbled pile of books now lying in a heap at the foot of the stairs.' Out of curiosity I asked what kind of books they were and was told they were mainly on philosophy, mythology, and the occult. We started to pick them up and noticed that the one I had used at university had indentations on it which went quite far into the book. They looked like marks made by adult human teeth. That really freaked us out.' The incident left them with a horrible feeling of anticipation which lingered for days. Dave began to talk to neighbours and was in a sense relieved to find out that his flat was not the only one singled out as other residents also began to recall their experiences though they were thankfully less dramatic. The third, and least easily explainable incident occurred years later, in which Dave had a frightening encounter with what he took to be an Undine or water spirit. He recounts:

'It was early evening, and I was lying on my three-seater settee. I was resting with my eyes shut but was not asleep. I was clear of mind and not stressed but I began to feel the atmosphere change and felt there was something coming into the room. I thought at first, I was being stupid but became very wary of opening my eyes. After a while I slowly opened my eyes and let them glance to the wall behind me. Lying along the back of the settee was a posed female form. She was right next to me. She had large black eyes like a fish and was staring down at me. I felt there was malevolence there. I was frozen with fear but let my eyes travel as best they could down her body. The top half was that of a normal woman, but the lower half was like that of a mermaid with what appeared to be fish scales across it. I was terrified and willed myself to close my eyes and just lay there in shock. After a while, the atmosphere slowly changed and returned to normal. I knew then whatever it was had gone. I sprang up instantly thinking I had lost my sanity. I touched the sofa and realised it was both cold and damp but not slimy as I thought it might be. I still can't explain this nearly twenty years later though I have thought about it over and over again. I thankfully never saw it again. In retrospect I felt it could have been an elemental, but I honestly don't know.'

We finished the interview and I left with the previous hour's conversation spinning in my head. Was it an elemental that Dave had seen? To be frank we will never know. Spiritualists and those interested in the paranormal argue that these forms are sometimes taken by spirits that were never human and therefore difficult to rationalize. In conclusion, Dave put forward his own theory that this experience could have been connected to his past occult practices, though again it is just conjecture. Despite ruminating on it, the answers remain elusive however I think you will agree that given the wide range of activity from poltergeist to residual those buildings could well rank as one of the most haunted in the city.

Peacocks Close

The next story, again from the Castlegate, concerns the spectre of a hanged man seen in nearby Peacocks Close which happened many years prior. The witness, a former colleague explained that the incident occurred one summer's evening while walking across the deserted Castlegate en route to the Beach Boulevard. For those familiar with the area there are still a few 'closes' remaining, one being Peacocks' lane. On passing something drew her attention and on glancing across was horrified to see the figure of a man dressed in old fashioned clothing hanging by the neck from a rope. She described the man's face as pale with a protruding tongue, the neck obviously broken. Stopping to stare for a few seconds, assuming it was a macabre prank, she noted that the rope hung from the ceiling at the entrance to the close. A second later his twisted expression elicited a yell and she bolted.

To conclude our interview, she explained: 'I was so shaken I ran to the phone box on Justice Street and phoned my dad, asking him to come and get me. I was almost certainly in shock and so he told me to wait there for him. When he arrived we went back to the scene of the incident which of course was as normal.' I am in no doubt that this sighting left an indelible mark on the witness and as we stood at the spot of the hanging, I noticed that there was nowhere for a rope to be attached, even if someone been intent on pulling a prank.

Bosies Charity Shop: Justice Street

Time for one last stop this time at the iconic Salvation Army Citadel on the corner of the Castlegate and Justice Street. Historically there has been shops at street level for many years which included the Salvation Army charity shop. What a place for a rake, dusty and a little decrepit, but the prices were low and the expectations high. Others may remember Castlegate Frames in its original location or The Oriental Emporium. In more recent times, Bosies, a breast cancer charity now calls it home and to a degree it has been gentrified. The shop operating from two premises sells both furniture and general charity shop goods, but its' below into the basement we head next to catch up on reports of a mischievous spirit. Why she is there remains a mystery, though by all accounts she appears to be playful. Debbie Hamilton takes up the story:

I was working in the basement of the furniture shop which is number 6-8 Justice Street. It would have been near Christmas time as I was raking in the far end of the basement looking for some lights. I distinctly remember it being very cold but becoming much colder instantly. I could then see my breath. I quickly found the lights and so headed towards the stairs. As I approached them, I caught the site of a figure walking across in front of me, which went through one of the walls. This was accompanied by a strong smell of tobacco and the odour of an old wet overcoat.' She continued: 'I often had to work in the basement as there was forever stock that need sorted and rotated. One time I was looking for men's T-shirts, this was in the basement of number 12-14 Justice Street. I remember piling up clothes and there was a huge mound of them. I turned my back from the rail after grabbing some more when suddenly I heard something rolling towards me. When I looked down there was a Christmas bauble rolling on the floor which began to bounce as it got nearer. I got a bit of a start but decided to roll it back. I am laughing now but I half-expected it to be rolled back, but it didn't. I left it where it had settled and headed back upstairs. Sometime later when I returned it had rolled to the other side of the room again. On another occasion, I was sorting through some clothes rails when I felt the back of my sweater getting tugged. I assumed I had caught it on something, perhaps the rail so tried to tug myself free. Again, I felt the tug but this time the strength had increased. I pulled back, but again it happened but this time it was insistent. I glanced backwards only to find nothing.' She laughed saying that afterwards, 'I legged it back up the stairs.'

Though nothing particularly unpleasant has happened, it can still be a little unnerving working in the basement with the thought of a mischievous spirit for company. I have been down there myself and it is crowded with stock, rails and boxes, making it difficult to get uninterrupted views in any direction. It has a claustrophobic atmosphere and not the kind of place you want to start imagining things in. Sightings indicate there is more than one spirit present, though one may have been identified, at least according to fundraiser Val Morrison. Described by her colleagues as being psychic, Val is convinced that the main culprit is a young girl called Abigail, who appears to like interacting with staff, whether they like it or not. She is small in stature, has ringlets in her hair and has been seen running and laughing in the basement area. According to staff, the sound of laughter is one of the most common phenomena reported. It is also assumed she has a connection to the building and so likes to visit on occasion. But is she alone? Not according to Debbie, who is convinced of what she saw. The male figure, only seen fleetingly appears to be more furtive, though causes no harm, and like all good ghosts doesn't need the use of a door.

Religious Figures

Some of the most fascinating stories I have heard have involved sightings of religious figures, who it would seem are quite prolific in Aberdeen. This comes as no surprise given the number of religious orders which were active in the city during the Middle Ages. Friars, unlike monks did not remain closeted from the world but rather followed their holy principles by preaching and helping the community. They lived humbly and practiced chastity and obedience relying on charitable support and donations to allow their work to continue. During this period, many wealthy citizens were more than happy to support them, perhaps hoping it would guarantee them a fast track to the promised land.

Identifiable by their coloured mantles or 'Cappas' orders included Trinitarians or red friars, who were based in what is now the Guild Street / Trinity Street area. The Carmelites or white friars operated in the same area and of course we now have Carmelite Street as a reminder. In the Schoolhill area of the city, behind Aberdeen Art Gallery there also resided the Dominicans or Black friars, nearby Blackfriars Street being a nod to its previous occupants. It goes without saying that the church played an important role during the Middle Ages, but we begin our journey not at the harbour, but in historic Kincorth.

The Kincorth housing estate at first look is much like any other, but it has a rich hidden past including its ownership by Arbroath Abbey and I am pleased to say is an area rife with paranormal activity. In the late 12th century King William, the Lion founded Arbroath Abbey and gifted it various pockets of land throughout the Northeast of Scotland. The Abbot of Arbroath was overseer of these lands and money raised by leasing areas to various parties went to the church. Many years before the current urban sprawl crops were grown in its rolling fields, tended by the monks who lived and worshipped in the area. Current street names reflect this, some of the most notable being, Abbotswell Crescent, Arbroath Place, and of course the 'Abbot', a local hostelry.

Unsurprisingly, tales of hooded figures have already found their way into the public consciousness, most notably through Peter Moss's book 'Ghosts Over Britain,' where he recounted the tale of a cloaked beckoning figure. This incident took place in 1970 when local resident Mrs Gladys Ewen was taking her usual route to work at Morningfield Hospital. It was a quarter to six on a cold winter's morning when she left her home to wait at the nearby bus stop and as she approached, was shocked to see a figure standing in a nearby patch of grass. The tall, cowled form beckoned towards her with an outstretched arm and hypnotized by the sight wandered towards it fixated by its looming presence. When she was around six yards from the figure it began to evaporate and dissolved into a mist which drifted off. The hypnotic spell now broken she took off towards her bus stop. On arriving at work colleagues were shocked to see her distress though whether anyone believed her is a matter of conjecture. After the initial shock she fell back into her usual routine and mercifully never saw the figure again, however similar figures have been seen in nearby Kincorth Circle, causing another local resident to flee in terror. The witness, a former community worker told me that one evening she had a memorable encounter, one that she has never forgotten.

She explained: 'I have had a few strange experiences during my life particularly around the Kincorth area which I would say have been of a supernatural origin. Some have also occurred in my place of work. But on this occasion, it took place in nearby Kincorth Circle. On the evening in question, I was walking along the street towards my home. I remember it being a very cold crisp night. It was dark although the lights illuminated certain parts of the road and you could clearly see your breath due to the cold. I was the only person about, and the streets seemed unusually quiet. As I passed a block of houses something moving caught my eye and I glanced in between them into the 'backie' area. I clearly saw a cloaked and hooded figure which appeared to have no feet. It was floating along in the space between the houses. I was startled and not knowing what it was I quickened my pace. When I came to the next break in the buildings the figure was there again keeping abreast with me. I began to run and again glancing towards the garden at the next break in the buildings I saw the figure moving faster and keeping up with me. I panicked and bolted as fast as I could. I did not bother to keep looking for the figure, and by the time I reached home my heart was thumping in my chest. I still maintain it was the figure of a monk and can never forget the fact it floated rather than walked.' The witness then shared some more of her experiences, but I will return to those later.

Once Aberdeen boasted over twenty picture houses. Today, I am sad to say we now have only three and with zero individuality, the majority show the same fare, their sole purpose it seems, to provide a venue for a good 'guzzle'. With only the Belmont or 'flechie' Belmon providing an alternative. It is sad to think that all these wonderful buildings have gone and like many Aberdonians I have great memories of proper cinemas. Speaking of cinemas, our next sighting took place in one, the ABC (Vue) to be precise. During my research, I was put in touch with a former projectionist at the cinema who prior to his retirement had a strange encounter with a monk-like figure. This occurred prior to the cinemas closure when the mood among staff was somewhat downbeat, and the custom was sporadic. Dave takes up the story:

'The building was quiet as a showing had finished and the audience had just left. If you remember the layout of the cinema, there was a corridor from which you could access all the screens. I was in the corridor, sitting in one of the chairs when I caught something out of the corner of my eye. I looked down the corridor and there was a shadowy figure that looked like he was wearing a kind of robe. He walked or glided briskly across the corridor and disappeared through the opposite wall. I did not have time to react as it happened so quickly. I would describe it as a monk-like figure due to what he was wearing. I had never seen a figure like this in all my time there, however there were always rumours about the building being haunted and people claimed to have seen or felt presences in the various corridors. It was a bit of a maze and at night when everything is quiet a cinema has a peculiar feel to it. Perhaps it was imagination on other peoples' part, but I know what I saw on that occasion. It was also alleged that someone was killed in the cinema during its construction but again I have no proof and it would not explain the strange attire.'

Moving down the Shiprow from the old ABC you soon find yourself in the Green, a historic market area once home to both Trinitarian and Carmelite Friars whose remains have on occasion been uncovered. It goes without saying that spectres have been seen in the vicinity who are described as having the general appearance of men of the cloth. One such story was covered in Norman Adams' great read 'The Haunted Neuk' and involved a sighting that took place in 'Shirlaws,' a motorcycle shop. In one memorable incident a member of staff was taken by surprise at the appearance of a friar, standing at the counter as if waiting service. The shop assistant busy stacking under the counter, was taken aback to see the figure as he regained his feet after assuming a customer had just walked in. On another occasion it was noted that an array of very heavy bike tyres, were suddenly 'flung' from a shelf by an unseen force. I spoke briefly to the owner of 'R n' B Music,' who now owns the premises. He confirmed that stories had circulated about the building for years but had no personal experiences other than the time he thought he saw a figure out of the corner of his eye.

Moving on we arrive at Nelson Street, situated in the city's east end. A nondescript street once home to the Oldmachar poorhouse. Spookily it sits near the site of a medieval leper hospital and though the site of the hospital is in the nearby 'Spital' there have been sightings of figures dressed in the attire of monks nearby. Going back to the 1970s and 1980s much of the larger tenements you see today were used as student housing and by then were dilapidated. I personally knew many people who resided there at the time, and some had tales to tell. Elaine was one such person who had flatmates, but at the time of the incident was alone. The main room was typical of the period and contained an old range and scullery as they were known. Opposite there was an alcove which housed her bed but again this was nothing unusual for properties of this age. She recollected that one bright morning when straightening out her duvet, she felt a sudden and powerful chill run down her spine. Glancing up towards the wall of the alcove she noticed her shadow was clearly defined by the bright sunlight streaming in behind however she was shocked to see a second shadow, she assumed of a man, standing motionless behind her. She stood stock still fighting the urge to turn round until the second figure vanished. The obvious conclusion would have been that the second shadow had been cast by someone at the window looking in but as she lived on the second storey this was quickly discounted.

Another student told me of a similar incident in which he woke to see a dark shrouded figure standing in his room and when he let out a startled yelp the figure vanished. In the same block but one floor up another resident was surprised to see an old statuette he kept on a nearby table begin to glow a luminous green. When questioned he claimed that at the time, he was wide awake and lay watching the strange phosphorescent glow, his reverie interrupted when it began to vibrate before toppling over.

A short walk from Nelson Street brings us to the Gallowgate and though not exactly a ghost story the following is certainly ghostly and worthy of inclusion. The following incident was told to me by the late Stanley Robertson when I interviewed him some years back. It concerns a recurring nightmare he had, which involved a priest committing murder which still makes me shudder. Stanley was a gifted psychic and was able to sense things that others couldn't which at times could be unpleasant. He relates the following which he describes as a dream but could potentially be a vision.

'There used to be an old church, which I called the Jacobean Church, it was a strange building. When I passed the archway leading to it, I always got a cold shiver going down my back. I began reading about it because I always used to have dreams about it. When you are tuned into things you will dream about them. In this dream I would always go inside, into this old oak church and would always see an Irish lassie there. She was only about sixteen and she lived there for some reason. I would see her being murdered by this young minister that was there. He was tall very slim and wore a long black outfit. I saw him in my visions clearly and he would always murder this lassie. I even saw the spot where she was murdered. Later in my dream folk ripped the ground open and found her remains deep down in the foundations. I used to mention this to folk and one time mentioned it to the minister at St. Nicholas. He said to me it was a most evil place and it was a gateway to hell. The church is now demolished, and I remember at the time wondering if they would discover a body when it came down. I never heard if they did.'

Given that 'the church' played such a prominent role in society up until recently, it is not surprising that so many religious figures of different denominations have been seen. Many of these appear to be ghosts or residual impressions who have no awareness of our presence and as such do not interact. Their appearances are fleeting and are therefore impossible to delve into further but there are the odd exceptions which the following demonstrates.

This story was told to me recently by Eileen Clark who I met at a local history group. The incident involved a visitation that was not alarming but rather life changing and provided the recipient with solid evidence of the continuing of life after death. The witness to this event was Eileen's grandmother and took place many years in the early 1900's at 64 Constitution Street Aberdeen. What is most fascinating about the following is it involved the spirit of one of Aberdeen's most respected historical figures that of Priest Gordon.

Charles Gordon was born in 1772 the youngest of nine children, he studied for the priesthood in France but was forced to leave due to the outbreak of the revolution returning to Aberdeen. He continued his studies until 1795 when he was ordained into the priesthood. By all accounts acts of kindness came naturally to him, a fact that did not go unnoticed among the people of the city. He was described, as being down to earth and seemed to possess a missionary zeal in his work in the most positive sense. This was exemplified by his work with the city's poor, the level of which was daunting. There were no social services in place to help the hungry and it was only the tireless work of people like Charles Gordon that could mean the difference between life and death for the most vulnerable. His ecclesiastical duties were varied and included working in the Loch Street soup kitchen, building orphanages for destitute children and performing many other charitable acts.

In later life an ambition long harboured by Charles Gordon came to fruition with the founding of St. Peters Roman Catholic school in Constitution Street. The school had two wings added to it and acted as orphanages for the children of his congregation, providing much needed security. It was in the building adjacent to the school that he spent his remaining years until his passing on the 24th of November 1855. At the time of his death the public outpourings of grief were unprecedented with thousands lining the street to pay tribute including the Lord Provost and many other dignitaries. It should also be noted that as a measure of his popularity his passing brought together many different denominations to mourn. The Aberdeen Journal of the time wrote, 'He took particular interest in the young and in educating and providing for them supplying to many the place of a parent.' On his passing the funeral procession went along King Street with his congregation taking turns to bear the coffin, to his final resting place in the Snow Kirk, Old Aberdeen. After the school relocated to Nelson Street the building was used for housing, became home to the Polish club and the 'Shiprow Tavern', providing food for homeless men which no doubt Charles Gordon would have approved of. Eileen takes up the story:

'Grandmother woke up and was immediately aware of the smell of pipe tobacco being smoked, she sat up in her box bed and saw a figure sitting in an armchair at the fireside, smoking a pipe, the time of the occurrence was the middle of the night. She was a little shocked at what she saw though it convinced her that there was life after death. It was not a subject she talked about very much. The figure she described was very distinct, had a slightly less than solid state, smoky but not see through and was dressed in his priests' robes. He was sitting in an armchair smoking a pipe. He did not speak or acknowledge my grandmother. He remained visible for a sufficient length of time, for my grandmother to become aware the figure was indeed, that of Father Gordon. My grandmother was a schoolteacher and was never anything other than a very down to earth person. She was a Catholic and the subject of ghosts and paranormal activities would have been very much of a taboo subject hence her reluctance to relate her story to other than a few. I believed her implicitly as she was never given to flights of the imagination.'

I was impressed with this story, given that it was told to Eileen many years ago by her grandmother when she was in her youth it still seemed fresh. Of course, I did a little background checking to clarify a few points and found 64 Constitution Street was Charles Gordons home in later life.

Next on our tour is Aberdeen Art Gallery on Schoolhill, which having recently undergone a major redevelopment, houses an excellent collection, worthy of repeated visits. Located next to Blackfriars Street, recent work uncovered skeletal remains whose unquiet spirits may well haunt the area. To back this claim, I can offer up the following and knowing both protagonists well, I can vouch for their integrity. Like many buildings in the city, that are rumoured to be haunted, ghostly appearances can be inconsistent. They follow no set pattern, and the phenomena can be sporadic, sometimes years going by between incidents. The same could be said of the Art Gallery, where apart from rumours there have been a few genuine incidents. But is it permanently haunted? The question remains open to debate. The following though random and unlikely to be repeated, is still satisfyingly spooky and involves our old friends, the Blackfriars. The event unfolded when former exhibitions officer, John Jardine, took it upon himself to prank, colleague Dorothy. Taking along an instant camera, he called her name and on turning she was snapped for posterity. She jokingly admonished him as they waited for the picture to develop but the hilarity stopped as a strange figure appeared on the image. When developed they were both shocked to see the image of a monk standing directly behind Dorothy. Blackfriars Street of course has undergone drastic changes over the years, and there are historic sightings linked to the street, which again mention monks.

Moving further afield, I was given quite recently two very brief accounts, one near the river Don at St Machar's Cathedral, the other at Stewart Park. At the former, the witness, then a child described how he and his brother were shocked to see a figure in a cowl floating above the ground as they were out walking their dog. The lower half of its body was described as having a 'smoke-like' appearance. They stood watching from a distance and it remained unaware of the children's presence, then after some seconds it faded away. The latter, again involving the sighting of a monk, took place at the entrance to Stewart Park in the Smithfield area of the city. The witness, a teenage girl, was heading home along the edge of the park, when she was stopped in her tracks by the sight of a figure wearing dark hood and robes. To her terror it began to move towards her at which point she ran. Her mother described to me that she was obviously very scared when she got home, which is understandable.

To finish off, the following took place over a prolonged period, six years to be precise and according to the witness still gives her nightmares today. The location was St. Clements' Street near 'Fittie,' the flat situated above the tiny St. Clements' bar. The year was 1993 and young mum, Leanne and baby daughter Lois were the tenants. According to

Leanne, the first sign that something was afoot was when baby Lois began laughing and waving at something unseen, in the room. Soon after objects began to move on their own accord, lights would flick on and off and the volume on both the radio and T.V would increase and decrease. This was accompanied by inexplicable temperature drops which convinced Leanne, they had an extra guest. Her daughter now slightly older then began to describe what she was seeing, stating that both a good man and a bad man were present. Terrifying as it was, it was also puzzling as the 'good man' apparently wore a brown dress. Some-time later a fortuitous meeting with a local historian provided a clue when he confirmed that a much older burial ground lay below nearby St. Clements churchyard and that monks had resided in the area. I assumed that Leanne had not found this news reassuring. She then went on to say that soon after, her daughter began admonishing her for trying to sit on a seat, when there was already someone sitting on it already. This was more than unsettling. Children of course are very sensitive and open to seeing spirit and there have been many documented cases, some of which we will look at later. Because of the situation, Leanne then approached a psychic, and this is what she was told.

'The good man, according to a psychic I knew, was there to protect the area, a janitor if you like who was looking after us. When the bad man appeared Lois, who could obviously see him would cling to my legs, though she said the good man would appear straight after. As she got older, she was able to take me to a grave in the churchyard which she described as being 'Johns' house.' Who John was, or whether he was the good or bad man I cannot say. We had so many incidents happen that it is hard to remember them all, though not all were negative. For example, one time a fire broke out and I felt we were alerted to it by something. On another occasion we had been in the process of being burgled when they left suddenly. Afterwards the police said to me that they thought something must have scared them off as they had left empty-handed, though what it was, I cannot say. It was an absolutely terrifying place.'

Leanne went on to explain that the haunting was not just confined to her flat as the pub below also had its share of phenomena. Co-incidentally she worked there behind the bar and like many regulars witnessed glasses moving along the bar by themselves and objects being thrown, while back at home her daughters invisible 'friends,' were continually around. It must have been exhausting. Leanne concluded that their guardian was most likely a monk, but who the other was remains unanswered. I suspect though she was grateful for the kindly intervention, despite having to 'sleep with the bedroom light on for six years.'

SCHOOLS OUT

Kaimhill Primary School

An unusual series of events were brought to my attention concerning the relatively modern building that is Kaimhill Primary School. The school, originally a secondary was built in 1951 and used as such until 1971 before becoming a primary school. Sightings of a figure have been reported in recent years however there is little to suggest what has caused this manifestation.

In the vicinity sits the Kaimhill crematorium where the 'Coffin Lids Case' of 1944 took place. Briefly the managing director James Dewar and undertaker Alick George Forbes concocted a scheme well ahead of its time when they undertook a programme of recycling. However, what they were recycling was coffin lids which were removed prior to cremation and turned into an array of household goods by various employees. This was enough to cause public upset but the discovery of unrelated bodies being cremated together, and the possible removal of personal effects sent the local population into a frenzy. The subsequent trial took place at the High Court in Edinburgh where James Dewar was found guilty of the theft of one thousand and forty-four coffin lids and sentenced to three years imprisonment while Forbes was charged with the reset of one hundred lids and sentenced to six months. This may have no bearing on the sightings at

Kaimhill Primary School, however the figure described appears to bear an uncanny resemblance to a mourner.

Jean Horne who worked as a cleaner at the school provided the following account which was experienced first-hand in April approximately fourteen years ago: 'I was cleaning the stairs at the far end of the building beside classrooms six and seven when I felt as if I was being watched. I looked up to the top landing and saw this black veiled face looking down, it immediately drew back behind a wooden board. It was a chilling experience, and I left the area immediately.'

Some days later she approached her supervisor and another colleague who mainly cleaned the top floor of the building and recounted her tale. To her surprise the supervisor turned out to also have had the exact same experience under identical circumstances. Her colleague then went on to describe the presence she felt in room seven and how she did not like cleaning there alone. It was only then she became aware of the similarity of the sightings, always described as being that of a head covered in a black veil, seen at the corner of the stair. It soon became apparent that nobody wanted to work in those rooms and so frequently they cleaned in pairs.

Soon after the activity stepped up a notch, when late one afternoon the supervisor became aware of footsteps coming up behind her. Thinking it was a co-worker she turned to speak only to find the corridor empty and on seeing no one left the area. Known as the 'red corridor,' no prizes for guessing why, it was by all accounts one of the most haunted in the building.

Jean continued to clean at the school for some years and the last time we spoke had not seen the figure for eight or nine months though was still wary of its presence. Out of interest she contacted a previous supervisor at the school who spoke about stories of a grey lady though she could not elaborate on this. Another cleaner who wished to remain anonymous reported similar feelings including extreme temperature drops in the corridor and an eerie feeling while in the gym hall. During my research I discovered some old maps that clearly show a building called Kaimhill Farm on the site of the current school. The building was in existence on a 1909 map and in others up until the 1950s when it appears to have been demolished to make way for school. Since the time of writing the old Kaimhill school has now been demolished and a new school stands in its place. I worked in both buildings over the years and in the latter for some considerable time and sensed nothing there. I suspect whoever it was moved on with the old structure.

Beechwood School

Beechwood School was known to generations of Aberdonians as a school for children with special learning needs. Situated near the top of Midstocket Road, it stood for over 50 years before its recent demolition. Subsequently a new school has been built on the site which now houses both Mile End and Beechwood pupils and is known as the new Mile End.

I visited Beechwood school on its very last day and was given permission to photograph the interior of the building prior to demolition. The trip was made to take a photographic record of its interior rather than to investigate anything paranormal. Not long after however I met Lynn who had cleaned there for many years and what she told me cast a new light on the building. This is what she said:

'I used to start my shift very early in the morning, before 6am. There were always a few of us in the building, however as it was a large space, we basically worked alone for part of the time. I was working with another cleaner, again early in the morning when we heard this strange crying sound. Initially we thought it was a cat that had been locked in and so we went looking for it. After searching the building thoroughly and finding nothing we looked outside but again we saw nothing. When we went back inside, we heard it again and the more we listened the more it sounded like a baby, or a very small child crying. We walked along the corridor following the direction of the noise which now seemed to be coming from upstairs and as we went towards the sound it became noticeably louder before it suddenly stopped. I can only describe the sound as heart-breaking but despite investigating thoroughly we found nothing. We were now a little concerned but put it behind us and carried on working. Suffice to say this wasn't the last time it was heard and on mentioning it to others it appeared that they had also heard it. We hated working in the upstairs part of the building. We began to talk, particularly to those who had worked there longest, and we were shocked to be told that these sounds were commonplace although usually heard during the autumn months. It was alleged that this recurring noise happened because a baby or small child had died there at some point. I can't say if this was true or not, but it was most definitely the sound of a child crying and was disturbing to hear. I am sure there was meant to be an older building here at one point and whether the alleged death was connected to this, I don't know.'

A second meeting was arranged, where she pointed out that herself and her colleagues had experienced many incidents across the city over the years, but Beechwood was the most potent. She told me the following. 'This incident again occurred in the top corridor which as I have mentioned, was an area unpopular with staff. I was walking along towards the end about to start working when my ear was flicked. It felt quite hard although initially I thought it was a fly or some other insect. I stopped and touched my ear before suddenly being prodded on my shoulder. I froze to the spot and must admit I was scared. The prodding happened again but this time harder. I willed myself to look round which I did very slowly though there was nothing there. I left the area very quickly to try and find someone.'

She went on to explain that despite incidents like these occurring from time to time you couldn't let it affect your state of mind, otherwise you would not be able to do your duties. It was also of some comfort to her that she was not the sole recipient as others appeared to get their fair share of the activity which became a talking point at work.

Despite unexpected 'clatters' and feelings of being watched the corridor was the spot where most activity occurred, though there were also other areas to avoid. One such place was the storage rooms, noted for having an unusual atmosphere. Lynn expanded on this: 'Below the storage rooms lay the swimming pool. I was told that there had been a fire there at some point and as it was unusable and so the school board decided to cover it over and use the space as storage. This was another area we hated working in due to the strange noises that were heard there. It was a strange, watery 'glooping' sound. You got the impression there was still water there as it sounded like movement in a large body of water. As far as an explanation for this goes, I was told that a child some time back had drowned there, but again I cannot verify this. All I know is that we did not imagine these sounds and it gave us the shivers.'

I was told in conclusion that the figure of an elderly lady had also been seen. She was described as wearing antiquated clothes and was seen walking through walls perhaps where a door had existed in the past. She was never described as interacting or even noticing any of the witnesses who were often shocked by her sudden if infrequent appearances. Lynn, again being one of the main witnesses gave me this statement.

'The old lady incident as I shall call it happened between six and seven in the morning. There was one other witness with me, but I lost contact with her a long time ago. However afterwards I was glad to find out that some other cleaners had also described seeing this lady. The old lady was quite rounded and walked very slowly. She wore a big grey shawl round her shoulders, and a long skirt which went almost down to her feet. The skirt wasn't very clean looking. I would describe her as being from around the 19th century by what she was wearing. She never noticed us on the occasion we both saw her. She just walked across the room and disappeared through the wall. The hair on the back of my neck stood on end when I saw her. I was spooked.'

Built near the site of the demolished Raeden House, could this figure have been a former resident still wandering the area? Raeden of course, has now changed beyond recognition and the ghost it would seem disliking modernity has made no further appearances to my knowledge.

Hazlehead Academy

Situated on the outskirts of the city this school is allegedly home to a spirit which appears to enjoy treading the boards. I first came upon the story when I was undertaking research at the Gordon Highlanders Museum. I got chatting to one of the volunteers, a teacher from Hazlehead Academy who proceeded to tell me about his colleague in the drama department and who believed the drama department was haunted. He suggested I give him a phone if I was interested in finding out more, and I did not hesitate.

Chris, head of the drama department is rightly proud of being involved with the school's youth theatre which was formed in the 1980s making it the longest running in the city. It also appears to have become something of a magnet for the unwanted attention of a spirit mainly active during production time. According to most accounts it seems anxious to let itself be known especially when there are other children about, which in due course will make sense. Staff, during rehearsals would note feelings of depression within the vicinity of the stage, prop and staff room with the atmosphere described as charged. Small incidents began to occur, unexplained cold spots appeared. It was enough to get staff talking and people mentioned feeling nervous, especially when it was quiet. Loud knocks were frequently heard on the thin plasterboard walls partitioning the rooms, and when investigated no cause could be found. Things then took a more dramatic turn when during coffee break, witnesses saw a spoon 'jump' out of an empty cup, a sight which prompted one teacher to start taking her break in another part of the building. The curtains weighted with chains to stop movement during a performance began to rattle loudly of their own accord, normally too heavy to do so on their own. With all this in mind I arrived with high expectations.

After the introductions we were given a tour of the prop area which we were told was the most active. As if on cue I was instantly aware of someone with us, and my colleague remarked how cold and shivery he felt. As Chris continued to show us around, the feeling remained as if someone was close by listening. It lasted until we walked onto the stage area when the temperature became as before. Once in the scenery room we were told that pupils had on occasion complained of being touched by something during rehearsal times. It was also noted that ironically during a production of 'The Little Shop of Horrors' a female pupil was changing costume in the privacy booth when 'a small freezing cold child's hand came over her shoulder.' She described the hand as appearing to be stretching. As she was putting on her 'beehive wig,' the mirror afforded a clear view of the disembodied hand. Surprisingly, she did not feel overly frightened by the incident. Later, during a production of 'The Crucible,' the image of what was described as the face of a screaming woman appeared amongst the scumbled paint of the backdrop. The teacher, on having his attention drawn to this by a concerned pupil noticed that in the vicinity of the face the air was icy cold, so much so that he stated that his throat was sore, like being outside on a raw winter's day. He immediately went and got a colleague, who also witnessed the phenomena which remains unexplained.

In 2005 perhaps the most baffling event occurred during the production of 'Blood Brothers' when an analogue camera (CCTV for the stage) showed a small boy leaning against a pillar with arms folded, watching the rehearsals. Picked up on the monitor and witnessed by eight different people including the stage manager. John (described as ex- army and not prone to flights of fancy) could offer no reasonable explanation. The boy in question was seen clearly and described as 'wearing a 1960s Paisley top and shorts and appeared completely solid. the strangest aspect of it however was he could only be seen through the monitor for when staff looked directly at the stage, he was invisible to the naked eye. The event was described as disturbing for the witnesses. I left soon after with the intention of returning.

And so, in early 2007 I felt the time was right to pay another visit and was rewarded by meeting two new staff members who by their own admission had been sceptical at first but soon changed their point of view after Chris suggested a little icebreaker. He told me that soon after their arrival, as a bit of fun, they were invited to go into the prop room and ask the ghost to turn on the lights. Everyone agreed to do this and once inside he jokingly called out for any spirit to let themselves be known. Getting no response, they were on the point of leaving when suddenly three bright balls of light appeared from nowhere which then shot past them. They were noted as disappearing through the outer wall, leaving behind a residual blue light which for a few seconds caused the contents of the room to glow. The bewildered staff then left hurriedly. On arriving the next day, Chris was shocked to find saws, normally hung on the studio wall, had been intricately placed in a slot on the workbench. He stated that there was no way they could have fallen on their own and land so neatly into the slot, they would have had to have been placed. I was very grateful for the courtesy shown to me during my visits and was convinced that there was something unexplainable going on. The volume of evidence was too great to think otherwise. I spent many days poring over old press cuttings in my attempt to solve the mystery but nothing of substance was found until a chance conversation changed everything.

During break, a colleague began chatting about her childhood and went on to talk about her school. It had been Hazlehead Academy, which she had attended in the late 1960s. I mentioned my recent visits and though intrigued could not provide any further information. She did however tell me, that a young boy she had known, tragically lost his life in a farm accident. Apparently very close to where the school now stands.

Victoria Road School

There is something about schools particularly old Victorian schools that are a breeding ground for urban myths and tall tales of spooks. Despite the many tall tales that abound there are some buildings which can be legitimately described as haunted. One such location is Victoria Road School. It closed in 2008 despite a campaign to save it and today lies empty its future open to speculation.

Victoria Road School was essentially a school of two halves, the first part being built in 1878 after the Fisherman's Association of old Torry voted to pay £1400 towards the costs. And so, on May 2nd the Torry Public School as it was once known opened. The first headmaster, Mr. William Yunnie, had according to records the unenviable task of teaching 100 pupils in the main room. As the population increased accordingly, so did the need for space and by 1904 the renamed Victoria Road School opened with the original part of the building now delegated as a base for teaching children of nursery age a tradition which continued until its closure. Once closed many former staff members and pupils have come forward to relate sightings of a lady in Victorian dress who they named 'Lizzie,' thought to be a former headmistress.

It must be said, that during my research, I have reached the conclusion that cleaners are probably best placed to have a paranormal encounter. Whether you might consider that a perk, of course depends on your point of view though most I have spoken to think not. First in and last out, they have much to contend with, including bumping into things, quite literally, that should no longer be there. Victoria Road School is no different in that respect as you will hear.

I first became aware of the rumours concerning the school while in conversation with my wife. Having spent many years working there she had heard stories concerning the building particularly near the central gym hall. Carol mentioned on one occasion she was in the old nurses' room moving boxes when she had an overpowering feeling that someone was standing behind her. So tangible was the feeling that she left the area promptly. She found the experience unnerving and her colleagues began to tell similar tales. Strange noises, footsteps, disembodied voices and an actual full-bodied apparition was described and so I contacted those willing to talk for the record. My first interview was conducted with Maureen a former administrator who furnished me with the following.

She stated, 'as a former pupil of the school I cannot remember any mention at that time of a ghost while I was there so I cannot believe that what happened three years ago was in any way influenced by my childhood memories. As the school administrator I was spending the first week of the summer holidays working in the office. I had of course heard from other staff members of their experiences in the building but can honestly say that I took it all as nonsense, being quite a sceptical person myself. That day I was entirely alone in the building but was in no way bothered as I had worked alone in the holidays for many years. I was packing up and getting ready to go for the day. I picked up my handbag and had just started to put my jacket on when I had the most uneasy feeling. I saw nothing and heard nothing but had the most overwhelming sensation that there was a presence outside the large office window. I got out of the building as quickly as possible and felt extremely uneasy for a few days after.'

When I asked if she had heard of any similar occurrences, she stated that the school cleaners had always claimed to be aware of something, but this had always occurred in the old school. This, as I have mentioned was in the original Torry Public school before it was renamed and extended. Not long after I was given an account by a long serving school cleaner who told me the following.

'The first time I felt anything was at the bottom of the school, the old part. It was an intense cold feeling that went away as quickly as it arrived. This happened several times. I just got used to it until one day while cleaning the gym my "hoover" was switched off at the wall. I immediately thought it was one of my colleagues trying to get my attention but on turning round to speak was shocked to see a woman who was dressed in what I thought was early 1900s clothing. She looked very real, so much so I began to speak to her, but she just went on through the gym door going towards the bottom part of the school. She literally vanished before my eyes. After that I began to hear footsteps quite regularly usually around 5.30 in the morning. Although I sometimes felt apprehensive, I just carried on as normal. One day when I was buffing the back corridor at around 6.30 in the morning the buffer went, what I can only describe as funny, turning by itself and pinning me against the wall. At the same time the temperature went very cold. I got it shifted and then I shouted out to whoever was doing this, to stop it! It was very alarming. At other times, doors would open and close. That didn't bother me though, as you got used to it. Another strange thing is that you would also hear a lot of footsteps coming from certain areas as though children were walking through the corridors.'

When I asked if she had any other experiences she would like to share, she described an incident that happened during the 'big clean' at the end of the school term. 'I was late one year with the big clean and had to go back to the school gym area again to put on polish. I took two of my dogs with me. I got as far as the top area which leads to the gym when they both stopped and started to pull back and shake. One darted up to the top of the stairs while the other just lay down frozen to the spot and shook. I had to just get on with the polishing and leave them there till I had finished. It was very cold at that point and my dogs would not come back into the school. I would often feel someone was watching me and used to say 'hello Lizzie' when it got cold however, I did not feel threatened apart from that time with the buffer. A funny thing also happened in the main corridor about a week before the school closed. The grandfather clock started to tick quite loudly but as you got nearer, it stopped. Also, in the last week there were more noises than usual heard all over the school, footsteps, doors banging, and certain areas seemed to be abnormally cold. Those cold spots seemed to appear all over the school and were very random. It was worse at the bottom end where the head teacher would have stayed. This used to be the old medical room.'

I concluded the interview by asking if she remembered anything else pertaining to her experience. She described the lady as looking like a teacher and stood approximately five foot three to five foot five inches in height. She was very slim and had black hair all tied up on the top of her head and wore lace up boots and a long skirt to her ankles. She also had on a white shirt and long black cardigan coat and seemed to be carrying something in her hands which she could not make out.

My luck continued as not long after I had a chance meeting with Mary who as a former worker at the school had been tasked with locking up the building. She told me the following which occurred at the end of her shift.

'Everyone knew about 'Lizzie' and she was seen several times over the years. This never happened in the newer part of the school but always in the original part. As you know there is a long flight of stairs that connects the two buildings and staff would always notice a difference in atmosphere and temperature between the two. I remember my friend having her "hoover" switched off at the wall while cleaning and after switching it back on turned round only to see a figure of a woman in old fashioned clothes standing behind her. The building had cold spots which would sometimes follow staff around which indicated when something was going to occur. The main thing that happened to me, was seeing the figure of a man in the building, which gave me quite a start. When it happened, I was about to switch the lights off at the top of the stairs and noticed a figure standing at the bottom. Thinking it was the janitor, I shouted down and asked what he was doing. The figure never moved and so I shouted again and started to walk towards it. I got part way down the stairs when I noticed it wasn't the janitor at all. The figure instead, was that of a small skinny man wearing a flat cap. As I approached him, he just vanished before my eyes. I was scared and I turned and ran from the building. The first thing I did when I got outside was to phone the supervisor who took the whole thing in her stride. The thing I remember most afterwards was that I was perplexed as to who he was, as most of the stories I had heard connected to the building, seemed to relate to a female figure. I still wonder who he was. The funny thing is that we all knew about the sightings of 'lizzie' but were told not to speak to the kids about her even though many parents asked questions. Apparently, they did not want the kids finding out too much as they did not want to scare them. Now that the buildings are closed, I have often wondered if she's still in there. I would have loved it if we could have gotten a medium in to help solve the mystery, but I would imagine that would never have been allowed. The building had an atmosphere, and we knew who was responsible for this though I might add there was never a bad feeling.'

So, for now Victoria Road School lies sadly empty and although I visited it frequently in the past its secrets now lie dormant. Despite this, my aim is to continue to gather evidence about this building as I have been told there are many other people out there who have experienced similar sightings. But who was 'Lizzie'? Interestingly, one of Aberdeen's old Post Office Directories from early last century contains an entry stating that the person residing in Torry Public School was Miss Elizabeth Nisbet, occupation Headmistress.

North Silver Street

Set back from Golden Square, North Silver Street is now a congested road, and with its resultant parking issues far busier than in 1980 when this story took place. The former house still stands near Ruby Place though according to former occupant Mark, it is likely more salubrious now than when he lived there. The flat at the time, described as being cramped, contained five tenants plus other assorted guests. The house itself had been a fashionable abode at one time and had been the home to a succession of relatively wealthy Aberdonians but was now considered cheap student housing.

As Mark pointed out during our interview that as students, their flat was something of an open house which at first was fun but soon began to get on the nerves of some of the residents trying to hold down jobs to supplement their meagre grants. Given that their neighbours were also 'studying' the constant movement of those staying up late to burn the midnight oil began to manifest itself in arguments. The peculiar layout of the flat also played a part in the increasingly volatile situation and because certain rooms could only be accessed through others, privacy became a distant memory. To this day Mark questions whether the constant stream of visitors also added to the strange vibe of the place.

The first indication that something was amiss was when Mark was accused of standing at the foot of the bed of one of the female students early one morning grinning at her, an accusation he flatly denied. The fact that he had not been in the building at the time, later confirmed by his girlfriend did nothing to persuade their flat mate, who remained adamant that he had been present in her room and began to look on him with suspicion. This further soured the already strained relationships within the group and after confiding in his girlfriend they decided that the flat mate was either delusional or had dreamt it and so they tried their best to put it behind them.

It was not long after that something more sinister occurred when Mark and Susan, on arriving home from visiting a friend were pulled aside by another tenant. He seemed agitated and stated that on passing their room he noticed that the door was ajar and from within the blackness had heard a soft chuckling and mumbling. It was with some trepidation that they entered room that evening which was jokingly referred to as the tomb. The tomb derived its name from the fact that it did not contain any windows and without natural light was constantly in utter darkness when not in use. After receiving this information, the couple became increasingly paranoid about spending any time there especially when alone.

Mark admitted that the flatmates soon became too scared to visit the bathroom at night unless accompanied as it involved a torturous journey up the communal stairway where in the semi-darkness imaginations ran wild. To add to the tension cold spots now began to be reported appearing randomly throughout the building and again the sound of laughter could be heard from the tomb.

Due to the lack of finances a move was out of the question, so the group decided to wait till the lease expired and tried to make the best of an unfavourable situation. This included upgrading rooms when given the chance. One such opportunity arose one weekend when as sole occupants they decided to bed down in the living room. Given that this was the cosiest room in the house they gladly dragged their mattress through and sat up watching television. The evening passed uneventfully and in the early hours they decided to call it a night.

When interviewed, Mark did not recall when he first became aware of Susan murmuring in her sleep, but he was immediately awakened. He described lying awake in the gloom listening as the murmuring soon became words which then became a frantic babble. Mark by now fully alert propped himself up as Susan tossed and turned next to him before waking in fright. Their attention was now drawn to the further end of the room, transfixed by the sight of a grey mist which floated in the corner of the room. They clung to each other in fright as the mist continued to move though it never formed a discernible shape. The experience lasted around 30 seconds before it slowly evaporated and with that they dove for the light switch. It was only then that she became aware of sudden pain along her back and on examination, red welts were noticeable. To add further horror, she described to her terrified boyfriend that she had a terrible dream in which a monkey sat on her shoulders hampering her breathing and scratching her. The couple did not sleep for the rest of the night. I was told that thankfully the incident was never repeated but they never used the living room again. Not long after the first of their flat mates announced their departure which prompted the others to follow suit. The house has since been upgraded and sold on to private owners. On passing today, one can only wonder what caused the manifestation to take place.

First Bus King Street

The King Street bus depot has undergone numerous changes in its long history from army barracks to tram depot and in more recent times headquarters for the First Bus group. Through all this time, the spectre metaphorically speaking, of a certain 'Captain Beaton' has loomed large. His earliest alleged appearances, recorded back in the 1920s, continue to this day. But did he ever exist? Or have people attached a random name to this unquiet spirit? The answer remains elusive, but first a little history. The King Street Militia Barracks as it was known was built in 1861 housing the Royal Aberdeenshire Highlanders later to become the 3rd Battalion Gordon Highlanders. Prior to the start of World War One Aberdeen Town Council purchased the site for the development of a tram repair shop but with the outbreak of the war those plans were put on hold. The barracks then reverted to military use becoming home to the Gordon Highlanders and remained in their hands until the end of the war. A massive housing shortage then forced the council to convert the King Street building and those adjacent into temporary housing. These abodes, many consisting of single rooms became home to returning soldiers and their families and continued to be occupied until 1932 when the residents were re-homed. This allowed the barracks to become the repair shop for trams and buses for which it was intended and thus it has remained so for many years.

The story of Captain Beaton is unusual in that there are substantial amounts of hearsay concerning his exploits available in the public domain, yet the lack of hard facts, are glaringly obvious. Despite this, the sheer volume of sightings is astonishing, and his name was most definitely on the lips of the first tenants back in the 1920s. So how did it all start? And what evidence do we really have to attest to his existence? In truth we have practically nothing apart from persistent eyewitness accounts that have spanned almost ninety years. So, can they all be imagining it? The answer I believe, is no!

The story which has often been repeated is that during the Great War a Captain with the 3rd Battalion Gordon Highlanders received head injuries in France, 1915. He was then described as being treated in France at one of the many Red Cross stations before being sent back to Britain to aid recuperation. Hospitals at the time were unable to cope with the vast numbers of injured men and therefore other buildings were utilised turning them into temporary hospitals. Aberdeen like many other cities, utilised temporary hospitals, and it was to the music rooms at The High School for Girls (Harlaw Academy) that he allegedly returned.

I have read varying accounts of what happened next. Some state that he was sent to the military hospital at the King Street Barracks to recuperate, circumventing the High School for Girls completely. Others provide a conflicting account, suggest the opposite. Which is accurate, remains unclear. Incidentally, the military hospital at the King Street Barracks still stood until quite recently but has since been demolished.

A hugely atmospheric building, it had its fair share of ghostly goings-on through the years but has now been replaced by more functional structures.

According to written accounts, Captain Beaton's name then crops up in 1918 when it was said he was due to be posted back to France. Apparently not able to face the prospect, the unfortunate Captain then took his own life by hanging himself in the south turret, once part of the officers' mess. The body on being discovered the next morning was then cut down. But what happened to it has never been disclosed. It is common knowledge that suicide was considered a 'crime' during this period and frowned upon by both the church and society. The very fact they could not comprehend why someone should commit this act is a measure of their lack of empathy. Sadly, this was illustrated by the fate of many returning soldiers during this period, when the number of suicides rose dramatically. Perhaps then it is due to the nature of his passing that no one had been able to find out the exact details of the case?

Soon after, the Barracks were decommissioned, and it was around this period that the rumours began to circulate about the shadowy figure of a soldier in uniform being seen in and around the building. Almost eighty years later two former residents of the Barracks, Mrs May Cooper and Mrs Helen Leiper recalled their experiences, in both the 'Leopard Magazine' and the 'This Is North Scotland' forum respectively and this is where we begin. Both witnesses, then young children, grew up hearing rumours of a ghost and painted a vivid picture of life at the time. Strange noises and cold spots were commonplace however what happened next was not.

Mrs. Leiper explained, that during a visit from friends, she got bored so wandered upstairs. In the drying space she came across a room containing a cot bed and on it sat a soldier wrapping a bandage round his hand who wore a khaki uniform. The soldier rose and vanished leaving young Helen looking at the empty cot. She hurriedly told the adults who assumed she had imagined it. It was not until many years later when bus drivers reported seeing the figure of a soldier at the depot that she felt vindicated about what she had seen.

Despite the occasional sighting it was not until the 1960s and 1970s that he made his dramatic comeback, with a string of appearances leaving employees unwilling to be alone in certain areas. These accounts first recorded in the Press and Journal are to be found in Central Library reference section and contain some interesting eye-witness statements. These include drivers reportedly feeling cold breath on their necks or being touched by icy hands while in the staff canteen. In one well documented case a kilted figure was also seen climbing stairs. The staircase, which led to the toilets. It became something of a no-go area for staff according to the article. In more recent times incidents of a figure seen walking through the wall where apparently a doorway used to be, had also been reported. This was verified by a current employee John who on showing me round the building, stating that during building work in the 1980s the original doorway was blocked off and ever since then a shadowy figure had been seen walking through it. Better still I soon received a personal invite to see around the building the details of which are below.

Having heard of Kings Streets most famous ghost since a child I was very keen to look around and had the opportunity to do so in 2006. During the tour I visited the area where the canteen stood though since conversion it bears little resemblance to its former self. The building has of course undergone many changes since the 1970s, and it was impossible to imagine what it would have looked like all those years ago. We continued onto the top floor where I found myself in the cold grey granite surroundings of the infamous south turret, apparently unchanged since 1861. Instructed to shine my torch upwards I saw to my surprise a wooden cross beam from which a filthy, frayed rope hung which on closer scrutiny appeared to have been cut through. Allegedly the instrument of the captain's demise, it had hung there for around 100 years until a recent misplaced decision consigned it to the skip.

Four months later I asked permission to return to the barracks with my colleague Duncan with the express purpose of interviewing as many staff members as possible. Jim McDonald who had volunteered to take us round made the introductions and it was gratifying to speak to so many open-minded people. First on the list was Alexander Leslie, an administration assistant who pointed out that there was period in the 1970s when things were happening on a regular basis. He mentioned that during that refurbishment, the canteen was moved to another part of the building and the company boardroom created. He described how a friend and colleague had witnessed a full figure which wore both a kilt and greatcoat. Around the same period another employee working in the coaching office apparently kept hearing a tapping noise at her window. She turned round to see who was there and came face to face with a shadow which then vanished, leaving her in a state of alarm. Alexander went on to say that 'In the evening you do hear taps and different noises which I put down to pipes cooling down.' He said that as a sceptic he felt there was in all probability a natural explanation for many of the reported incidents and some he thought were due to fertile imaginations. Before leaving he mentioned that in the 1970s his colleague Dougie who 'was heavily into spiritual things' had brought a Ouija board down to King Street to try and communicate with the ghost. Messages were allegedly received from a Captain or Corporal Beaton during one of the sessions which begs the question, did the use of the Ouija board somehow encourage some dormant energy to manifest? More recently I had the opportunity to speak to Jim, who as a former driver told me of an incident that happened to one of his colleagues. This is what he said.

'Once the buses stopped running at night, at about 11.30pm you had to get back to the depot and deposit any cash into the night safe. In the evening there were usually two inspectors around but once they had gone you just put the money in the safe and went. The person I am going to tell you about experienced something and never lived it down. He came back to the depot at night and went into the locker room to put in some clothes. He was going to use them the next day. When he got there, he noticed two figures out of the corner of his eye but as he was busy putting away his belongings, he did not pay them any attention. Anyway, he made some incidental comment, but they just ignored him and because of that he thought, well, F*** you! and being annoyed glanced over but the pair just vanished in front of his eyes. Well, he got such a shock he just wet himself there and then. Of course, he made the mistake of telling folk at the depot and they just pulled his leg. He must have gotten a real scare.'

Another equally scary occurrence took place on Christmas Day around fifteen years ago. I was told that at the time a lone security guard had just started his walk-around. It was a freezing night by all accounts, so he was grateful to escape the elements on entering the old tram shed. From the back of the building, he could distinctly hear voices. Thinking someone had left a radio on he went to locate the source of the noise. There was of course no radio, yet the sound of voices appeared to be coming from a locked part of the tram shed. He stopped, hearing two male voices in deep conversation coming from inside the old military hospital, behind a locked door and he held the only key. The tone of the voices indicated an argument and somewhat alarmed he left quickly in the realisation that whatever it was, was best left alone.

Keeping with the tram shed I was told of a cleaner who had handed in their notice because of something they had witnessed in the same area and so I interviewed them soon after. This is exactly what I was told:

'I worked for the corporation as it was called, cleaning buses. I enjoyed the job as we used to have a laugh. Basically, we were each given a bus to clean, a double decker and you boarded it with a mop and bucket and scrubbed it down at the depot. We worked when all the buses had stopped running and there was a team of us including my mate Andy who used to work with. One night I was on the top deck of a bus mopping the floor when it started to rock back and forth. It started off quite gently but in a matter of seconds it had become violent. I remember falling onto a seat and the bucket tipped over sending water everywhere. The first thing I thought, was it was Andy and some of the others playing a trick. Well, I'm not going to repeat what I said, but I swore and shouted out of the window at them as I was fuming. That was when I noticed Andy walking through the door at the end of the shed, looking perplexed and he had no clue what I was on about. He looked shocked when I told him. Of course, we had all heard stories for years and strange things would happen. It was a creepy place at night. Anyway, I didn't last long after that.'

Next on my list of interviewees was Dave whose job was to co-ordinate bus movements. He told me that many of the workers maintained a healthy scepticism and tended not to jump to conclusions though a baffling incident happened to his colleague quite recently. He conceded that after the incident he was a little nervous about being alone in the building. He takes up the story:

'I was in the depot on my own when someone from accounts, a new start, came by asking to be let in as she had some important work to finish. I found out later she knew nothing of the buildings' history at the time. She went upstairs and while in her office heard someone running along the corridor behind her. She thought nothing of it even when the footsteps continued as she sat working at her desk. After finishing up she came downstairs and said to me I had better check if everyone has left before locking up as there is someone moving around up there. I knew there was no one else there but said nothing as I did not want to alarm her. I was nervous about locking up, doing it very quickly that evening.'

Nearly ten years have passed since I first wrote about the depot and a lot has happened in the intervening years. A radical upgrade took place a few years back resulting in most of the surviving infrastructure being removed. The old tram sheds and the military hospital are all gone now replaced by a more functional yet uninspiring depot. Even the alleged rope was discarded despite some protest. Though much of the original features have now gone there is one remnant from the past that refuses to budge, and it would appear has shown displeasure at the changes. I spoke quite recently to Joe Mackie one of the senior management team and was secretly pleased to hear that the captain had been up to his old tricks. Joe had worked from the depot since the 1960s and was well acquainted with the stories, and though he had never seen anything himself had a healthy respect for those that had. This was apparent during the recent renovations when a raft of phenomena was reported including a builder being nudged on the stairs and a 'brickie' having a brick taken from his hand. The brick then floated to the ground and bounced which the 'brickie' assured everyone was impossible.

His sightings it would seem are not solely confined to the barracks as the following testifies. The witness, now an adult, was at the time a child and travelling along King Street by taxi with her mum. As they approached the depot, she witnessed what she described to me as a man in full battle dress walking across the road in front of their cab. He vanished just outside the building. She remembered, asking her mum why there was a soldier there but her mum assumed she had imagined it, as there was no one to be seen. She explained that as a child she had no knowledge of the building or its history and therefore was at a loss to explain what she saw, but the memory is clearly imprinted today.

I am happy to say the file on the King Street depot is ever growing, but before we leave for now there is one more tale. This, literally hot of the press was passed on to me as of 2021.

The protagonist who I have known for over 40 years disclosed the following information, pertinent to his time as a bus driver with Grampian Transport where he worked from 1986 to 1989. The exact location was near the main reception door where a set of two flights of stairs led to the 1st floor. On the landing was a large window with views to the outside yard, and from it the stairs were illuminated when dark by a large orange light, which was positioned just outside. He wished to remain anonymous, but these are his exact words.

'It was 1989, around February and still dark in the early evening. I was working late in the office, working on a programme of summer tours. I was the only person working at that side of the building as I had been upstairs earlier and noted that all the offices were completely empty. The cleaner had also long finished and left for the night. Finishing up I cleared my desk and went to the reception, where at the foot of the stairs I switched on the light. I had forgotten something so went back along to the office only to find on my return the light was now off. At this point a sudden fear hit me, I don't scare easily but I felt a cold sensation, like the temperature had dropped. As I entered the landing, I noticed the light switch was positioned at off and it was freeing. At this point I could literally feel the hair on the back of my neck stand up and as I looked up the stairs, just before I put the light on, I clearly saw a reflection in the window from the light in the yard. It was the bottom half of a kilt and it swirled round the top of the stairs before disappearing up the second flight. I put on the light but was rooted to the spot and was sweating yet freezing, I'm shaking just writing this now. Anyhow the temperature rapidly returned to normal, and I went to the control room where you exited once the building was closed. There were three people working there and I casually asked if anyone had left the room in the last five minutes but was given a resounding No! It still freaks me out to this day.'

And so, we come to the end of perhaps the most frustrating search I have ever undertaken, into one of Aberdeen's most enduring 'ghost stories.' Who was Captain Beaton of the Gordon Highlanders? The numerous articles on the haunting speak with authority, providing, names, dates and details none of which can physically be verified. Attempting to find his full name and death certificate I spoke to a retired Major at the Gordon Highlanders Museum who stated that his (Captain Beaton) name did not appear on the army list of 1914 or 1918. In his opinion this indicated two things, firstly that he may have already been in the army prior to the outbreak of the war or secondly that his name was never Beaton in the first place. There were a few Beaton's on the role, but none were ranked Captain, and none had passed away during that period.

In response to his much written about recuperation, I also contacted Harlaw Academy where they suggested I search Aberdeen City Council archives. After a short search they were able to locate a set of school magazines from 1915 which contained the headmistress' report inside. This detailed the school's usage at that time though the archivist described the contents as frustratingly brief. In it, the headmistress recorded that the school buildings had been taken over as the headquarters of the 1st Scottish General Hospital, while the pupils being moved out to alternative accommodation. The injured men, apparently housed in the music rooms, remained nameless.

In conclusion, I cannot help but feel the continual telling of the tale, has reached mythic proportions and the 'facts' though perfectly believable are part of the myth. A recent article for example, claims he was blown up in the war, adding further embellishments to the story. It is this layering of supposition, a need to add flesh to the story that has clouded the waters. Perhaps there never was a Beaton, but if that is the case, then who first came up with the name? There is paranormal activity, of that there is no doubt, but who is responsible remains an enduring mystery.

The Tolbooth

Aberdeen's museum of civic history is one of the city's oldest surviving buildings. The original Tolbooth a place where taxes were collected was also the Wardhouse a place where criminals were held while awaiting trial. Completed in 1629, it remained true to its purpose and served as a prison for around two hundred years. Today in its most recent incarnation it is known as the Tolbooth.

Justice in the 17th century was swift and brutal and the severity of the punishments usually outweighed the crime. The city records are testament to this and therefore it is only natural to assume some of those negative emotions may be stored in the fabric of this building. I first became aware of the Tolbooth through work, and in 2006 had my first taste of its unique 'atmosphere'. I had just finished taking a tour and we had assembled in the entrance hall prior to leaving when it was suggested I should take photographs of the group for posterity. I was asked if the children could use the camera also and I did not see the harm. The resulting image partially obscured by a white mist was intriguing.

And so, I began to visit the museum more regularly in the hope of capturing further phenomena but to no avail. This however changed in May 2007 when I was assisting a group write a report on historic crime and punishment. A tour of the museum was organised and as usual we started off in the main entrance hall before making our way up to the first floor. The group were obviously having fun and things were going well and so we ascended the stairs to the 'condemned' cell. This cell unlike the others, retained its original brick floor and housed some of the most tangible reminders of our bloody past. These included the blade of the 'maiden' (a precursor to the guillotine), the scolds' bridle (for punishing gossiping women) and various shackles. Being one of the smaller rooms in the building it also possesses a particularly oppressive atmosphere not helped by its sinister contents.

As there were eight of us in the group, the room soon became very warm. I stood to the left nearest the door, alongside four others. The rest were in the main body of the room. The temperature up till that point, nigh on suffocating suddenly dropped as the sound of shuffling feet ascended the stairs. An icy cold sensation crept into the room, and I glanced at my companions whose eyes had widened considerably. The footsteps continued and stopped at the threshold though the source remained unseen, then in the cell the sound of a chain being moved was heard. The group huddled closer and there was tangible fear in the air, but within seconds it had gone. As our guide led us from the cell, I whispered to my nearest companion: 'Did you hear that?' and she in return whispered: 'yes.' Outside, the sun was shining and in the following discussion it was apparent that all four students nearest the door had experienced the same thing as I had. Those further in had not, though on hearing what happened, they did not seem disappointed.

And so for the next few years I took every opportunity to explore the building. I was at this point in the privileged position of being asked to assist with public events and of course some of those were 'ghost hunts'. These events can sometimes be a little 'gimmicky' and perhaps cannot be classed as serious attempt to commune with the dead, however they did give me an opportunity to further my knowledge. Groups came and went, seances were held and occasionally some phenomena witnessed but as a rule the mob handed approach gleaned little evidence. Of course, even the slightest creak was enough to convince some that spirits were abroad but in truth there was little evidence found that could stand up to scrutiny. I have personally found that the best evidence is usually given to those who have not asked for it so perhaps there is something to be said for avoiding crowds. The following incident best sums this up.

In 2005 Mary Wood visited the museum with her husband and her friend's son, recounting the following: 'I went up the stairs and could hear a wifie greetin.' (a mannequin situated on the top floor). I was looking at the board (information panel) on the first floor and as I turned to speak to my husband, I saw a little man about 4ft. high wearing a brown striped suit and a brown hat from the 1920s standing behind me. It looked like a Trilby hat. He nodded his head at me but did not speak. I just ran out, jumped six steps at a time or so it felt and ran out of the building onto Union Street. The man at the door came after me asking if I was okay. I was then taken back inside, and I told him what I had saw and he replied that I wasn't the first person to have seen him. He then offered me a drink of water as I was sweating so much.'

As it transpired neither her husband nor the child witnessed anything unusual as they were looking in the opposite direction and remained perplexed as to the rapid exit. Mrs. Wood concluded by saying she had never been back since. She remains adamant about her experience and having spoken to her on at least three occasions her story has never varied. Soon after I spoke to some of the workers who look after the building who verified the story saying that she almost ran into the road in her fright. The Tolbooth became a record office and wine store for the council once ceasing to hold criminals so the sighting of a man in a trilby hat is feasible.

Despite the amount of negativity surrounding a building of its nature the phenomena is sporadic. There have been many attempts capture evidence by paranormal groups, some more successful than others. I have personally, heard whispering directly in my ear and witnessed a passing shadow caught on camera, yet solid evidence remains somewhat elusive. Saying that I did spend some time in one of the cells on my own during a Halloween event, and it's an experience I don't care to repeat.

Provost Skene's House

Being one of two 16th century buildings left in the city it would have suffered the same fate as the others had it not been for the intervention of the Queen Mother who voiced her disapproval at plans to demolish it. It was renovated and then run by the City Council as a museum until its closure some years back. It has a direct link to the Jacobite uprising which in my opinion should have been exploited, however its now set to be home to a 'hall of heroes' attraction. With a colourful past from family home to common lodging house the building has borne witness to many events over the centuries and in my opinion and that of former staff and visitors is haunted. Which makes me wonder what the spirits who reside there think of the current plans?

The building first mentioned in the Sasine Register of 1545 was owned by Alexander Knollis a member of a wealthy land-owning family. From 1585-1622 the house was then home to a succession of wealthy people including a Laird and a Bishop until latterly owned by a bankrupt. Initially a three-storey rectangular tower it was subsequently added to by the Knollis family and then by Baillie Mathew Lumsden who owned the building from 1622 till around 1641. Wealthy merchant and Provost, Sir George Skene created further changes during his subsequent ownership by changing the window elevations, flattening the roof and building the east staircase and turrets. He also created the beautiful plaster ceilings that remain to this day. The house continued to be occupied by Skene's family relatives until 1732. Later still, the infamous Duke of Cumberland occupied the house on his way to defeat Bonnie Prince Charlie at Culloden. Afterwards being known as Cumberland House.

The next owner of note was Walter Duthie owner from 1844 to 1870 a writer to the signet of Edinburgh it was during his ownership that the building became a house of refuge. Philanthropist Miss Elizabeth Duthie who gifted the Duthie Park to the city then owned the property and in 1879 leased it out as the renamed Victoria Lodging House. Despite changing its name, the house remained a lodging-house until its closure in 1951. Co-incidentally I worked with one local man some years back, who used to visit there in the 1930s. His best friend at schools' dad was apparently a caretaker and helped look after the men. He was told that some of them slept sitting upright, supported by a rope which rested under their armpits. In the morning it was common practice to loosen the rope which led to a very rude awakening. He indicated that the room this took place in became the painted gallery.

Speaking of which, it was during the 1951 refurbishment of the Long Gallery in the Lumsden wing that a series of tempera-painted panels were uncovered depicting the Life of Christ. They are considered among the finest of the remaining examples in Scotland and were lucky to survive. The house is of course ironically situated in what was the residential part of Guest Row. It was first mentioned in a charter from 1439, referred to as 'Vicus Lemurum,' Latin for 'street of spectres.'

This name was apparently given due to its proximity to the nearby kirkyard as opposed to what follows.

Of all the locations I have researched I would say that this building has more than earned its right to be called haunted. The range of phenomena is impressive, and I can assure the reader the following are genuine experiences. The first incident I will recount happened right under my nose, though I did not learn this till many years later. I had been delivering a drawing class and was unaware of an argument taking place in another part of the building. The culprits, a mother and her grown-up daughter were in full flow and the attendant on duty had the unenviable task of trying to restore order. The daughter was convinced her mother had 'barged past her' on the stairs and she vocalised her grievance, while the other denied it vehemently. Despite the presence of the attendant, the commotion escalated and a third party, innocently sitting nearby was then accused. The situation was eventually diffused much to everyone's relief. Though who the pusher was remains a mystery. Years later I chanced upon one of the students, Amy, who had been present that day and she mentioned that during the class she had been the third party accused of pushing the complainer. She was completely innocent of course but after I explained the full story she seemed quite taken that the guilty party was possibly a ghost.

The next incident took place in the early evening when Stevie, a former employee was descending the staircase. He apparently became aware of footsteps behind him and thinking a visitor was still inside at locking up time went back up to investigate. Finding no one there he descended once more only to have the noise of footsteps follow him downstairs. He ran for it, switched the alarm on and fled.

Continuing up the stairs you reach the painted gallery. Later, I was told that a rather vociferous tourist had complained to staff that she was unable to enter there as it was full of people. She had allegedly made a long trip just to see the room and on pushing the door found it only opened marginally. She peeked in and saw a crowd of people standing facing the end of the room. What sort of meeting was going on? she enquired, only to be led back upstairs to a now empty room where she was assured that she had been the first visitor that morning.

Returning to the 17th century parlour a former staff member recalled how she prepared to switch off the lights at the main fuse box before becoming aware of the sound of a swishing dress approaching. She swung round and faced what she described as the ghost of a woman dressed in old fashioned clothes with dark hair, coming into the room. She told me that the figure appeared to be solid as she was, going on to say she got the impression it saw her as well as it wore a slightly startled expression. Described as being very shocked she then questioned whether she really saw it as it had happened so quickly. She concluded by saying that there had been many residents at Provost Skene's House and therefore contains spirits but believes the most frequently seen is that of Elisabeth Aberdour wife of Mathew Lumsden.

Taking the staircase which leads down from the 17th century parlour you reach the old kitchen, and it was here that another apparition was seen by staff. This time, the figure observed was thought to have been someone who had secretly entered while it was closed to the public and so was confronted. Why they never questioned the fact she was wearing an old dress and crinoline bonnet remains unanswered, but they receive quite a shock when the figure suddenly vanished.

Sometime later I had my own experience on the top floor when I was surprised to see in my minds' eye a small man dressed in black with a very long grey beard. He walked towards me, bent over and appeared to be coughing though he did not notice me. It only lasted seconds but so clear was the impression that I still remember it vividly. I continued down the staircase and was aware of his presence and the accompanying chill until I reached the next floor down when he went out of the atmosphere. It was these impressions that lead me to conclude that the house was home to different spirit energies from different eras.

The house at the time attracted visitors of all ages and on one occasion I was told that two teenage girls were accompanying their younger sister who staff believed to be around six years old. They were asked on leaving if they had enjoyed their visit. They had, but for the fact the young girl complained of being followed by a man from room to room. The elder siblings kept looking round yet could see no one despite the youngsters' protestations. The young girl apparently claimed he was always there, though she seemed more perplexed than afraid. The older girls laughed it off saying to the museum assistant that it was her imagination getting the better of her. Though they thought otherwise.

Former attendant Eileen recalled a time she was on duty and stated: 'We were in our workroom preparing to open up when we both heard heavy footsteps echoing up the main staircase to the house. We both looked at each other and initially thought the door had been left open and that someone had unwittingly come in early. We went to check the door and as it was still locked went upstairs to double check and of course as we suspected the building was empty. This happened a lot.'

A few months later Sandy, one of the supervisors, was on the top floor when he heard someone walking around in an adjoining room. As the two rooms are connected by an open door, he went through to see who was there only to discover the room empty. He then went downstairs only to find the front door still locked. He readily admits that he is sceptical but has found his experiences baffling. During our interview I uttered the word 'cool,' when hearing of the footsteps incident to which he remarked, 'Well it wasn't cool for me.'

Moving to the east wing you would have found the Regency rooms. They contained more opulent furnishings as befits the period and connecting them was a small painted gallery. It has been noted that staff locking the connecting doors often feel this area to be particularly claustrophobic, a feeling I would concur. I cannot explain why, but it is very different to the rest of the building. There are of course various stories connected to this area including the following which took place during an evening function. The incident described involved an attendant who while patrolling felt the sensation of someone standing directly behind him. He initially froze, while his scalp crawled before managing to bolt from the room. His colleagues were shocked to see him appear downstairs and I quote: 'looking like a bucket of water had been thrown over him' and being 'completely soaked in sweat.' He refused to go back upstairs alone.

Perhaps though, more dramatic evidence came from the experience of a visitor during Christmas 2006. She was the only person upstairs at the time and apart from attendant

Sandy they were alone. Sandy recounts: 'I was in the office when a middle-aged lady came down the stairs who appeared to be flustered. She explained that she had been in the Regency room and had continued into the small painted gallery where she was confronted by the sight of a woman sitting on the chaise longue. The visitor got quite a shock and turned and ran before she could see what the figure did. She described her as wearing a long dark dress and lace cap. Of course, I immediately went upstairs to find the seat empty and no sign of the woman.'

All good things must come to an end and with the news of its imminent closure ringing in my hears, I attended an investigation with a local paranormal group. It was a bittersweet experience, as I had grown attached to the place and had made many good friends among the staff. Unfortunately, we found little evidence on the night, perhaps the ghosts were sulking and who could blame them. There was however one more incident of note worth mentioning. I had taken a photograph which had a strange shadow present. It looked a little like a terrier with pointed ears. I thought nothing more of it, filing it away for posterity until a chance meeting with the team leader some months later. During the conversation she asked me if I still had the image, as some intriguing evidence had come to light. Apparently, the results of their EVP session had just been uncovered and on those the sound of a growling dog had been heard. The recorder had coincidentally been left in the room where I had taken the photograph.

COMMUNITY SPIRIT

Powis House

Powis House or Powis Community Centre as it is known today was built around 1800 by architect George Jaffray and belonged to the estate of the Leslie family, before being bought by Aberdeen Town Council in 1941. It then became both a library and community centre making it the first of its kind in Scotland. It is without doubt one of the most spiritually active buildings I have ever visited, its reputation common knowledge among locals, yet has never been written about before. Powis was described at the time as a 'straggling estate' which is certainly true, covering an area which ran from Kittybrewster to Old Aberdeen. The entrance to the original estate is still marked today by two ornate towers. These stand in the High Street of Old Aberdeen and are known as Powis Gate.

I first became aware of the house while assisting a student, Melissa, who was writing a local history report on crime and punishment. We inevitably got onto the subject of haunted houses, and she mentioned that Powis House was well known for its ghost among the local community and that a close friend of hers had first-hand experience of this. It had taken place in 1996 just after the youth group had left for the night. The building now locked stood silently, while outside the group were in her own words, 'mucking about'. One of them, Kevin (not his real name) was facing the building when out of nowhere he let out a terrified scream and ran. Melissa, unaware of what he had witnessed and like the others was given a terrible fright. She later described his expression as being one of sheer terror. His friends left shaken and bewildered headed for the safety of their homes. Afterwards it took weeks to find out what had happened to Kevin as he refused to leave his house and even then was unwilling to discuss the matter further. But what had he seen, to make him react so? Call it coincidence but I already knew the answer, as Kevin had been one of my students two years previously and had recounted the very same story. It had obviously been a frightening experience and I remember clearly how he struggled to recall the incident. I was in no doubt it had affected him deeply and the following is what he told me.

'I was with my mates, there was group of us standing just outside the centre on the grass, after the club. Something made me glance up at the building. On the top floor is a large half-moon window which was illuminated by a bluish light. At the window I saw a female looking down at me, who looked like she was half-smiling. She had long black hair and a very pale face, it looked she was floating. I could see her clearly. She then turned and walked away, the blue light receding with her. At that point I just screamed and ran. When I got home, I locked myself in my room and didn't come out. I got my mum to answer the door afterwards as my friends kept wanting to know what happened. I didn't go out for a long time. I still remember it clearly to this day.' When we spoke after the incident I pressed for more details, and he described her as wearing either a light-coloured dress or night gown and that her face was pale with indistinct features. I knew by his demeanour he was not lying.

After hearing the above, it was with some trepidation that I accepted the chance of a visit to the centre and in due course arrived. It is an imposing building sitting amid relatively new housing and appears oddly out of place. The vast estate belonging to the house no longer exists, the tiny patch of grass it sits on being the sole survivor. I was told that many years ago, the Miss Leslie's still took tea on the lawn, served by a Japanese butler while all around the local children gawked in wonderment. I hope this is true as it paints a wonderful picture.

Once inside the interior proved to be surprisingly spacious consisting of large public rooms on the ground floor, what would have been the library upstairs and in the eaves, the old caretakers flat. The basement, accessed by a circular staircase is large and contains bathrooms at each end, a music room, assorted cupboards, and a washroom. There are also the remains of the original kitchen, replete with fireplace. I found it fascinating and spent many hours exploring the building, which undoubtedly feels quite foreboding. The basement, I felt seemed particularly eerie being isolated from the rest of the house and it is there we begin our journey.

Around twenty years ago my wife had been using the washing machines in the basement. These were for the use of the community and at the time she was waiting for the cycle to begin when she became aware of someone standing directly behind her. The hair on her neck stood on end and she froze momentarily before bolting upstairs where she recounted her experience. The community staff however seemed nonplussed and casually said 'that will be Annie,' which is what they have named the ghost. Annie by all accounts has become part of the fabric of the building. But who is she? No one knows for certain, but people have speculated she was either a servant or perhaps a relative of a former owner. Either way the figure of a woman, sometimes nursing a baby has been seen regularly though according to reports she's not the only spirit present.

A further meeting with Melissa proved fortuitous and we discussed the alleged haunting at length. Her grandmother, a former cleaner had worked there for years and both she and Melissa would meet up after school and keep each other company. Sometimes she would help clean and at other times would do homework in the library but either way she was able to describe the many incidents she witnessed while there. For example, she remembered on more than one occasion someone mischievously turning out the light in the basement or even worse in the attic, while her grandmother was working. I found the thought of this was terrifying as I remember on one occasion pushing one of the attic room doors open only to have something push back on it. It was an unpleasant experience. Returning to Melissa she claimed the activity was so prolific that it became almost commonplace, however one incident particularly stood out, resulting in her grandma handing in her notice. She explained: 'I was sitting downstairs having a snack when I heard a scream from above. I ran upstairs and saw my grandmother who was pure white and said she had just seen the figure of a small girl standing near the door that leads to the eaves.' I found out later that two of the Leslie children had died from scarlet fever in that location.

Some months later I was given the contact details of a further witness Mike, and on meeting he described his experiences while working there. As a keyholder he would sometimes work out-with office hours, running the music program and on more than one occasion got more than he bargained for. He takes up the story:

'I've had several experiences in the house, the first happened in the music room which as you know is in the basement. One evening there were three girls who wanted to record themselves singing. I had set up the equipment but before they could open their mouths, a male voice boomed out through the speaker. I could not understand what was said, but he spoke for a few seconds. The girls screamed and became upset, though I calmed down the situation by saying it was a passing taxis radio being picked up. I doubted the equipment was capable of this however that is what I said. On another occasion I was working with a group of lads and during band practice a loud bang from outside the door brought proceedings to a halt. On investigating we found that a fire extinguisher had been lifted off its' bracket, upended and then dropped, breaking the pin. It was impossible for this to have happened on its own. There was no one else in the building apart from us as the main door was securely locked.'

After explaining what had occurred, he took me outside where I was shown the replacement extinguisher and I concluded that it would have been impossible for it to fall unless lifted, therefore who was responsible? A sudden movement on the floor above drew our attention though we were pleasantly surprised (and a little relieved) to find it was just the cleaner. On seeing us she remarked, 'I thought it was the ghost,' which I found funny, although I was told later that she refuses to go to the basement on her own.

Next on our agenda was the large nursery room on the ground floor, where on entering he described seeing the spirit of a woman nursing a child. It happened without warning while busy stacking amplifiers, when the figure of a woman 'whooshed' into view. She stood there momentarily before vanishing, which he described as quite frightening. Later, other witnesses came forward claiming to have seen a similar figure at the window. After some time, and as it was getting late, we called it a night though agreed to re-convene later after Mike proposed an experiment. He suggested we re-enact the incident he had previously described, and I agreed.

Around a week later I arrived at the agreed time, and we stood in the creche room as before. The plan as previously discussed involved me standing near the door, camera at the ready, while Mike stood where the woman had appeared. He then asked out if someone would like to provide evidence of their existence, in classic ghosthunter fashion. After just a few moments the temperature began to drop rapidly, and an intense cold spot manifested itself in the far corner where he stood. He called me over and we were then able to step in and out of it at will. I took began to take photograph, which revealed a large plate like globe hovering nearby, which had moved further into the room on the second. The temperature quickly returned as before. Afterwards we discussed what had happened, and although I do not subscribe to the argument that all orbs are of a spiritual nature, the fact the temperature had altered so radically at the same time was quite persuasive.

After a while we called it a night and swopping numbers, he promised to call should anything else occur. I was secretly pleased when he did soon after and anxious to hear the news arranged a meeting. Michael takes up the story: 'I had set up some recording equipment in the music room, for two girls to record a song they had been practising. I had to leave them for about two minutes but left my assistant in charge. I went upstairs to do some photocopying. I must add that neither the girls nor my assistant had any knowledge of my previous trouble with the speakers. No sooner had I reached the office when they ran upstairs in a state of panic. Once I had calmed them down, they claimed to have heard a voice which shouted at them through the speakers which then began making breathing noises. They were obviously upset and refused to go back in the room. I went to see if there was anything wrong with the equipment of course, but there wasn't.' It is not uncommon for spirit to use technology to let itself be known I surmised but in Powis this was particularly hazardous. Not long after I was given the news that Mike had left his post and was now working elsewhere. I knew that it was unlikely I would be visiting again so had to be satisfied with my earlier findings. I had one more treat in store though when I was contacted by a local resident called Olive, who I was intrigued to hear had spent much of her childhood at the house. Her best friends' dad had been caretaker there some years previously and so it was with great interest I received the following.

Olive takes up the story. 'Growing up we were led to believe that the property used to belong to a Lady Burnett at one time. We frequented the house usually for activities such as the youth club and dances. My best friend at the time lived at the top of the building in what was then the caretaker's flat. Her dad kept an eye on the building which I remember at the time being used as a baby clinic and home to a pensioners' club and a women's guild. Very often I would stay with my friend at the top of the house and when everyone was accounted for it was not unusual to hear footsteps climbing the stairs and walking along the corridor. My friend's father would immediately go out to check but there was never anyone there. Her mother, realizing we were scared, used to say, "Och, it's just Lady Burnett paying a visit." Her father swore at one point, that he saw a monk in the basement of the house and looked at it for about ten to fifteen seconds before it disappeared. After he told me this my feet would hardly touch the stairs when I visited. They used to leave the front door off the latch for me and I would pelt up the stairs.' She finished off by saying. 'I would love to go back to the building and see if it still has the same unique atmosphere.' I could not agree more, as out of all the locations I have spent time in over the years, this one does without a doubt, possess a singular atmosphere. Difficult to describe adequately but the word potent comes to mind.

Rosemount Community Centre

This community centre started life in the late 19th century as Rosemount Secondary School before becoming the annexe of the Aberdeen Grammar School. The building as you would expect from the Victorian era is a formidable granite structure which eventually incorporated the nearby villas as a means of coping with the rising population. A proposal to build a fourth floor to meet those needs met with resistance and in an article from the Aberdeen Journal was described as a 'fantastic and mischievous proposal.' The author's acidic pen went further describing the proposal to add a fourth floor as 'an emanation from the fertile brain of Mr. Hugh F. Campbell' (presumably someone on the school board) and that 'the man who proposes such a scheme deserves to be drummed out of Aberdeen.' Whether he ever did remains unclear. After its life as the annexe, it lay semi-derelict for years before finding a new lease of life and I am pleased to say it has thrived in recent times. Having worked there periodically for many years I was in a great position to hear of any unexplained incidents, and it did not disappoint.

The activity has been noted to range from the sensation of being followed to full figure manifestations and lights being switched on once the buildings shut. My first meeting was with community workers Lil and Fiona who described their experiences while working there. Though neither had personally seen anything Lil was keen to point out that when she worked in one classroom, she was aware of a 'spooky feeling' and did not like the atmosphere. She went on to say that some members of staff complained of being followed but on turning saw nothing. The building of course is large with a maze of corridors and stairways, and it is not inconceivable to suggest that flights of fancy may responsible. But can one put down the movement of furniture during the night as fancy? Or lights switching back on after the building is locked, for the night? I intended to find out more.

Some weeks later I returned and met with Frances who explained that early one morning she was sitting at her desk when she caught a glimpse of something near the office door. Glancing up she was confronted by a 'solid and real looking figure of a woman of African appearance.' She noticed that the women kept looking around her though assuming she was a mum waiting for the crèche to open, continued working. A few minutes later she glanced up and saw the woman heading towards the staff toilets. She kept working, but as a considerable time had now passed Frances assumed the lady had fallen ill and so entered the toilet to check. The room was found to be empty and the tiny widows impossible to exit by were also locked. On being asked what she thought about the incident, Frances stated that she was not normally a believer, but what happened on that day had left her shaken. She went on to say that it was not unusual to hear doors closing and footsteps echo in the corridors, to which her colleague Averil, testified and on speaking to her she recounted a very similar experience.

'l saw a figure go by and went out to ask if I could help in any way only to find the corridor empty. She was wearing something coloured red, perhaps a cape but was moving too quickly to ascertain exactly what. Perturbed by the incident she spoke to a colleague who said her description matched that of a Red Cross nurse as they wore red capes. It came as no surprise to find out later that the school was once used as a hospital for soldiers during World War One which may explain the 'nurse.'

As mentioned, the building lay derelict for many years and having worked there I was privileged to explore the building at leisure and in doing so met with numerous people who were only too willing to share their experiences. At least three people have for example been surprised to see the old gym lights switch back on by themselves once the building was locked at night, my friend Fiona being one of them. She told me that on that occasion she decided just to leave them on till the morning, which I think sensible.

In more recent times two workers Rachael and Mandy both witnessed the same incident when a pair of heavy fire doors swung open and then shut as they stood at the reception desk. Having worked there for years I can assure the reader that they took a great deal of effort to push open, being very robust, and a draught could not possibly cause them to swing open with such force. They described it as being like someone had walked into the reception. Incidentally, a quick check afterwards found there were no doors open anywhere on the ground floor at the time. Of course, swinging doors do not necessarily make a good ghost story make but perhaps what follows does.

I had known Anne for many years as a community participant and student, having undertaken classes there. One day we got onto the subject of ghosts, and she told me about things both she and her son Malcom had experienced. Once the term ended, we lost touch for a while until one evening when I received a phone call. I recognised her voice immediately and it was quite clear by her tone she had been given a scare. She explained the reason for the call was that she had just seen a ghost, which of course caught my attention. With little prompting, she explained that earlier in the day she had been attending a class and had gone to the coffee room as usual prior to starting. On entering she almost bumped into a man who was standing just inside the door and so apologising, side-stepped quickly. A backward glance brought the realisation that he had vanished. Had he just left quickly? Unlikely, as he was gone in a split second. Later she struggled to describe him in any detail, though this was not helped by the sunlight streaming in from behind. We had often discussed the alleged activity there and agreed it was a fitting end to things. At least for the time being.

Sunnybank Community Centre

Sunnybank school first opened in 1906 and like most schools of its age has been used for a variety of purposes other than education. For example, in both World War One and World War Two the school was used for training purposes by the military. In 1939 the school was extended to cope with an increase in pupil numbers and it was in this extension that I chanced upon, community workers Carmen, Sarah and Carol who enquired if I had heard about the 'ghost'. I co-incidentally had, well at least had heard some vague rumours, but that was the sum of my knowledge. During our conversation it turned out neither had they up until their own experiences and therefore were not 'primed' to jump at their own shadow. They were quick to stress this point and stated that unlike Powis House which many people knew about, Sunnybank did not have a reputation. Carmen told me the following:

'A little while back we were sitting in our office on the top floor. The office door was open, and we both noticed a large dark shape which moved swiftly past the door. We both looked at each other and stood up at the same time thinking someone was wandering about unattended. We poked our heads out of the office and finding nothing shrugged and sat back down. Not long after the same thing happened again but this time, we looked out of the office more quickly only to find the corridor empty again. We sat down and as we chatted, we thought we saw the dark mass again fly past the door. We darted after it and searching the corridor, stepped into what I can only describe as a cold spot. It was beyond cold as the temperature was freezing. The hairs on my arm were on end and I moved back from it. As I stepped out of the space the temperature became normal. I asked Sarah to step into the space and the exact same thing happened to her. It was very strange as we could put our hands out and feel this icy column obviously invisible to the eye and when we stepped back instantly the warmth of the corridor came back. We left the area and quickly returned to the office.'

Convinced that something out of the ordinary had taken place they began to ask if anyone else had experienced similar phenomena. They had of course, and the cleaners began to share their experiences which proved interesting. For example, persistent rumours of seeing the spirits of soldiers came to light, and of the disembodied sound of footsteps.

For those working in the community area there was other phenomena to contend with most commonly light sensors being activated. The sensors operate by movement, so what can be turning them on if a room's empty? Something invisible to the eye it would seem. But what that 'something' is remains elusive, though it appears to detest bad language as demonstrated by the following.

Knowing the building well I am acquainted with the scene of our next incident, which was the stationary room. The incident involving a member of staff, who wished to remain nameless, gave them quite a fright though it is not without an element of humour. As you can appreciate for those who use photocopiers, there is nothing more frustrating than trying to pick random shreds of paper from the feed. This was the scenario for one member of staff who in frustration, hissed an expletive. In response the stationery laden shelf behind her collapsed without warning causing a near heart attack. Alarmed colleagues then rushed to her aid alerted by the terrific noise. Unsurprisingly no fault could be found and so the shelf was then re-attached securely. I was told it then repeated the process under similar conditions sometime later, no doubt prompting calls for a new copier or at least a swear box.

On a more serious note, the cleaner mentioned that someone had hung themselves from the rafters in the attic many years ago. She had been found by someone using the cupboard, hanging above the spot where the copier now stands. It was a grim story but was it true? Rumours abound in old buildings, where restless spirits are assumed to lurk or so it would seem but without further research it will remain a rumour. Despite this, it has been noted that staff both past and present associate the area with having a strange atmosphere.

The Ghosts That Never Were

When I was young, I liked nothing better than settling down in bed with a ghost book. Factual or fictional it did not really matter as the accompanying thrill was what I was after. Those 'thrills' caused no end of sleepless nights. I was particularly drawn to those set in the Edwardian era, when good manners were always requisite to being invited for a weekend stay in the country house by an old Etonian. The friend due to some unnamed malady had usually aged and we the reader eagerly awaited the denouement. I was drawn to many writers, M R James, Burrage, Wakefield and Elliott O' Donnell the self-styled ghost hunter of the Edwardian era who wrote prolifically on the subject. Of Irish descent he would appear to have had many admirers and was continually invited, well at least according to his books to various homes across the country where he catalogued his findings. His books were fascinating covering all aspects of the supernatural from haunted trees, and rivers to haunted castles and haunted people. He appeared to suffer from the most horrific visitations from the beyond prompting, author M.R.James to tartly remark: 'I sincerely hoped the ghosts described by O'

Donnell were fictional, since life might otherwise become an extremely hazardous business.'

Of course, the fact he had spent some time in Aberdeen was the clincher for me, but the question remained, were they true? So as the naivety of youth evaporated a shadow of doubt began to form. Evidently, he despised spiritualism yet promoted the idea that ghosts were able to interact with people. He omitted names making research an impossibility and his tales grew taller.

After his death, the 'Evening Express' ran a series of articles recounting his exploits in Aberdeen which were published in the mid -1960s. One for example, made mention of an alleged haunted house on the Shiprow where he stayed overnight. He apparently suffered a frightening visitation though was able to tell the owners of the possible source, but again the basic details of the house and protagonists were omitted for anonymity which is of course very convenient. Two of his most well-known stories are connected to the city and both appeared in 'Haunted Scotland' and though they may not be true they certainly deliver on the fear-factor.

The first account featured the shade of an apparent suicide in the region of Great Western Road the second concerned, 'The White Dove Hotel' or 'The Hindu child' as its sometimes known. This tale reprinted in numerous ghost books is a staple of the 'true haunting' variety,' yet it would appear no one has ever questioned its veracity. This story was supposedly told to him by a nurse engaged to look after an ailing actress residing at the titular hotel. The address was noted as being either on St.Swithin Street or in its vicinity depending on which version you have. It was described as an old building which no longer stands suggesting it had to be

Georgian or older as the uniformity of the street today is decidedly Victorian. The date of the incident was given as early 1900s by which time the new street had been laid out and any other structures gone. According to the story the nurse was subjected to visitations by the apparition of a young girl while she tended her patient Miss Vining. The young girl eventually revealed herself to be a corpse much to the horror of the nurse while the patient suffering from an unspecified illness passed away. I loved this story and as a kid used to walk around the area trying to guess which one was the 'White Dove' therefore it was a little disappointing to have my illusions shattered.

My first port of call was the local studies library where I looked through archival material but of course there were no buildings in the area prior to those today. Out of frustration I then went to the births, deaths, and marriages office to search for the name Vining and of course there were no records of anyone with that name. I then paid for an assisted search on the database for the name 'Ann Webb', another restless spirit in the O' Donnell canon, named as the tragic suicide in the second story. She according to the tale returned from beyond to protest her innocence in a case of wrongful fraud. A thorough search again found nothing and with that I accepted defeat.

Elliot O' Donnell may well have had paranormal experiences in his life. He was obviously regarded as an expert and had influential friends who appeared more than happy to allow him to investigate their properties. So, in a last-ditch effort to be proved wrong I contacted the Maryland Library where they hold an O' Donnell archive and in which I hoped his Aberdeen exploits hopefully lay. A few weeks later I was contacted by the archivist who having searched the memoirs could find no reference to the 'White Dove Hotel' or indeed Aberdeen. And so mildly disappointed I resigned myself to the fact that although a good writer he was an even greater storyteller and though his true ghost stories will be enjoyed by generations to come, please take them with a large pinch of salt.

View Terrace

Built in 1872 by architect George Brown and initially known as View Place House, its' notable first owners included the Reverend John Mearns and the Reverend J. Stewart of the North United Free Church. It was also known to have been a 'boarding establishment' run by a Mrs W. Gillanders but by 1911 it had become known as View House and remained thus until the 1940s when it became a pre-school day care centre.

Today it is used as a nursery and so I was unable to personally visit but the following was related to me by former employee Anne and involved herself and her colleagues. What follows took place between March 1980 and April 2000 during Anne's tenure and it became apparent that she believed their workplace to be haunted. Her colleagues were quite open about their experiences, they recounted tales of furniture being moved, strange unaccountable noises and sightings of a 'Green Lady.' It must have been a delightful induction but all credit to her for taking it in her stride.

Asking her to elaborate, she explained. 'Sheila (the cook) and I were often in the building on our own, when we would hear someone singing (it was a woman's voice) but on searching the building there was no-one there.' The singing came from the ground floor (there are three levels to the building with an attic area) We never felt frightened, and I used to call out good morning as we came into the building, to let her know we had arrived. Jenny (the kitchen assistant) spoke to us at length of an experience she had when she was opening the building one morning, but I only found this out later after having seen the figure myself. She told me it was still quite early and as she approached the building, she noticed a woman's face at the window looking out at her. The figure was there long enough for her to provide a vivid picture, being described as in her thirties with fair coloured hair hanging loose in ringlets and wearing a light-coloured dress. I saw the same woman myself some-time later when I was busy cleaning. I heard a sudden a noise and on turning quickly noticed a woman with light coloured hair. She wore a beige two-piece outfit and had beads round her neck. She was walking through the laundry room with a cup in her hand which appeared to be made of delicate bone China. I could see her clearly through the open door and on saying hello she turned and smiled back. I thought at the time she had come from the parent's room and was using the urn to get water for her tea and so went through to introduce myself. But of course, there was no one there. I was taken aback to say the least and when I described her to my colleague Jenny, she looked shocked. It was then that she told me about the woman she had witnessed staring from the window. It was obviously the same person, and we were both stunned.'

This however was not the end of the matter as Anne recalled. 'In the top floor of the house there was a small room on the right which had previously been the milk room. This was where babies' bottles were made up and babies were fed but it was then used as a toy cupboard. One afternoon a group of us were standing outside the office which was on that floor too. We were chatting about the imminent closure of the building when suddenly boxes of Lego and Stickle bricks came flying off the shelf onto the floor with an almighty crash. We got a fright and after recovering could see it was impossible for them to do so without assistance. We thought that it may have been the 'Green Lady' upset at our conversation about the closure.'

Strangely once they had moved, I was told some presumed missing files were found carefully placed on their desks after a long and fruitless search. This led to the belief that the spirit had followed them but there was nothing to indicate it had been permanently.

I thanked Anne for her time and in the preceding days conducted a search in the local library. My head now buzzing with all manner of rumours began concocting scenarios, but my research drew a blank. My hope was soon reignited by an email from Anne who explained the following. At a recent work event she had been introduced to a former worker at View Terrace being based there in the early 1970s. Both were amazed and were soon chatting like old friends recounting work experiences which included stories about the 'Green Lady'. It turned out that the worker had borne witness to some strange events herself. For example, on one occasion, when about to leave the office, she could not locate her house keys. She assumed her colleague had hidden them for a joke and questioned her, but she protested her innocence. The banter continued until the keys, materialising out of nowhere were flung at her feet causing them to jump back in alarm. The former employee went on to say that as far as she knew the 'Green Lady' was allegedly once a cook at View Terrace house who 'had died in a gas explosion that took off her arm.'

An intriguing building, I would have loved to have visited but as it is currently a nursery, I thought my request might not be regarded as prudent. At present I have been unable to further my research but hope one day to be able to find out a little more. Perhaps there was a fire and explosion, but then again it could simply be a case of a former owner happily wanting to spend a little time there.

Kincorth Tales

Kincorth is a large council housing estate which lies to the south of the city and as mentioned earlier the area was once home to monks. Rife with activity, my investigations found unsurprisingly, that the shades of those monks and soldiers from the Great War, are the most frequently witnessed. The monks of course have a long association with the area as does the army, whose soldiers billeted and trained there using the 'Gramps' for their exercises. I received the following from Maureen, whose close encounters of the paranormal kind were gratefully received. Two of the incidents occurred when she resided in Kincorth with the first taking place in Covenanters Drive. Maureen told me the following.

'Before I was married, I used to sleep in the same bedroom as my Granma up until I left home. Years later I returned to the family home now with my husband and we both slept in the same room I occupied as a child. It was early one morning soon after moving that I awoke to the sound of someone poking the fire. Confused I sat up and looked across to the fireplace. There was a distinct white haze sitting in the chair which appeared to be poking at the fire. I said Granma! out aloud and the figure just disappeared. I did not feel frightened, but I did get a start.'

Maureen continued: 'Another incident I would like to tell you about also took place in Kincorth, this time in a flat on Webster Road. I had in fact just moved in and was sitting down to have a coffee in the living room. I was not really thinking of anything when I was suddenly aware of a presence behind me. I turned in time to see a tall man who was staring at me. I asked out aloud what he wanted and at that moment he vanished. I saw him a couple of times after that, and the same thing happened when I called out. Once I got to know the neighbours, I asked them if there was ever a man that had lived there. I described him as accurately as possible, but they said there had never been anyone of that description. I was puzzled but not frightened only wishing to know more about him.'

There is of course ample evidence to show that a ghost or spirit may appear in any number of locations, though more likely to be witnessed in ones' own home, which may be of little comfort to you tonight. But what if you knew someone had died there before you moved in? Statistically of course any home of a certain age is likely to have witnessed this scenario. But what if the passing was more tragic and you knew of it? Would you still want to live there? I know I wouldn't but perhaps I dwell on things too much. The more pragmatic might be unconcerned as in our next story. Told to me by John Dow it concerns a couple residing in Gardner Crescent, Kincorth, the number of the home I will omit. John recalls:

'Dougie, and his wife knew before they moved in that an old man had been found dead in the bath, it hadn't put them off though and they just shrugged it off. About six months after they had moved in, I got a phone call about seven in the morning and I knew instantly something was up because they would never have phoned at that time. She was howling and greetin' saying he was ill and unable to speak, so I went round immediately. I took my dog which is an ex-police dog. When I got to the house it wriggled and started to howl and it refused to come along the lobby and curled up. I had to take it back out. Anyway upstairs, he is sitting upright in bed with a fixed stare, not blinking or saying a word. Opposite the bedroom lay the bathroom and he was just staring into it. The ambulance arrived and he was taken to hospital. We thought he suffered a stroke or a fit, but it was not the case, and he came out of it soon after. Nobody could work out what caused it. When he was able speak, he told us what had happened. That morning he was sitting up in bed and something had caught his eye in the bathroom. When he peered across, he saw the dead body of an old man with his head peeking above the rim of the bath. The shock was too much and that is how he ended up in the state he was in.'

Moving on we venture into Kincorth Community Centre. I spent a pleasant afternoon around twelve years ago speaking with staff. Sometime later I attempted another visit however due to staff changes this was ruled out. What you will hear are accounts given on that visit and I might add staff were delighted to share their stories.

Lorraine who was to be my guide and wasted no time in mentioning the activity had been ongoing for over a decade and has included sightings of both a soldier and a child as well as classic poltergeist phenomena. Again, I was told there were many witnesses to corroborate events and so wasted no time in getting there. First stop was the oldest part of the building home to the play group room and toy store. This was the alleged epicentre of the activity which I did not doubt as a sudden drop in temperature made my skin crawl. Someone was tagging along. Lorraine opened the door to the toy store and explained that the activity in the room mainly involved the battery-operated toys. She explained:

'As you saw there are plenty of them and we make sure they are all switched off at the end of the day for health and safety reasons. The most common occurrence here is that the toys will suddenly switch on randomly which can be unnerving. Some of them have also been noted as moving after the room has been locked up for the night. We used to put it down to forgetfulness, as you would, however it kept happening, so we began to keep a careful eye on where things were placed. On some occasions we would open the door in the morning and find them scattered across the floor, knowing the night before they had been neatly stacked. Sometimes a toy would completely vanish only to turn up unexpectedly in another part of the building which no one could explain. How it got out of a locked room is anyone's guess. People also complained of the room becoming icy cold while tidying in there, so it was not a task folk enjoyed. It got so bad we eventually called in a friend who has mediumistic abilities, who agreed to walk round this area. She told us that there was a spirit of a small child in the building who was gravitating towards the toy cupboard. She was not sure who he was but appeared in her minds-eye to be around four years old. He was mischievous as many children of that age are and enjoyed playing. He was just doing what kids do she said.'

During the conversation I mentioned my findings regarding the Great War and Lorraine acknowledged that a soldier from that period had also been seen on occasion in the same area we now stood. I was told his most conclusive sighting so far, occurred when a teenage visitor bumped into him inadvertently one evening. His mother, also a worker at the centre swore that what he had witnessed was in no way exaggerated. On the night in question the lad was waiting for his mother to finish work and was killing time by wandering about in the building. In the corridor he was taken aback to see the figure of a soldier, who stood looking at him. He was described as wearing the uniform of what he thought was a 'sapper' and appeared solid in appearance. I was then told that the soldier had spoken to him, whether literally or psychically, I have yet to discover. Many believe that thought transference is not uncommon in such cases, so we must assume this is the case. Either way the soldier had stated, in no uncertain terms that his name was 'Samuel,' and not 'Charlie,' the affectionate name then given to him by staff. At that point, the youngster ran to find his mum and by his demeanour was judged to be telling the truth. He was according to those who saw him afterwards, scared. On enquiring, I was told that although the soldier has seen by others over the years, this was his most dramatic appearance to date. Strangely enough the aroma of home cooking and apple pie has also been noted in the same area, so perhaps it was used as a mess hall in the past as had been suggested.

Continuing with the tour, stories included numerous incidents related by the then janitor. Much like cleaners, they have a greater chance of seeing a ghost due to the unsociable hours they keep and here was no exception. Phenomena described, included, feelings of being followed and loud noises from no discernible source. Sometimes the sound of coughing had been heard and more alarmingly the sound of a man's voice uttering words, into the janitor's ear when working alone. It was also noted that during recent refurbishments the building had a particularly oppressive atmosphere and that the activities appeared more prolific. Perhaps the spirits were unhappy with the changes, displaying their ire by creating the sound of heavy banging doors despite the doors having been replaced with newer and quieter ones.

To finish we reconvened in the office where I was told of an incident which left me in no doubt as to the veracity of their claims. Witnessed by multiple people it remains unexplained to this day. Lorraine takes up the story: 'I remember the incident clearly as it involved a group of us. As you know we seem to always be having things moved around and this can be very frustrating especially if it's important. On this occasion one of our youth workers had literally put her keys down on the desk over there (she indicated a desk in the far corner) and had then turned to talk to us. On turning back to pick them up again they were gone. Of course, nobody had really paid any attention up till then, so we assumed she had mislaid them. We raked through pockets and searched the office and by now she was in a bit of a state as they were her only set of keys. We were standing in a huddle facing each other and all talking at once about where the keys had gone, when they dropped from above our heads and landed at our feet. We got such a shock and jumped back. Obviously, we were glad to get them back but were also annoyed and a little scared as whatever it was seemed to be playing around with us. We always got that feeling that whoever was still in the building liked to muck about and wind us up.'

Lorraine finished by stating that she believed spirits are still around us as we go about our daily lives and can at times appear mischievous. Before I left, I asked if they believed the building to be haunted, which they did, believing there to be more than one active spirit. They thought however that they were not permanent residents, which based on the evidence I was inclined to agree with.

Before we leave Kincorth I must mention one last thing. As you have read there have been sightings of soldiers in the area, which have been ongoing for years. I was recently in conversation with former resident Leanne who told me a very interesting story concerning her brother. Apparently when they were growing up in the family home at Covenanters Drive, her brother was plagued by the re-occurring dream of a soldier. Spookily the soldier would enter his bedroom at night, through the wardrobe. Obviously disconcerting, it was made worse in the aftermath of a conversation with their upstairs neighbour, who admitted to also having the same dreams. This begs the question, was it a visitation?

Reading over my notes, I am in no doubt that the area has many more secrets to share, which will become apparent as time goes by. Its rich past, now hidden beneath a modern exterior is all but hidden from the eye, though who knows what you might find, if you scratch beneath the surface.

Nazareth House

The Poor Sisters of Nazareth were a religious organization formed in Hammersmith in the mid-19th century. Their mission was to take care of both young and old and in subsequent years many of these so-called Nazareth Houses sprang up all over Britain. Perhaps well-meaning in principle, unfortunately some of these houses did not live up to their ethos, with certain individuals being accused of creating a harsh and brutal regime for their charges. Many of the children sent to these houses were either orphaned or were from homes where parents were unable to cope as was the case in Aberdeen where children from all over Scotland took up residence. In recent years Nazareth House in Aberdeen came under the spotlight for this reason when charges were brought against several of the sisters, accused of both mental and physical abuse. It is incredibly sad to think that these young voices went unheard for many years, and it is only in recent times that the full story of their plight has been recognised, some would say too late. As a child I remember walking by Union Grove on many occasions and thinking how dark and foreboding the building looked little realising what had gone on inside its walls.

The sprawling collection of Victorian buildings that make up Nazareth House in Aberdeen is now a care home for the elderly and as such has been impossible for me to visit. However, I met up with some former employees who were quick to let me know that the echoes of the past still reverberate through its corridors. Maureen, a lifelong care worker, explained the following:

'Carers at Nazareth House always said that they felt there was something unpleasant in the atmosphere of the building and particularly in one room which they did not like entering at night. This room was noted as being occupied by children long ago and it was not uncommon for people to say they could hear the sound, of children crying. This happened to me personally. You would feel an icy chill, and then hear crying when there was obviously no one else there.'

I asked Maureen if there was anything more, she could remember and she continued:

'I remember one time in the evening when I was in the kitchen with another colleague. I was working at the dishwasher emptying out some plates when the air turned icy cold. I remember remarking to the other carer how cold it had become. A few seconds later I saw what I can only describe as two clouds of blue/white smoke floating through the air towards us. The clouds came right up to where we stood. At this point the other carer let out a yell and ran from the kitchen. Strangely, I personally was not fazed by this as I have experienced things such as this in the past. The two cloudy shapes vanished as quickly as they had appeared and so I just kept working.'

I remarked how impressed I was with her fortitude and wondered how I would have coped in a similar situation. Naturally, I would like to think as stoically. She then contacted an old friend and former work mate who kindly volunteered the following and as before this incident took place near the kitchen.

'I remember there was one room which people had to pass on the way to the kitchen. The door to this room was sometimes open and although used in the day, was usually empty at night and therefore in darkness. I remember distinctly there were a couple of chairs near the door that could be seen quite clearly. One evening I was walking by this room, heading towards the kitchen. It was quite late, and I was on my own at the time. As I passed the open door, I did a double take and looking back I saw a blue vaguely human shaped object. It appeared to be sitting in the nearest chair. When I went to investigate it vanished before my eyes. In truth I was slightly nervous but curious as to what it was. A few days later and again in the evening the same thing happened as I walked by the open door. This time however the shape had moved and was sitting in the opposite chair. As before, and on my approach it quickly vanished. I wanted to get to the bottom of the matter, so I spoke to other colleagues who had worked there longer and who knew something of the history of the building. I was then told that one of the residents had died a little while back and these were her favourite chairs to sit in, she used to always wear blue. My colleague remarked that perhaps she was still around, being close friends with another resident who still used the room.'

Union Street

Aberdeen's Union Street is an impressive feat of engineering. In 1796 Charles Abercrombie an engineer and surveyor proposed a plan in which he would remove the top of St Katherine's Hill then the epicentre of the city and build a viaduct over the Denburn Valley. And so, in the early 1800s a series of arches were constructed above the undulating older medieval roads including a 60ft span over the valley which allowed the city to expand. Gradually the buildings we know today or at least the ones that have survived, began to appear while the buildings at the east end of the city had to be 'butted up' against these spans creating a series of vaulted chambers. Many of these chambers have now been blocked up however there are some that are still used for storage, and one hopes that the city takes a leaf out of Edinburgh's book and opens them up. I can't think of a better location to tell ghost stories in. Perhaps one day.

Ghost that allegedly haunt Union Street include the 'clencher', an invisible entity supposed to grab passers-by though who these passers-by are remains a mystery. Also noted is a white figure seen in the St. Nicholas Kirk graveyard. Information is scant with the latter only making one appearance and the former having all the hallmarks of an urban myth, so with this in mind, these next morsels have at the very least been genuinely witnessed in recent years.

Where better to begin than in the east end of Union Street where it all began just over two hundred years ago. The first building on our list is the Town House built by Peddie and Kinnear in 1865. Many years in the making this iconic structure houses both council offices and civic chambers and as with any building of its age it comes with a fair number of stories attached. These include objects moving of their own accord to the obligatory shadow figure seen lurking in the corridor near the magnificent central staircase. If you have been inside the building, then you know that it would not be too hard to let your imagination run riot in such surroundings. Cleaners have also reported hearing voices while on an early shift, with one being cheerily greeted by a disembodied voice which had wished them a good morning. Speaking recently to one of the town solicitors I was informed that one of the most common phenomena people talk about is the fact the swing doors are pushed open when there is no one present, well at least no one living. This happens continually and again cleaners tend to witness this while on early shift. I have been in the building while working and have tested those very doors, which are old, narrow, and extremely hard to push open, suggesting a natural explanation seems unlikely.

Perhaps more disturbingly I was told of an incident which took place in the same location some years earlier when a cleaner was forced to leave their position due to seeing something in the basement. Just what that something was, has never been disclosed, however a friend of mine who works there stated that the incident was common knowledge amongst staff, and so must have terrified them.

Five minutes' walk from the Tolbooth sits an innocuous building, formerly 'British Home Stores'. A bit of an architectural disaster it sits atop the Aberdeen New Market which replaced Archibald Simpson's, original New Market. Despite the building being relatively new (circa 1963) there are rumours that it is haunted. Coming in at 33,000 square feet the notion of being alone in its cavernous interior would be enough to cause anyone's imagination to work overtime. I spoke to members of staff at the time including Commercial Manager Sandra Currie and her colleague Eamon Mitchell, who kindly provided me with the following accounts.

'Eamonn and I were locking up the store. We used to go around together checking all the exits and entrances were sealed and ready for closure. The time was approximately 5.55pm. We have a radio in the stockroom which Eamonn remembers switching off at the plug point. The next day was the fourteenth of January 2010 which I remember clearly. I was opening the branch in the early morning and when I got into the stockroom, I found the radio on and blaring. There was no one else there and no one had been in during the night. I distinctly remember the radio being off. The timing of this incident was at 7.15am. I was not scared but rather intrigued. Having shared my experience with others I was quickly informed that other people in the floor above had seen a shadow which moved across the wall on more than one occasion. Someone mentioned the name "Maggie" which I suppose is associated with the alleged ghost.'

Eamonn Mitchell also added: 'I was in the building on my own responding to an alarm call out. I had already checked both the first and second floors and was just checking the third when the lift was called and began to ascend to the bottom floor. You need to push the button at the bottom floor to do this, so I was extremely perturbed.'

Perhaps one of the most beautiful buildings to grace Union Street was the Palace hotel. A grand traditional Victorian hotel it succumbed to a ferocious blaze in 1941 lingering on as a forlorn shell before eventually being demolished. In its place the ghastly C&A block was built which despite having no architectural merit still survives to this day. The building is now a Travelodge hotel and is rumoured to be haunted. Before looking at some of the stories associated with this building, I think it would be useful to look at the tragic history of the Palace Hotel as I am convinced what transpired there, has a bearing on the current manifestations.

The Palace Hotel was opened by the Great North of Scotland Railway in 1891 and quickly became known as the most luxurious in the city. Passengers entered a large reception room accessed from the joint station and were transported by a lift, courtesy of the American Elevator Company, to the upper floors. From Union Street guests were greeted by the sight of a well-proportioned vestibule decorated with tiles and polished marble. It was not known as 'the Palace' for nothing. It even boasted a heating system which was second to none piping warmth to every corner of the building. As an aside my grandfather worked there as a 'boots' after his return from the 'front' and would have had the unenviable task of polishing the shoes of the well-heeled if you pardon the pun. Like many others who worked there he would have seen luxury that would remain tantalizingly out of reach.

On the morning of Friday, October the 31st 1941, Aberdonians were greeted by the shocking headlines that a huge fire had destroyed the opulent landmark though given its ferocity many would have already been aware of the unfolding tragedy as flames lit up the night sky. Even during wartime with people being accustomed to tragedy this was a cause for deep sadness as six hotel employees, all women died after being trapped in the staff sleeping quarters despite the heroic efforts of the fire service. In the aftermath of the tragedy only a shell remained as a stark reminder of that terrible night and though it continued to dominate the corner of Bridge Street now instead of welcoming lights there were only empty windows. What could be done with such a building? There was talk of rebuilding but at what cost? And so, remained frozen in time as outside on the streets people came and went. An offer was eventually made by Dutch clothing retailer 'C&A Mode' and soon afterwards the remains were demolished. The new building as you can imagine was a workmanlike affair and has since that time housed numerous businesses and as mentioned is now a hotel.

Author James Warrender has a special interest in the building as his mother Carol-Ann witnessed an apparition there, so I was grateful for his contribution. I also spoke to current staff members, who I am pleased to report seemed more than happy to share their experiences though I have omitted some names as requested.

Below the hotel sits a car park, and on the tour, we found ourselves in a long corridor leading to an open doorway. On entering I found myself in a large barrel-vaulted room, one of a series of vaults that lie beneath Union Street. It was of a significant size and from the ceiling a pulley hung above a series of granite steps. I was told that this was once used for taking goods into the hotel. The brick walls were blackened at many points whether from age or from the fire I do not know. In one corner lay a large tangle of metal which looked like the remains of machinery that had been partially melted by fire. We returned to the upper floors where we bumped into a long-serving cleaner. After the introductions she mentioned she was in no doubt that something peculiar was going on in a certain room. The room in question was on the third floor and in it a figure had made frequent appearances, possibly due to an alleged suicide. Guests had also commented on this area and naturally staff had become wary whilst undertaking their duties. Of course, belief in ghosts is purely subjective and one lady made it abundantly clear she thought it was all nonsense. It was suggested that I leave and stop asking questions. I of course obliged only to sneak back once I had ascertained her shift pattern. I was rewarded by meeting cleaners keen to divulge their experiences. Suffice to say the belief that the building is haunted is a view shared by most.

Contacted by James, he told me the following: 'I spoke to my mum over the weekend, and I got as much information as possible from her. Apparently, many of the staff at the time were aware of these things happening and the owners had called in representatives from the church to perform an exorcism in the room that seemed to be troubled. It was all done in secret however people had an inkling of it happening though were told not to ask too many questions. I was told it was a Christian church that performed the exorcism rather than a spiritualist one and that it did not work as the activity continues. I was told the exorcism took place in the room and on the nearby landing due to poltergeist activity and because figures were being spotted in the vicinity'. He concluded by making the analogy, 'it's beginning to sound like the hotel from The Shining.'

Carol-Ann added: 'I was covering for the bar manager who was off at the time and my duties included cleaning up at the end of the day. On that occasion I was hoovering and knelt to pick up a coaster from the floor. I glanced up and saw a man sitting in one of the chairs. I noticed he was bald and appeared to be around fifty years of age though I do not remember what he was wearing. Just as I looked at him and he disappeared leaving an empty chair. I remember the day was a Wednesday at around 4pm and I was alone at the time. He was totally solid and had a drink in his hand. He was as clear as you or I am, and I did feel scared at the time. Many members of staff have heard and seen things in this building over the years. One place I did not like is the original kitchen from the Palace Hotel which is still there underground. It has a strange feeling to it although I have never seen anything untoward there. I believe the fact that some of the rooms are haunted is due to the number of incidents that have occurred over the years particularly on the third floor.'

I found the building intriguing, not just because it contained the remnants of the Palace, but also due the exorcism having taken place there. Of course, it is not unique in that fact as I have been told of two others in the area which have had similar issues. The first took place in a social club and the other in a former orphanage. In both cases employees were threatened with dismissal if they ever mentioned it. I was told that in the latter a priest was called in due to a raft of paranormal activities such as the sound of crying babies, unfortunately they were unwilling to say more. Suffice to say the building is now used as a residential home.

Another fascinating report comes from 'The Hydro Electric Shop' situated at 156 Union Street. Our main protagonist, Cathy, worked there for many years and her experience is quite unique due to the clarity of what she witnessed. Tasked with opening in the morning, staff would access the building by the back door, entering by the basement. In the basement lies the entrance to a tunnel which leads to Millburn Street, and it was in this area that the sighting took place. Duncan, a fellow enthusiast kindly arranged for us to visit Cathy's home and where she provided me with the following details.

'When I worked there several of my colleagues had remarked on the strong smell of Lavender that occasionally permeated the shop. We used to speculate as to what was causing this. There was a consensus that the building could be haunted. Anyhow, if you were opening in the morning, you let yourself in by the back door. At the rear of the shop there is a metal staircase leading to a small room and in it we kept our stock, such as kettles and irons. I had just put my coat into this room when I became aware of something behind me. I turned and noticed a shaft of light coming down the stairs. I was only a couple of foot away and I stood mesmerised as a figure began ascending the staircase. It was the form of a young woman I would guess around eighteen years of age and she floated rather than walked. I can still picture her very clearly. She wore a long flowing dress which was dark underneath but light on top. It was Lilac in colour and looked almost like a nightdress and petticoat. There was a lovely light emanating from her which I remember vividly. She was quite beautiful with porcelain-like features and had lovely blond hair with ringlets falling down her back. All the while she was smiling, I hoped at me, but perhaps that's wishful thinking. I noticed she had the most delicate hands and that she wore nothing on her feet. She continued to float by me towards where the entrance to the tunnel was. I was mesmerised.'

I asked at this point if she had felt scared? 'I was never scared, in fact quite the opposite. There was a great feeling of peace in the air. I just stood there and felt relaxed and at ease. She continued heading towards the entrance to the archway before disappearing. I mentioned it to a few folk and although some were intrigued others laughed it off as a bit of a joke. Anyhow I know what I saw and still feel lucky that I was witness to it. Some of my workmates, those who had smelt the scent of Lavender, naturally believed me. I am sad to say that I never saw her again'.

I left intrigued and soon after secured a visit to the shop. The current staff, all very helpful, gave me permission to photograph the location of the sighting. The steep metal staircase where the figure was seen leads to the basement where I was shown the tunnel which leads to the bottom of Crown Street. It looked like a very unappealing walk, but I was told it was inspected regularly. Sometime later I found out the upper floor had once been a function room where receptions were held. Perhaps the beautiful visitor had attended one in the past?

In June 2007 I had arranged to photograph the interior of the old Trades Hall on Union Street which sits within Primark. The hall built in 1848 was the original meeting place of the Seven Incorporated Trades of Aberdeen. More recently it housed a restaurant for Littlewoods' store. I met the assistant manager and was shown the hall which is now entered through the store. She mentioned that staff had for years maintained that they had felt a presence in the building particularly in the basement area. The basement lies within one of the arches that exist under Union Street and although sounding mysterious, their purpose was storage. She mentioned that rumours had circulated for years about the spirit of a ghostly piper who had been killed in the vicinity and that strange noises had been heard in the sealed off area but could not elaborate further. She then stated that some of the stories had existed from when Littlewoods owned the store. As there was no more to be gleaned, I left and after looking into the history of the area found that in proximity to the current building lay the 'kidnappers house.' Situated on the Green at the foot of 'Boots staircase,' it was eventually demolished in 1916, being then over three hundred years old. The kidnappers allegedly kept children there, before being shipped abroad as slaves, and were thought to have employed a piper to help mask the sound of their distress. This unsavoury practice was supported by council officials who turned a blind eye to proceedings and is part of the 'Indian Peter' story. I passed on the information to the assistant manager, and she seemed genuinely surprised as she knew nothing about the kidnappings. Incidentally I read recently that a former Café 52, employee had taken a photograph of the 'Boots' staircase at the end of his shift and was astonished to see it showed a series of orbs surrounding what he described as a clear image of a piper. I have not seen the image but of course would love to. It is intriguing to think that perhaps there was some truth in the stories though not meeting anyone who had first-hand experience of this I cannot in all honesty say. Perhaps it is only an urban myth, a fantasy bandied about for years as a means of unnerving new members of staff, but I did read a story recently on Facebook which would suggest otherwise.

The post was discussing the abandoned lower storage area under the Littlewoods building and the story recounted by a former butcher who had worked there. On delivery day, two porters had arrived with a consignment of meat destined for the storage area, which backs onto the Green. They were from Newcastle and Liverpool respectively and the butcher, Kevin, got chatting with them. According to the report behind two sets of steel doors is a long tunnel which runs under Union Street ending up at 'Bakers' (a former glassware shop) The men having some time to kill decided to have a poke around the abandoned area and fetching a torch they entered the tunnel. This was the only means of illumination as any attempt to install working lights had so far failed, leaving it unusable. Once inside they crept forward, describing seeing a large granite wall at the far end with bricked up windows on it. As they went further, they were suddenly alerted by the sound of running feet coming towards them. The footsteps came closer, getting louder, but the men now frantically shining the torch saw nothing. They turned and fled in terror, bolting through the doors before slamming them shut. It was stated that all thoughts of further exploration ended after the incident. As a footnote a former porter at BHS, also recalled how he heard footsteps and strange noises coming from an area, generally avoided by staff. I must admit the idea of exploring 'secret tunnels' sounds very appealing despite the possible hazards.

Speaking of tunnels, I was contacted by Debs who related an interesting experience which took place in the Tunnels nightclub. Having been opened for some time, its' an established music venue which sits within a few of the smaller spans at the east end of Union Street. This took place around 2005 and although no ghost was seen, there was sufficient spookiness involved to warrant inclusion. This is what I was told:

'I thought I would share, an uncomfortable experience I had around 15 years ago when I was attending a gig at the venue. I took some time out within the nightclub to cool down and sat at the table and chairs provided in the inner foyer. Construction was still apparent within the location, including the last tunnel on the left-hand side, which was still open but covered with wire fencing. I was completely alone and as I sat there myself, I began to feel the most intense and very strong feeling of evil, emanating from this large dark hole. I got up and went to find my friends as I had to get out of there. I am not easily scared but it was an absolutely, awful experience, and one I cannot readily explain. I've since been back, years later, and the end tunnel was thankfully walled up.' Deborah, after researching, mentioned the various uses for these tunnels in days gone by, including storage and even perhaps an ancient walkway to a long-gone Monastery. Of course, the area around the Green is rife with stories of deep ancient tunnels, burials and massacres, what place of such age is not? and perhaps we would feel cheated if there was not the odd 'ghost story' around.

Heading towards the west end we arrive at number 263, former home of Jones the bootmaker, another Union Street casualty. I visited the premises twice, the second being prior to its' closure, another casualty of Union Streets sad decline. Above the shop lies a derelict flat which I had the pleasure of photographing also and from my findings it would appear, that Union Street is full of such gems. Of course, this begs the question, who owns these properties? Why are the empty? Could they be put to some use? Perhaps one could prove the existence of ghosts more easily than the riddle of the absentee owner.

I had passed the shop for years and on occasion bought my kids shoes there but had never entertained the possibility of it being haunted. It looked too new, too bright. But appearances can be deceptive and behind the façade lay a much older building full of character among other things. Of course, I was delighted to hear that the building might 'haunted,' after receiving a tip off, so wasted no time in securing a visit. On arrival I was hugely impressed by their openness and for the courtesy they extended. They recounted numerous experiences which took place on the shop floor, the flat and in the stockroom, my first stop being the latter. In it I found rows of shoe-laden shelves and I imagined how eerie it must have been to retrieve a size six there, when all alone. At the end of the stockroom a steep staircase led to a stout door where next to it a heavy padlock hung from a hook. Behind the door a flight of stairs led to Langstane Place while upstairs lay a flat. The flat had been home to an elderly lady for years but since her passing had lain empty.

Derelict buildings can of course exude a certain atmosphere as did this one with its large empty spaces and creepy bathroom straight out of the 'Shining'. Believe me when I say it was the kind of place in which you would not like to linger. I did some filming while I was there and even looking at the footage made me nervous; it had that vibe. So that was the setting but now to the stories. There are three contributions which took place in the areas I have described. The first are from Julie who unluckily had three experiences to boast of.

She explains: 'I was unpacking a delivery downstairs while both of my colleagues were upstairs on the sales floor. I was kneeling on the floor busy unpacking boxes when I heard a friendly voice bid me hello. I could sense them in front of me as they walked by, but I did not look up but rather pulled the boxes to the side to allow them to pass. When I glanced up there was no one there. I then looked in both stockrooms expecting to find my colleague, but no one was there so I ran upstairs only to see them there. The second incident happened again in the stockroom when I was hoovering one morning. I was in the corridor when I felt my shirt get tugged. I ignored it at first, but it happened again but this time I clearly heard a child's voice asking me what the hoover was? It was an inquisitive voice, and it repeated the phrase 'what, is it? what is it?' Again, there was no one around. The third incident happened while I was going up the back stairs. This is the stair that leads to the old recording studio where we also keep stock. As I stood at the bottom an object dropped from above and landed onto the step, in front of me. I picked it up and found it was an old padlock and it was very heavy. The strange thing is the padlock hangs on a hook at the back of the door and it would have been impossible for it to fall off unless assisted. Incidents two and three were very strange, but I am still not sure about the first one. It may have been possible for a voice to have carried from elsewhere and perhaps a passing lorry caused a vibration which felt like someone walking past me. But not the others they were very odd.'

When visiting the flat afterwards, I was told about the padlock incident, and I can verify that it would have been impossible for it to have landed where it did. If it had dropped from the nail on which it hung it would have landed straight onto the top step due to its weight, rather than float out for around twelve feet before dropping. It was as if something had thrown it from the top step.

The next incident took place in the old recording studio which is directly outside the flat. Nobody knew when it had been a studio but the room, sectioned off into booths is now used as a stockroom. This area felt remote from the rest of the shop and not a popular place to be sent according to what I was told. The following was provided by Fiona.

'I was moving stock from the flat down to the shop floor, I took down a pile of boxes and when I left the door to the studio it was held open by the carpet. I came back soon after to find it fully closed. There was no way it could have closed by itself as the carpet prevented it from moving when open. There were no other people about, so it was difficult to explain. The place used to give people the creeps.'

Directly below lies the shop floor and it was there that Kieran experienced the following: 'I was standing upstairs in the full price section. It was Thursday evening and Fiona was downstairs. There was no one upstairs as the doors were closed. Suddenly I heard a bang, and I turned round and saw a child's shoe on the ground in the middle of the children's section. It could not have fallen of the shelf as there was a lip holding it in place and it certainly could not have made such a loud noise. Even more strangely it had landed a considerable distance from the shelves.'

Afterwards I wondered what the building had been used for in the past, and what would happen to it in the future for that matter. I heard later it may have once belonged to a doctor and was perhaps his home? I have been unable to pursue this further but hope to gather some historical detail as soon as practicable. Like other empty buildings, I often wonder if the spirit is still there, hoping to find someone new to play with, only time will tell.

Old Aberdeen

Picturesque Old Aberdeen existed as a separate burgh until being incorporated into the adjacent city by an Act of Parliament in 1891. Notable as a conservation area it is one of the only places in the city where there is still a proliferation of historical buildings, some dating back to the Middle Ages. Buildings of note include the late 15th century King's College Chapel, St Machar's Cathedral, the Old Town House and Powis Gates as well as numerous others sitting quietly on its leafy streets. Visiting the area is like stepping back in time and on quiet days it is easy to forget that mere yards away lies busy King Street and St. Machar Drive with its constant drone of traffic.

Given the age of the buildings it is considered by many to be the perfect location for ghost stories and certainly the area is rife with half-whispered tales. These include haunted graveyards, the wandering shade of a suffragette allegedly seen by police officers and the sighting of a ghostly hand in nearby St. Machar's Cathedral. As many of these tales are already public knowledge I have instead focused on those, that are more obscure, including one particularly creepy incident involving a cellar, where better!

As we approach the Spital we reach the back gates of St. Peter's Cemetery. Just opposite lies a building which I first read about some years back and the owners experiences were very intriguing. After a little research I found that others nearby had witnessed similar sights though if they continue right to this day I cannot say. The homeowner Patricia Reith mentioned that both her and her husband had been in the process of renovating a very old four storey building which had two derelict buildings on either side of it, one of which was an old doctors' house. One night she inexplicably woke only to find the figure of a woman standing near the bed staring at her. The light from the streetlamp outside illuminated the room and she could see the figure very clearly. Described as being severe looking with hair tied back in a bun, she wore a high-collared blouse and a long dark skirt while around her waist she carried a set of keys on a chain. She was convinced the woman was aware of her as she continued to stare before eventually turning slowly and walking off. Disturbingly, the figure then began to walk upwards as if on non-existent stairs. The witness spent the rest of the night awake in fear of her return, which to her relief did not happen, though afterwards her presence was occasionally sensed. Speaking to her neighbours sometime later, one of whom operated the bakers' next door, she was told they had also been visited by her. The buildings opposite still stands to this day however the old bakery has since gone.

Many years ago, I was intrigued to read the story of how some schoolchildren in the late 1960s witnessed what was described as a hand with purplish fingers protruding from the door of St Machar's Cathedral. There were no further details given or indeed what the outcome was, though I suspect if it were true, they would not have enjoyed the experience. This however is the location of our next story and the witness Eddie explained in our meeting, how a nights' drinking ended on a sour note.

'On my way home one night me and a friend decided to stop off at St. Machar Cathedral. We had been drinking, but not excessively, so we probably were braver than usual. On entering the cemetery, we decided to rest for a while and sat on a nearby bench. We began chatting and proceeded to put the world to rights. The interior of the churchyard was dark, but we quickly grew accustomed to the gloom. We could see the gates quite clearly for example, despite being seated some distance away. Out of nowhere we became aware of the approaching sound of heavy footsteps and noticed a tall dark figure walking along the path towards us. The figure continued past us and because of the dark we could not see his features. I called after the passing figure and asked if he had a light, having lost mine earlier in the evening. The figure did not acknowledge me, so I stood and repeated the question more loudly. Again, it did not reply but instead broke into a run. We then froze as it ran full pelt towards a row of headstones and vanished just at the point of impact. I can tell you we both instantly sobered up and ran for it. To this day I am convinced I saw a ghost.'

The nearby Chanonry is the location of our next story. Beautiful during the day with abundant trees nestling gently against the surrounding buildings, but when darkness falls, well that is a different matter. I was told the following by Mrs James, who walking one evening in 1968, was passing the back gates of the Old Aberdeen School. Despite the passage of time, she remembered clearly it was on the 2nd of January at around 8.30 on a cold winters' night. Earlier in the evening she had been visiting relatives in nearby Seaton and on her return took a short cut through the Chanonry. There was no one around and the air was frosty and still. Footsteps approached and looking up she saw an elderly couple walking towards her with their dog. At that moment, her gaze was drawn to a large wall about fifteen feet ahead. Leaning out from the wall was the figure of a man whom she took to be around fifty years of age. He was wearing what she described as a white fisherman's jumper and was looking directly at her. Nothing unusual you would think except there was not an aperture in the wall. She explained: 'He was looking at me as if he was leaning out of a window. It was only the top part of his body though as the bottom half did not exist only the wall. The hair stood up on the back of my neck and I began to shiver uncontrollably.' She went on to say that at that moment her only thought was to make some distance between her and the figure. Despite over forty years passing she remembers that night with great clarity.

Moving down onto the High Street the spires of King's College now come into view. As with the Chanonry it has numerous buildings vying for one's attention: the Powis Gates, the tiny and much overlooked Snow Kirk last resting place of Priest Gordon and nearby King's College. Directly in front of the latter, lies the tomb of Bishop Elphinstone and it was on this spot that a passer-by allegedly witnessed a ghostly duel. The witness asked his name be omitted for personal reasons, however he was adamant that what he saw was genuinely paranormal. Returning home through the stillness of the High Street, the usually bustling streets were bereft of students being out of term-time. It was approximately 11pm and though getting dark the sky had enough light left to illuminate the surrounding area. In the gathering dusk he noticed movement on the grass directly to his right and glanced over. He was shocked to see two men in what he described as 'musketeer type clothing' engaged in combat. They whirled and parried with long thin swords and although appearing solid he noticed that there was a certain 'wispiness' to their forms. He stopped and stared transfixed, initially thinking it was either a prank or a re-enactment, though retrospectively he concluded that it would have been a strange time to indulge in such activities. He stood for some seconds before realising that when their swords met there was no sound, the spell broken, he now ran from the scene. He stated that he did not feel scared as such but was unsure of what would have happened had they noticed him. I reassured him that in my opinion if they were ghosts then they would have likely, been completely unaware of his presence.

Other tales associated with the area that I have heard of include that of a ghost seen coming from the Snow Kirk, but for the moment exact details are scant. It is without doubt an area rife with tales and of course given its age it is the least one can expect. Sticking to the High Street, this next story was sent to me very recently and was a genuinely terrifying experience for the unwilling participant, which I am sure you will agree.

'Many years ago, I had a friend called Jean who lived on the High Street, and she told me this story which I believe to be true. When she and her family first moved into the house, she was continually woken by the sensation of someone touching her head. She asked her family if they were responsible, but they denied doing it. One night when it happened, she woke suddenly to see a figure at the end of the bed beckoning to her, to follow. She followed it downstairs into the corridor where the figure lifted the carpet to reveal a trapdoor. This was opened and Jean walked down some stairs to the basement. There she witnessed the most horrific murder. This vision or whatever it was, terrified her so much that afterwards she could never bring herself to tell anyone exactly what she saw. After the incident Jean returned to her bedroom. She told me that from that day on, she never again felt the strange sensation on her head. Of course, when she woke the following morning, she rushed downstairs lifting the carpet to find the trapdoor, but there was no sign of it. She then questioned whether it was a horrible dream or if it had been something stranger. Some time passed and one day she called into the local corner shop. It started to rain so she lingered in the shop and began chatting to the shopkeeper. During the conversation, the shopkeeper said: 'you live at number.......don't you? Did you know that a murder was committed in your house?' Jean, unwilling to hear any more about it, sped out into the rain.'

Was it a ghost trying to tell her something? And was it at peace once the circumstances were revealed? According to her friend, Jean was witness to some horrible replay from the past, the content of which she could not bring herself to describe. I hope one day to find out the exact details of the crime, if indeed there had been one.

Just along the road in the Crombie Johnston Halls, Laura, a former resident, and graduate recalled the following. 'I lived there in my 1st year, and we all saw odd things. One of the wardens would point out the nearby Snow Kirk, claiming it could be responsible for some of the activity and I believe to this day I saw something while staying there. The figure was that of a young man, dressed in what I would describe as out of date fashions. The first time I saw him was in C wing and when I was coming back from the library. I remember it was just before ten as the doors had still to be locked by the warden. The figure was as clear as day and as I did not recognise him as a resident, I said hello, asking him if he lived there. I received a very soft hello, in response before he vanished right before my eyes. He was quite tall, had brown hair, a handsome face and longish hair, a sort of 90s boy band look. I saw him a few times during my 1st year and again in my 3rd and 4th, when doing ad-hoc reception work at Crombie.

One of the security guards now retired, also told me he had seen him. I have never seen an entity as clear as him in all my life, he was so close I could have touched him. I did ask around the halls in my 1st year if anyone else had seen him, as I could not quite believe what I had witnessed. No one recognised my description, and in fact I got a lot of stick about it until one of my neighbours saw him too. They got a real fright. During my time there I did a little research to see if there were any deaths at the halls but there was none, however an old copy of the Press and Journal which I found in the library, mentioned a male student who died in a car accident had lived in the halls. That was as far as I got with it.'

Old Aberdeen has many more treasures lurking, of that I am in no doubt. Stories continually crop up, some just rumours, some often repeated and others that have real substance. The witnesses to those we have just seen were all credible and the experiences were life-changing in some ways. Given the opportunity, I would love to be able explore some of the buildings in the area, as I am convinced, I have just scratched the surface.

St. Katherine's Centre: Shoe Lane

The quaintly named Shoe Lane is a small, blink-and-you-miss-it thoroughfare off Queen Street. Once home to numerous businesses it now contains only a handful of buildings including the Lemon Tree venue, a crèche and above it an office space, once rented by the Workers' Education Association. The Lemon Tree situated in what was once the St. Katherine's Centre, or St. Kay's as it was affectionately known is haunted as we have already discovered, but what of the surrounding buildings? The office space for example is modern and of no historical significance though it sits near to both Marischal College and the original Greyfriars Church. Does this have any bearing on matters? Maybe, maybe not, but having once worked there, I can categorically state, it is haunted. What my colleagues and I experienced over the course of two years prompted us to seek help and only then some clues were found. In short it oozed a feeling of dread which sent more than one person scurrying for the exit myself included.

I had for some time, like my colleagues experienced feelings of unease but my first solid experience occurred one winter's afternoon in November 2009. The building was accessed by a steep double staircase and was literally a box like structure. On the right-hand side of the stair was a door that led through to the Lemon Tree while below sat the creche. The interior was cramped and consisted of a long narrow corridor leading to a kitchen and meeting room. Off the corridor were two more meeting rooms and two bathrooms. The first contained a broken shower while the second just sinks. It was all very 1970s, a bit tatty and depressing to be truthful. It all began at around 8.30 one morning when I unlocked the building as usual. Heading towards the coffee jar, I passed the second bathroom and glancing in, was startled by the fleeting glimpse of a woman with long dark hair. She was bent over the sink and appeared to be washing her hair. My momentum carried me past the door, but I quickly stepped back only to find the room empty. The impression of the figure stayed with me for some time after and I mentioned it to my line manager Annie on her arrival. Though not overjoyed to hear the news, she wasted no time in telling me that I was not alone in experiencing something. She went on to say that fellow workers had also felt uneasy in the corridor, sensing someone was behind them while locking up. One morning as I opened the building, I met with Fiona, who worked downstairs. She asked me who had been working late last night. I of course said, no-one which was true as we had all left at 5.30pm. She looked surprised and informed me that on many occasions she had heard footsteps walking back and fore from above and assumed we had been working late. I half laughed assuring her that we were not that diligent. The feeling of unease intensified.

Things came to a head on Thursday 17th December 2009 when myself, my line manager and five others witnessed what can only be described as extreme poltergeist activity.

The word 'poltergeist.' as you are no doubt aware is of German origin and means 'noisy ghost' and the description certainly seems apt for what was to follow.

Because of the strange phenomena I had taken it upon myself to try and find out why it might be happening. Was there something of historical significance causing this? What kind of buildings had existed there? It was an impossible task given the areas' vast history, but I produced a grab bag of facts which I hope would help. I should mention that it was the day of the end of term party which we always held for our students. It was an opportunity to catch-up informally and talk of future plans and the conversation quickly turned to ghosts. I mentioned to Annie some of my findings, which included evidence of a Victorian plumbing shop in the vicinity. She jokingly made a comment about a phantom plumber being the culprit which we found quite funny, but our laughter was curtailed some minutes later by the sound of loud footsteps on the stairs. It was Fiona from the crèche below who then announced that there was water pouring in through their ceiling. The source located seconds later, was the shower and despite having never been used during our tenure was merrily spraying water onto a rapidly expanding puddle. On entering the cubicle, the handle was found to be obstinately rigid despite the combined effort of both me and my colleague. A brief struggle ensued in which we received a soaking, but eventually it was cranked to, 'Off.' But what could have had the strength to turn it on in the first place? The unanswered question hung in the air as did a palpable sense of brooding, so the following mop-up was done rapidly. Whatever it was had obviously reacted to our throwaway comments and taken exception to them, therefore we agreed to be a little more respectful in future. Fearfully we returned to the meeting room and after making excuses the six witnesses left. The party was over.

It was because of this incident we decided to hold a vigil in the building to try and get some closure. We gathered a team consisting of my co-workers Annie, Ross, and Stan as well as a medium, Linda. Meeting in the early January we waited till evening and having decided in advance to concentrate on three rooms we set up our recording equipment but within minutes something had drained all the batteries rendering our attempts to record proceedings as futile. To this day I cannot explain why two recorders, a hand-held camera and recording camera all failed at the same time. Answers on a postcard please. Despite this we decided to carry on and so Linda asked us to sit in a circle and join hands. Very soon she appeared to be communicating with someone and as the temperature dropped, she began to receive a steady flow of information. The person communicating, she stated, was named Charlie, and was a former caretaker who had worked in the building. She went on to say it was a derogatory nickname given to him by some previous centre users who didn't respect him. He communicated certain practices had taken place in the building which he had not agreed with, though what these practices were remained unclear. Linda then went on to say she was picking up an image of two woman who were in a relationship. One was older and she could plainly see her bullying the other. She paused before continuing, stating that the elder of the two was shoving her partners head into the sink forcing her to wash her hair. This revelation was met with stunned silence and the atmosphere both heavy and depressing remained until Linda called a halt to proceedings. It was probably just as well, some members of the group felt very emotional and one person, who by his own admission was very sceptical of proceedings became very upset. Afterwards when questioned he could not explain why. Incidentally, a full glass of water left in the bathroom was retrieved soon after and found to be unaccountably drained.

We reconvened in the main student room, a feeling of relief amongst the group. Linda carried out the promised blessing and once done we left, everyone deep in their own thoughts. We had found some answers it seemed but would the blessing work. Only time would tell. I left the job soon after but kept in touch and was informed that for quite some time the atmosphere felt lighter and less ominous but as the year wore on and the dark nights returned, the gloom slowly manifested. Perhaps what hangs in the ether will never truly go away, and though we caught a glimpse, there may be worse things still to be uncovered.

The Gordon Barracks

The Bridge of Don, an area to the north of Aberdeen City, is a large sprawling suburb consisting of housing and retail parks. Although many of the houses are relatively new there are some interesting buildings in the area including the Gordon Barracks. After the closure of the original barracks at Castlehill the soldiers were moved to their new headquarters in Bridge of Don. The year was 1935 and much was made of the event as the massed ranks marched along King Street to take up their new residency. Most of these B listed buildings are still in existence today but are now used for a wide variety of purposes including home to the Territorial Army, the Sea Cadets and 'The Northern College'.

I had often passed these buildings and never gave them a second thought until a chance meeting with a former tutor from 'The Northern College'. During our meeting I was told that in the middle of a lecture she became perturbed after being poked sharply in the back with what felt like a finger. Turning as surreptitiously as possible, given the room was full of students, she saw no one. She carried on with the lesson only to have the same thing happen a few minutes later and again stopped. Soon after the sharp prod was again repeated. By now she was extremely uncomfortable with the situation but thankfully whatever it was had gotten bored and stopped. During our conversation, she described to me the immense relief in being able to wind up the session without further interruption. This incident was not repeated in her classroom however she did state that for the next few sessions there was a palpable feeling of expectation that it would happen again. Despite claims that other tutors had experienced something similar it was years later before I heard of anything further. This time from a former nurse Wendy, whose mother had worked at the barracks. This is what she told me:

'My mum was a nurse at the barracks, and she had to work an overnight shift at the M.R.S building. She could not get anyone to stay with me and my brother, so we had to go with her. My brother and I had a room each in the old isolation ward and we also had our dog with us for company. He stayed in the room with me so I had to keep the door closed so he wouldn't wander about during the night. The beds were typical old fashioned hospital beds and were quite high. Along the top of the wall there were glass windows running the length of the room to where the door was located. I remember thinking I hope I can get to sleep, because of the light coming through the windows and the door. I prefer a room to be pitch black to get to sleep in, but despite this I eventually did. In the middle of the night, I woke suddenly and saw a glow in the shape of a head and shoulders at the side of my bed. It immediately started to fade and as it did, the dog put his front paws up against the side of the bed and started sniffing round the edge of the head and shoulders until it disappeared. I was not alarmed or scared, and the dog sniffed round the room for some time afterwards until I fell asleep again.'

I asked her if she knew of any other stories connected to the ward, but she had only heard that male nurses did not like the atmosphere in that part of the building. She did however mention the following: ' I used to babysit for one of the medic's sons and anytime we were in the M.R.S, he would consistently toddle up to the isolation ward. He seemed fascinated with the door leading to it. No matter how many times I picked him up and took him back to the other end of the corridor he would always go back despite there being no one there. Our dog was also fascinated with the isolation ward both before and after my experience and would continually sniff around the door. I was not upset in any way, just slightly shocked.' When I asked if she had any thoughts on what she had seen that night? she replied, 'I believe it was a ghost.'

Not long afterwards I was pleased to receive a story concerning a now demolished part of the complex. I met Kenneth Rae through work where he attended a course and when mentioning my interest in the paranormal, he told me the following story. Again, I have written it in his own words.

'The building I am going to tell you about was known as the 'house' or at least that's what we used to call it. I believe it used to be the Officer's Mess and was situated at the back of the barracks. The area has changed since then, and now flats are built there now. We experienced many incidents in and around there, which began when we were around 14 years old and continued even during its demolition. It was a massive building and had two back doors one on the far left and one on the far right. Both led to a very long hallway with rooms going off it. It had a large staircase on both the left and right sides and one in the middle which led to the second floor. There were a further two double doors at the back which were both locked. All the windows were boarded up and all the floors empty of furniture and fittings apart from the kitchen having a few sinks and units and the odd fireplace. The other rooms had the occasional mirror or wardrobe. Due to the boarded-up windows it was in permanent darkness apart from little bits of light which came through the gaps in the windows. Most of the time you needed to use a torch even during the day and most definitely at night when it was pitch black. It was an adventure to sneak around the deserted building and myself and three friends visited there on numerous occasions, as did many other kids from the local area. My first experience happened one afternoon. I can't remember the time exactly now, but I remember there were four of us in the building. My friend and I were chatting at the foot of the main staircase while the others were upstairs. I remember we were standing by what I think was a living room though it had no door. The window on the staircase was boarded up but there was some light coming in from a skylight window. Suddenly a shadow-like figure appeared on the wall right beside me. It had a strange triangle shape and was around five feet tall. Strange as it sounds it appeared to have no limbs or head. It was very odd. It started to slowly go across the wall past the living room entrance then disappeared at the room which had no door before moving up the stairs at what I would describe as walking speed. It went to the first stair landing where the boarded-up window was, it then turned and continued up to the second floor. It reached the wall there and disappeared. What was odd, was that initially we carried on chatting and did not find the incident scary though we wondered what was causing it. About five minutes later it reappeared and followed the same pattern as before disappearing when it reached the wall near us. This time we began to feel nervous. Our friends were still upstairs and when it appeared for a third time, we shouted for them to come down which they did quickly. We left the building immediately.'

I wondered at this point if perhaps some light source from outside or reflection from a passing vehicle could have caused the appearance of the shape, like a light passing across a ceiling at night, but I did not mention this. Kenneth continued: 'At the time I heard about this guy at school who was pretty tough. He had been there himself poking around with his friends. They decided to go upstairs and came across some rooms with closed doors. He went into one of these rooms on his own and saw an old man sitting there, wearing a waistcoat and hat. All his clothes were dirty and were described as glowing bright blue. He was meant to have run out of the house crying his eyes out. That is what I heard but not what I saw though'. I asked Kenneth to tell me more about his own personal experiences and he continued with the following which occurred at the time of the demolition.

'It was around eight in the evening, and we found ourselves standing in the dark nearby. This was at the time when it was getting demolished so there was a lot of scaffolding round the building. There were also large mounds of earth and rocks everywhere as they had started digging up the ground. There were only two of us out and as we approached, we noticed a small fire burning in the front of the building. There were only some small bits of wood on it, and we wondered if some workman had left it burning and it had been kept alight by the breeze. As we crept nearer, we could hear a strange 'tinging' noise which got louder and faster the nearer we came. Perhaps it was the wind making the scaffold produce the noise, but we weren't sure and the fact that the noise kept getting louder made us nervous. Something made us turn round at that moment and we saw a very bright white looking figure. Again, I would describe it as being rectangular in shape though this time it had a round-looking head but without features. It was totally white and around five feet tall. It seemed to be floating and moved behind a large mound of rocks. We stood and waited but it did not come out from the other side which freaked us out. I wanted to see what was behind the mound but my friend being too scared refused and left. I walked towards the mound determined to find out what it was but lost my nerve before I got there and ran from the site. I caught up with my friend at the gate and to be honest we had such a bad feeling from the incident we never went back. I have never shared these experiences with anyone before, apart from (obviously) those that were there, but believe them to be paranormal. I will never forget what I saw, but I do regret not being brave enough to see what was behind the mound.'

I have not visited the site for many years though I am aware of the changes that have taken place. It was interesting to get some stories from an area of the city that up till then had been bereft of ghost stories. Perhaps there are others waiting to be told after all it is a very old building which I suspect, has a colourful history.

Ouija Boards: Just Harmless Fun?

The Ouija board is widely recognised in Western culture as an aid for automatic writing supposedly when a spirit imparts messages from the other side. But does it produce genuine results or is it as many believe, just a bit of harmless fun? In this chapter I have looked at both sides of the argument and in doing so will provide a few examples of why its perhaps best not to meddle.

The roots of the phenomenon of automatic writing were first seen in China around 1100 BC and it was stated that the use of a planchette or wooden- movable indicator was used in producing a series of scripts. These scripts were in essence communicated by those in the spirit world to scribes on the physical plane and it is interesting to note that many other scholars in diverse locations such as India, Greece, Rome, and Medieval Europe were thought to have practiced this type of spirit communication as a means of transcribing religious documents.

In more modern times planchettes were sold as novelties until the year 1891 when two American businessmen Elijah Bond and Charles Kennard patented the idea of a planchette sold with a board on which the alphabet was printed. An employee, of Kennard William Fuld, took over the production of the talking board as it was known and in 1901 gave it the name by which it is known today: 'Ouija'. The name derives from both the French and German words for yes. Kennard claimed it was given to him while using the board and initially stated that it came from an ancient Egyptian word meaning good luck. Either way the board's use became increasingly popular. At first the act of using the board was regarded as a harmless parlour game until American spiritualist Pearl Currans began using it for her experiments. This occurred around the time of the Great War, when the use of the board took on a new meaning, accepted by many as a means of communication with the dead. It comes as no surprise that interest in the spiritualist movement was at its peak during this time due to the tragic loss of so many young lives. Despite a waning interest in spiritualism after the war the boards continued to sell well, right up until the 1960s when toy manufacturers, 'Parker Brothers' bought the rights.

Mainstream Christian religion has criticized the use of the board for its reputation for enticing evil but whether this is true or not, is debateable. The scientific community on the other hand always on the lookout for a rational answer have concluded that it is the unconscious movements of those controlling the pointer, that is giving the messages and have christened the psychological phenomena, 'the ideomotor effect'.

The volume of evidence I have personally collected would be enough to fill a book therefore I have picked out a few of the most interesting stories which if nothing else should provide the curious with a note of caution. Both parties are close associates whom I have known for many years, so again I believe their testimony to be truthful. Incident one took place in the early 1970s in the Springhill Road area of the city where Dave was involved with a group of friends who regularly used a board. This is his story:

'When my friends parents went out for the evening this was the signal to meet up at their house where we would use a board. One night we were having a laugh, it was all light-hearted at first. The glass was moving around the board getting yes and no answers but then the atmosphere changed, and an intense feeling came over everyone. Suddenly the door opened and in walked my pal's parents. Normally they would be out for hours but the person they had gone to visit was not in. My finger was still on the glass and as I pulled it away in surprise there was a flash and I got what felt like an electric shock. There was a mad dash to hide the evidence. They would have been furious if they had known what we were up to, so the board was quickly hidden away. We were all trying to act normal and so had a cigarette with his folks before making our excuses and leaving. We parted company outside the house, and I began the walk back to my house. I headed back towards Byron Crescent and thought nothing more of the evening's events until I heard quiet footsteps behind me. I glanced round and saw nothing so carried on my way. Again, I could hear the sound behind me and looked back again seeing nothing. I must admit I was very nervous and began to walk faster. I always remember that I was wearing brand new white plimsolls which obviously make very little noise while walking, so was convinced the footfalls behind me were coming from a much harder shoe. I started to run and could hear the steps which were right behind me also speed up. Out of breath and scared by this point I rushed past the terminus and reached my gate. I ran up the path, fumbling with the key. I was in a panic to get in the house and did not dare look back as I had heard the gate opening behind me. I rushed in and slammed the door. The speeding footsteps continued up the path before bang! something struck the glass part of the door. I was very scared and standing by the inner door noticed something dark behind the frosted glass before it slowly began to recede back down the path before disappearing. To me it looked like the figure of a nun. I remember trying to get my breathing back to normal as I entered the living room where my dad was watching telly. I remember him asking if I was all right as I probably looked as white as a sheet. Anyhow I stopped using the board and thankfully never experienced anything like that again. My friends of course thought I was winding them up.'

The second story I was given is possibly even more disturbing and took place in 1985 when Robert was invited to a party by his then girlfriend, situated in Cults. Nearby sat, 'Netherley,' a house which had been lying empty for some time, which is an important element of this story. It had over time, become a magnet for local teenagers fascinated by its large empty rooms and basement. Adding to its mystique, was a miniature pet cemetery which lay at the foot of the garden. Being remote and well-hidden the basement area was used for all sorts of clandestine activities, and it was common to hold Ouija board sessions there away from prying eyes. Robert being older had never participated in any of these sessions but knew from his girlfriend that they had taken place. The fact they were held in a deserted and spooky old house only added to the thrill. Not long after, the group attended a party at a mutual friends' house. It was, by all accounts low-key and Robert decided to retire to the spare room, where he soon fell asleep, subsequently suffering from a terrible nightmare. This is what he told me:

'During the night I had this hellish dream. I dreamt that two figures were coming out of a mist towards me. The two figures a male and a female both had malevolent expressions and a terrible feeling of anger radiated from them. By their side was a large black dog which was growling. In my nightmare the dog appeared to now be in the corner of the room in which I was sleeping, and I awoke terrified. At that instant I could hear the loud scraping of paws on the bedroom door which at that point literally burst open. Two dogs bounded into the room and my heart nearly stopped. After a few moments of stark terror, I realised that these dogs were the hosts pets and were perfectly friendly. It was just a strange coincidence, but it gave me a great shock. I decided to wait until the next day to tell my girlfriend about the incident. She looked deadly serious as I explained what had happened. Hesitantly she told me that for many years she and various friends had not only been holding séances and Ouija board sessions in the old basement at Netherley but also in the spare bedroom which he had slept in. She went on to say that at the time of the sessions they thought of them as just harmless fun, until one day something came through that changed their outlook. She described that during this session the alleged spirits of a young couple killed in a car crash relayed a message describing in no uncertain terms that they were angry because of their fate. Their dog had also been killed in the accident.'

For every horror story there will always be many who have found Ouija board sessions to be nothing but fun. And while the scientific community damns it all as codswallop, I personally have serious reservations. Perhaps too I am being superstitious, but the weight of evidence suggests otherwise, and am aware of the possibility of the long-term psychological damage that can be brought on by the obsessive use of the board. To illustrate my point perhaps the following sobering account told to me by Stanley Robertson will suffice.

Around eight years ago I had the privilege of interviewing Stanley Robertson who by his own admission was in possession of great psychic abilities. Such was his reputation as a writer and singer he was frequently asked to host events around the world. On this occasion he had kindly offered to help with a local history project and so over the course of two fascinating hours we were treated to numerous anecdotal tales and songs which reflected his interests in the travelling community and the supernatural. This what he told us:

'A ghostly experience is not necessarily a frightening one. The thing is they have never really left us but are just in a different dimension. Sometimes our two worlds cross over. The old travelling people used to say there was a time in 'the deid ceilings' of the night when heaven and earth pass by close, and this is when ghostly occurrences were likely to happen. The thing is ghosts don't hurt you. Some are sad, some are happy, and some don't want to leave, but the thing you must worry about is demons because that is nothing to do with them. The demons are those that walked out with Lucifer before the world was. You can read this in the Old Testament. They chose Lucifer so they would never be born. So, all ghosts are folk that have lived and died, so their activities are still there, but they do no harm. Demons have always been here they have been liars from the beginning and will always be liars. So, when you play about with Ouija boards you are tapping into that. I had a real, real bad experience once. I never tap into these but when my second book came out, I was asked to do a psychic programme on the radio. There are all these psychics of the land, but they are as psychic as a flea. I was invited onto a programme. It was a Northsound radio program, and they were having a phone in. This man said to me what kind of psychic are you anyway? I said I am a natural psychic. He said that is the best one to be and I laughed. Some man phoned in and said he had bought this beautiful table which he cleaned up and painted it with runic signs, which he said was very beautiful. He went on to say that he shared a flat with his girlfriend and another lad called Gordon on King Street. He said the only thing is with the table, is that he really enjoyed playing with it. His girlfriend and Gordon also started using it and it began to tell them little true things. Just little things it was telling them to start with. Every night they would play with this table, they would even have little parties. One night, Gordon was asleep, and the lassie was playing with the table when suddenly what they described as a puff of smoke came off the table. She claimed that the figure of what looked like a witch appeared, who claimed she had been summoned by the lassie dabbling with the board. She disappeared but despite the scare they kept tinkering with it and this thing would appear. The lassie was terrified, but Gordon remained unaware of this happening. One night the lad claimed that the figure was in the room when they arrived home and told him to get the machete which they kept in the room. Gordon was in his room asleep, and it demanded that they bring it Gordon's head. The lassie was terrified and ran and dragged Gordon from his bed and took him outside as the boyfriend seemed to want to do this. I told him at this point that he had opened a gateway to hell, and it was very, very dangerous. Folk don't realise or want to believe how dangerous it is. He asked me what my advice would be, and I told him that first off, you must destroy the gateway, which was the table. He refused to do this, but I said that if he didn't, this thing would always be able to get through. I then said once he had destroyed it he should go find a priest. I didn't want to get involved in any of this, but he said he needed to see me face to face. I've a big family and am very careful of whom I meet. Anyway, I told him I was having a book launch at Waterstone's so if he wanted to see me it had to be there. Anyhow a heap of people attended and when I looked over there was a guy and a gothic looking lassie, and I knew right away it was them. So when they came about me, I noticed the guy had a briefcase. I asked him if he had gotten rid of the Ouija board, and he told me he had sanded it and took off the symbols and was now using it as a card table. I said you still have a gateway. He told me that they still feel a presence, but she does not appear. He then opened the briefcase and took out a photo of the board, which really was the most beautiful thing it was a piece of classic art but as soon as I saw it, I felt myself going through and insisted it must be destroyed. He said he did not have the heart to destroy it but said he would put it away where it could not be seen. So, you see, folk tap into these things and just don't realise how dangerous it is.'

Stanley naturally never visited their home so had no way of verifying the events though his reaction to the photograph, and how it made him feel was real. As for me I cannot say either how much was true or embellished by the owner of the board however it would seem to me that they had gone to great lengths to tell their tale which would suggest there must be some element of truth attached. One could come to any number of conclusions about their story, possible mental illness brought on by compulsive behaviour, a need to be listened to or possibly overactive imaginations. Yet again there may well have been a demonic manifestation in the flat, and if so, would you want to use the Ouija board again?

Twenty-four years after the incident in Cults I am taking my colleague and his friends for a ghost walk around the Castlegate area of the city. In the pub afterwards the conversation turns to the paranormal. The participants all attended Cults Academy and my colleague Ross mentions the deserted house in Cults where many years ago they used to hold séances.

'We used to muck about with boards and being teen-agers' we did not think much of it. On one occasion we were in the basement larking about when someone suggested we hold a séance. My dad had died recently, and someone suggested that we try and speak to him. I was cynical, however I asked out anyway. I thought I would ask something that nobody would know to try and find proof, so I asked some questions about his first wife. They lived in Glasgow, and I had never met her. I asked what was inscribed on a necklace that had been given to my dad, by his first wife. I had never shown this necklace to anyone but had kept it as a memento. The glass began to move around the board very deliberately and spelled out 'Always Yours.' I was completely shocked as were the others when I showed them the necklace, as those were the exact words inscribed on the inside. We stopped afterwards as everyone was freaked out. Like I say the building was used a lot by school kids to hang out in and using the Ouija was a common occurrence. Strangely enough I heard from someone recently who knows the current owners and allegedly there are still odd things that happen there periodically. The building of course has been modernized since I knew it.'

I then mentioned the incident involving the terrible dream and the dogs. One of the group Jane coincidentally remembered Roberts' girlfriend, indicating that a vague story concerning a couple being killed in a car was also circulating at that time, at which point I shuddered.

Personally, I have had no real experience of using the Ouija board and certainly do not feel the need to rectify this. I recently took a tour of the Castlegate area of Aberdeen, and the subject of the Ouija came up as it invariably does. The person in question mentioned incidents concerning both friends and family who had 'dabbled' in the past. This included her brother who many years back had been using the board with friends and had received a terrible fright when they had allegedly and inadvertently contacted the spirit of Jack the Ripper. If true, I think that would be reason enough to leave well alone.

Strange but True

Over the years I have collected a wide variety of tales and experiences from people from all walks of life, many unexplainable. But how do you go about investigating those that go beyond, the bounds of a traditional haunting? The following provided by, and I stress, normal, rational people, begs that vey question. You will read of creatures whose existence has up till now only existed in myth. I will let you make your own mind however I think you will agree they make for fascinating reading.

The first story was passed onto me by my colleague Mike who witnessed the appearance of a strange animal while holidaying in the Grampian Mountains in 1981. The exact location of the occurrence was north-west of Braemar, in Glen Lui, an old drover's road at Creag Bhalg. The area is one of immense beauty, rugged and remote. Mike was accompanied by his wife and children at the time of the incident and told me the following.

'It was mid-day in early June, and we were about to set off on a circular walk from our camp in Glen Lui through the narrow Clais Fhearnaig, down to Glen Quoich then returning by Mar Lodge. I was standing admiring the view at our campsite, basically waiting for the rest of the family to ready themselves. I was looking towards one of the tops of Creag Bhalg when I noticed a very large animal. I asked my wife Yvonne to pass the binoculars to me and on doing so got the surprise of my life. What I saw seemed like a very large badger but with no markings on its body. It was low to the ground with long greyish hair and thick paws. As the beast moved, with what I can only describe as a floundering motion I noticed it was moving at a quick pace. We watched it for around ten minutes before it disappeared over the hill onto the Glen Quoich side where we were soon to be heading. We started our walk and talked about what we had seen but could come up with no explanation though we saw no further sign of it.'

I then asked if he had heard of any similar occurrences in the area and he replied, 'I have heard of many strange stories about the area but the only reference to a large creature like the one I saw was on an internet site about the Cairngorms. This article described sightings of a large mole like creature in the area. After thinking about it I realised that this description certainly suited the kind of animal I had seen. The animal was very large, much bigger than anything that should exist there and was noticeable without the aid of binoculars even at that distance. I could see dust rising from the ground as it floundered along being propelled by its large paws. I had never seen anything like if before or since. It was too big to be a normal animal from the British Isles. The funny thing was the children did not seem in the slightest bit concerned, 'It's a giant badger so what!' was the comment. We on the other hand were concerned that we would meet it at some point on our walk.'

I looked a little further into this and discovered that an animal roughly matching this description had been seen by others in the region and this legendary creature had been given the name of the 'Famh'. In an article and talk given by Raymond Bell for the Edinburgh Fortean Society he mentioned the poet James Hogg, who referred to the 'Famh' in his work, the 'Queens Wake.' wrote: 'Oft had that seer at the break of morn/beheld the Famh glide o'er the fell.' He also mentions it in 'The Shepherds Calendar' in which he claimed that an eyewitness, Mr McQueen, stated that he had also seen a creature of similar description. Whether this is true or not is open to question however Mike was in no doubt as to what he saw. Lastly, I chanced upon another forum in which the members discussed the very same creature allegedly linked to the Cairngorm region. The creature was described as "an evil and ugly monster known as the Famh (Gaelic for mole) which reputedly haunts the Cairngorms around Glen Alvin. It possesses a head twice the size of its body and legend says that to cross its path before sun-up will result in your untimely death.

Speaking of strange creatures and as a slight aside I recently read an article on mystery beasts and came across another oddity, the Earth Hound or Yard Pig which allegedly lives off interred bodies in graveyards. It has been closely associated with the Banffshire region of Scotland though one was noted as being killed nearer to home circa 1915 in the Mastrick area of the city. The chronicler, Mr. A. Smith describes how the creature was uncovered by a farmer while ploughing and was subsequently killed. It was said to have the appearance of something between a rat and a weasel with mole-like feet, prominent tusks, and a pig like nose. Another creature of similar appearance, with a head somewhat like a hound, was allegedly slain in the 1860s despite the circumstances not being written down until 1917.

Elementals are described as being mythological spirit beings associated with the elements of earth, fire, air, and water. They appear in classic literature as either an aid or hindrance to humans. This however is not the only definition as there is a school of thought that suggests that elementals are also spirits that have never been born. These are thought to be made up of an amalgamation of dark energies either created through the subconscious or as a direct result of negative actions. They have been associated with buildings or land known to have a bloody history, an example being where witchcraft or black magic has been practiced, leaving a dark residual energy. These thought forms can take on the appearance of any manner of things and I have heard of examples where half human creatures have allegedly made themselves known to the detriment of witnesses. These have included the 'mermaid' story, discussed earlier in this book. Other examples include a friend who in the 1970s was woken from his slumber by the presence of something at the foot of his bed. Both he and his wife were terrified to see what he described as 'a gorgon-like figure standing staring at us.' I was told it thankfully vanished as they let out a cry. This happened in a nearby housing estate a place not normally associated with such strange goings on.

Another example I was told of involved a young man who resided in the Justice Street area of the city who awoke to find, a gigantic face staring down at him, which filled his entire line of vision. Again, his cries of fear broke the spell which had literally pinned him to the bed. In both cases there was no repetition of the activity however it did leave the recipients anxious to say the least. One Mastrick resident recently told me of another interesting encounter with what he described as a 'Green Man' type figure. As you are no doubt aware the 'Green Man' is a nature spirit which is prominent in folklore throughout the world and is associated with rebirth and the cycle of growth. Usually seen as a sculpture or carving it appears in many cultures and takes the form of a male face made up of vines, leaves or flowers. Highly decorative, these motifs can be found in many churches and buildings and became extremely popular during the Arts and Crafts movement. The witness told me that something which closely resembled the description of a Green Man was seen clambering up a tree in his back garden. He assured me that at the time there was nothing of any consequence on his mind and in fact he had been very relaxed, having a cup of tea at his door. It appeared to look in his direction before it blended into the foliage and vanished. Whether all are genuine paranormal encounters or perhaps misinterpretation will be for you to decided. Below is an example of a case that has puzzled researchers for near fifty years. The outcome is still open to debate not helped by recent revelations.

A case which has always fascinated me and certainly would appear to have similar aspects to an elemental haunting is that of the 'Hexham Heads'. Although the story does not originate from this area, I think it is worth retelling as an example of an elemental or of a living beast created from the subconscious. An answer has never been found and indeed the whereabouts of the heads themselves is now uncertain. The story begins in 1972 at the home of the Robson family in the village of Hexham when the homeowners' children uncovered a pair of carved stone heads approximately the size of oranges in their back garden.

Several nights after the discovery the Robson's' neighbour, Ellen Dodd, and her daughter were terrified when a 'half-man, half-beast' entered their bedroom. Despite their screams the strange creature did not seem to notice them but instead went down the stairs. On investigating they found their front door open. The beast appeared to have been walking on two legs.

The stone heads thought to be of Celtic origin were then handed over to a collector Dr Anne Ross, who having other similar items in her collection wished to compare them. A few nights later her inquisitiveness backfired when she was woken in the early hours of the morning with a feeling of dread, and on glancing towards her bedroom door she was shocked to see the very same creature standing there.

'It was about six feet tall, slightly stooping and it was black against the white door, and it was half animal and half man. The upper part, I would have said, was a wolf and the lower part was human, and I would have again said that it was covered with a kind of black, very dark fur. It went out and I saw it clearly and then it disappeared, and something made me run after it. That is something I would not normally have done but I felt compelled to run after it. I got out of bed and gave chase and could hear it going down the stairs then it disappeared towards the back of the house.'

Not long after this incident Dr Ross came home with her husband only to find their daughter in a terrified condition. She had allegedly entered the house only to witness the large black form of the creature running down the stairs before it vaulted the banister and landed with a soft thud. It was believed that the stone heads were responsible for these terrifying manifestations and accordingly Dr Ross passed her collection on to other interested parties. Eventually the British Museum obtained them, and story drifted from the public consciousness until a former owner of the Robson residence appeared. He claimed during a lengthy interview that he was responsible for the heads, having made them for his two children to play with, before burying them in the garden. This revelation of course has caused much debate. For one, if he had made them, then what had caused the wolf-like manifestations which academics claim represent the Norse god Fenris? My question of course would be, why make your kids such creepy toys? Either way mystery continues to fascinate the public and for those personally involved it remains both terrifying and baffling in equal measures.

Marchburn Crescent is the scene of our next story and again provides an example of the downright bizarre. I recently met with Jean who works for a local charitable organization and during a conversation about books I mentioned I was particularly interested in the supernatural. Her eyes widened as she told me of an incident one that is as fresh in her mind today as it was over forty years ago. Here is her story.

'It was in 1963 and I was eight years old at the time. I know I was young, but it had such a huge impact on me that I can still picture the events today. You can ask my family to verify this because they were all involved. I was hanging around one day with a friend who was a little older than me. For some strange reason I wanted to visit Allenvale cemetery where I knew my grandfather had been buried. Of course, being only eight and not having much clue how to find a grave we searched for ages. The older girl started to freak me out by saying that there was a grave over there that had a staircase in it going down into the earth. She kept saying, 'can you see it' and to be honest I thought I could. Again, I was young and susceptible but either way at the time I did see it and got very scared. The girl kept going on about ghosts and the like and so I said that I wanted to go home. We used to wander about all day and so on returning home I was given a row by my older sister. She was basically meant to be looking after me and had been worried sick about my disappearance. When I got in, she said that I was to go straight to my room and forced me to go upstairs to bed. The staircase had a double landing and as I walked up to the first one, she turned out the stair light as a punishment. I could hardly see a thing and so carried on up. I reached the landing and screamed out in terror as there was a huge looming figure on the landing. Its head nearly reached the roof and must have been around seven foot tall. It was covered in long brown hair which hung over its face. It vanished and my screams brought everyone else running out of the living room. I blurted out what I had seen, and I am not kidding when I say we all bolted out the door and into our neighbour's house who must have wondered what was going on. They immediately took us back to our house and went inside, searching it thoroughly as I suspect they thought someone had broken in. Anyway, there was nothing to be found. After the event I was terrified for weeks and could not sleep alone or in the dark. The figure as I have said was very tall and being covered in hair was quite unlike anything I had ever seen. Of course, no one believed me at first even though they all ran from the house but as it took me so long to get over what I saw, they began to realise that there may have been some truth to the story. Sometime later, I remember trying to draw it but because it was not a great drawing, I destroyed it.

It was not until years later in the 1980s when I was watching a documentary that I saw the same creature. I was absolutely shocked as the animal in the documentary was practically identical to what I had seen when I was a child. As unbelievable as it sounds the figure on the television was that of a supposed 'Bigfoot' or 'Sasquatch.' People have said that I must have seen a picture of one as a child and my imagination had done the rest, but I honestly knew nothing about these creatures, in the 1960's it was not something that people knew about unlike today. I was frozen and the memory of what I had seen came back instantly. Strangely though many years later I went to see a medium, the only time I have. I have seen my grandads' spirit on numerous occasions during my life and as we were very close, I suppose I wanted to see if any messages came through. The medium said that I had a spirit guide who was a Native American Indian who had always been looking out for me. I can obviously not verify this, but I thought that because of this possibility there may have been a connection. My sister also mentioned an interesting point, wondering if the figure was that of my spirit guide, wearing an animal skin. I honestly do not know but I have never forgotten what I saw and in fact when I think about it now, I can still see it clearly.'

Moving further afield we reach the rocky coastline near Peterhead and the village of Boddam.

Valarie and Terry Wright both then stationed at RAF Boddam had moved into nearby Earls Court a small row of houses at the cliff edge. The building still standing today looks entirely different than in 1964 having undergone some major changes. Back then the interior had an unusual layout. For example, the upper floor consisted of bedrooms on each side of central a staircase which led to an unused attic. The house was described as having an atmosphere and I was told that strange things would sometimes occur. These included furious jangling coming from an old clock in the hallway, which the tenants found inexplicable rather than frightening.

Apart from a general unease all was relatively normal until strange sounds began to emanate from the attic. The room, near derelict was secured by a latch on the outside, it had no electric light and only one grubby skylight provided illumination. They had no use for the space and having lain empty for some considerable time, it contained nothing more than two old sea chests and a thick carpet of dust.

The first incident occurred on what was described as an atypical night when the couple had not long retired. After a while they became aware of a series of 'heavy thuds' going across the

Attic, at which point Terry went to investigate. As he approached the door the noise ceased abruptly and finding the door still locked, decided to wait until daybreak to investigate further. In the morning however they were greeted by the baffling sight of their enamel bath now covered in large dusty animal prints. On inspection it was apparent they belonged to a cat, much bigger than a domestic variety, the prints being, the circumference of a coffee cup. They entered the attic but being unable to find any evidence of their mystery intruder they locked the door behind them. Praying on their mind afterwards, they questioned: What was it? Where had it come from? And more importantly how did it get downstairs? It was with some trepidation that they went to bed that evening and lay listening while the same sounds were repeated. Again, no evidence of entry could be found.

Some days later and with mounting concern, Terry approached a friend at the RAF camp and confided in him, persuading his companion to help resolve the matter. His friend was only too happy to assist, and the pair searched the attic thoroughly at the nearest opportunity. The search revealed the prints of a large cat but no sign of the culprit. They checked every nook and cranny, yet found nothing and debated how an animal, of some considerable size was able to gain entry. Even the skylight was found to be rusted shut and of course both chests contained nothing but some tatty clothes.

With very few options available they decided to set a trap to try and catch whatever was making the prints should it return. And so, the pair engineered a trap which could be sprung should whatever it was, attempt to leave the attic. They even left some food as an enticement, hoping if something attempted to reach the bait it would dislodge the plank causing it to plunge down the stair, to where three nail beds sat. Being engineers it was meticulously planned. That evening as Terry lay in bed clutching the ancient bayonet, they had found on moving in, the silence was deafening. Nothing stirred until at the point of sleep all hell broke loose. Suddenly without warning there was a terrible commotion and the most horrible sound like a screech, it was unforgettable like an animal in great pain. Terry then sprinted from the room to find the trap had been sprung but there was no sign of anything living or dead. They searched the attic again which was empty, returning for a restless night's sleep. In the morning they cleared away the debris and waited to see if it would reappear, but the noise from the attic was never heard again. Over forty years have passed since the incident, and it remains unexplained. If it had been an animal of flesh and blood, how did it get out of the house with no means of exit? The building itself has undergone major changes since the time of these events but still stands today. Ironically, the couple retired back to the village around twenty-five years later staying almost next door. They never did find an answer but apparently the house had belonged to a sea captain who was rumoured to have taken his own life.

An equally strange story to finish off this section was told to me by Seaton resident Edith Mustard who I have known for many years through community involvement. During World War two, a very young Edith was taking her younger sibling Jim for a stroll in his buggy. They were heading to a well-known Aberdeen landmark, the 'Gibberie Wallie' or Gingerbread well, where its namesake was sold in days gone by. Now forlorn and bearing the marks of recent graffiti it is a sad sight compared to what early photographs show. Today it can be found in Sunnybank recreation ground, and this is where Edith had her encounter.

' I remember taking Jim out in his pram and we went down to look at the 'witches house.' This was an old ruin, like a shack that sat behind the well and was surrounded by trees. Years before an old woman lived there and I suppose she was teased or thought of as a witch. The local kids were scared so used to dare each other to go near the house so it ended up as the 'witches house.' Even though she was gone we were all still wary. So, as I said I was near the house when a tall figure stepped out from behind a nearby tree. His face was indescribable and not human, and to this day I have never forgot it. He had this moon like face and a huge split mouth, thin and narrow and incredibly wide. He put its finger, up to his lips and went shhhhh! like it was telling me to be quiet. It then stepped back and was gone. Well, I never moved so fast in all my life, I was terrified. Even today I can't explain what I saw, it was just unnatural.'

I have known Edith for years and I am certain she saw something, but what it was remains unanswered. I visited the well recently and in that secluded spot I imagined how it must have looked all those years ago. It felt forlorn and unloved, so I left soon after.

Marischal College

Marischal College, one of the most iconic buildings in Aberdeen and the second largest granite building in the world, exceeded only by the Escorial Palace near Madrid, and was originally founded in 1593 by George Keith, 5th Earl Marischal of Scotland. It has undergone many changes since its inception, having originally been constructed on the site of a medieval Franciscan Friary. The frontage has recently been redeveloped as a base for Aberdeen City Council however it is in the older part of the building that our story takes place.

Up until its closure I spent many years visiting and working in the museum and through my work met up with two cleaners who had a tale to tell. I was asked to omit their names however both were long-serving members of staff who have since retired. The following events took place in both the Mitchell Hall and the Picture Gallery which at 6am in the morning were described as 'always eerie.' I was told that the following event occurred during exam time and both rooms had been set out with rows of desks. It was also noted as being around 6.30 am. At the time two cleaners were in the Picture Gallery and were walking up an aisle between desks. They chatted as they pushed their mops ahead of them. They then became aware of a very peculiar noise and turned nervously knowing they were the only people in the building at that time. They described it as sounding like leaves being blown along on a windy day, a strange rustling sound and worse of all it seemed to be following them. They kept moving along until the noise faded behind them.

It comes as no surprise to learn, that next to cleaners the security guard is usually best placed to have an encounter. In the wee small hours, when a building is empty, who knows what might keep them company. Historically proven to be the optimum time for spookiness, many might not regard this as a perk of the job which the following incident demonstrates. Taking place during a patrol of the Mitchell Hall, the guards' attention was drawn to the figure of a man standing beside the organ. Not sure whether to run or stay, he watched cautiously as the figure began to move slowly. It appeared not to notice his presence and walked towards one of the walls, through which it disappeared. The guard stood still for a moment, but the figure did not re-appear. It is of course impossible to say who this person was, not the guard but the ghost, perhaps a former professor a student or some poor unfortunate who ended up at the hands of an anatomist, in the rooms directly below. With buildings as old as Marischal College, many hundreds of people have been through its doors, some perhaps never leaving. This may be true of our next story which unfolded during a theatre performance, taking place below the hall in what is regarded as the spookiest part of the building, the old anatomy rooms.

There is something uncanny about the area and I can only assume it is because of the medical practices that took place, mostly legitimate though some perhaps not. The rooms had a massive refurbishment some years back and I remember noticing a skip being filled with old medical equipment, destined for the tip. I Shuddered at the sight of a neck brace on a pole once used for supporting corpses. Today it is used as studios for both artists and dancers and on occasion performances such as the one that took place in 2016.

The organiser, Dr Fiona-Jane Brown, director of Hidden Tours Aberdeen, herself an afficionado of the paranormal, described the following incident which took place at an event held in the anatomy rooms. It was during rehearsals for The Promenade Theatre Halloween event that footsteps were heard on two consecutive nights echoing in the empty rooms next door. On another occasion both Fiona and co-worker Chloe, had been covering windows with black bin bags for the upcoming performance. Once finished, I was told they switched off the lights and closed the door before undertaking a last check of the other rooms. They then left only to find someone had switched the lights back on. Neither of course could offer a rational explanation and so focused on preparing for the event.

The play, a 'Grand Guignol' style performance, took place the next night, which was Halloween. The story based on an urban myth, told of a drunkard who being found in the street and assumed dead is borne off to the anatomy rooms by over-zealous students only to awake as the scalpel cuts deep. In the climax the disembowelled man makes a frantic bid for freedom in what Fiona described as an 'almost Benny Hill scenario,' with the poor unfortunate running out of one door, only to appear from another, while clutching a handful of offal. The crowd no doubt loved it, and who wouldn't? On the second night however, the performance was disrupted by something very unexpected, the sound of a disembodied voice crying in pain. Fiona stated: 'I was annoyed to have missed this as I did not attend the second night but my colleagues waiting in the kitchen witnessed everything. During the skit, the actor who we named the 'guts man' burst into the kitchen and began demanding who was responsible for the ridiculous yelling and who was making that awful screaming sound.'

The assembled cast assumed that he had been responsible for the racket, thinking it was part of his performance, so were somewhat taken aback by the truth. A post event meeting shed little light on the situation with one person, a sensitive herself describing the screams sounding like someone was dying and not of this world. The audience thankfully heard nothing except what was happening on the stage and remained unaware. On hearing of the incident Fiona later theorized that perhaps the re-enactment of the anatomy had triggered off a recording from the past, which I agreed was not out with the realms of reason. It is also not inconceivable to imagine that in the days of public hangings, some poor unfortunates thought to be dead could potentially have revived on the 'table.'

Fiona went as far as to name a potential suspect, identified as that of George Thom, hanged for attempting to poison his family. What would have happened had he survived? And more importantly, what would have been the outcome? Would those present have tried to 'cover up' their mistake? It is an unpleasant thought. In the aftermath we are left to ponder what took place that night. Was it a replay from past events, triggered by a macabre re-enactment as many suggest? It is feasible though we may never truly know. I would be interested however to see if anything similar occurs in the future and considering the buildings history, I am convinced we have not heard the last of it.

Torry Tales

Once a Royal Burgh, Torry established in 1495 existed as a separate village until being incorporated into Aberdeen in the year 1891. Predominantly a fishing village, much of its unique heritage was sacrificed in Aberdeen's rush to capitalize on the burgeoning oil industry. In the late Victorian period, the need for housing was at a premium and plans were put into place for the creation of the tenement lined streets that we see today. Victoria Road and Walker Road are just two examples of town planning at its best both of which provided spacious accommodation for families to escape the overcrowded and cramped environs of the city centre. As a former resident I was well placed to gather a selection of creepy tales.

I met with a former colleague from Aberdeen Foyer, Wasif, some time back and he asked me if I would like to hear about an experience he had while living in Torry and I replied yes. During our conversation he explained that he had moved into Menzies Road some years back to number 64. On moving in he felt there was an unaccountable atmosphere of gloom about the place which he had not felt when viewing. He told me he was soon plagued by vivid nightmares in which a group of women of varying age, wearing long black dresses were present in his bedroom. He also felt the omnipresent sensation of being observed which he found very unnerving and even though he kept the heating on constantly, the flat was described as always being cold. Very soon after, he began to regret his move and quickly attempted to sell the property, which proved impossible. He explained: 'It seemed something did not want me to leave as every time the flat was about to change hands a problem would arise either from the purchaser or solicitor. This happened on several occasions when the sale fell through at the last minute which was very frustrating.'

Because of this he withdrew it temporarily from the market and tried to focus on work but not long after events took a more sinister turn. According to his testimony it started one morning whilst showering, when a shooting pain on his back caused him to wince. Looking in the bathroom mirror he was shocked to find long scratches on his back which 'would have been impossible to inflict on myself'. The one small crumb of comfort was that a long-awaited visit from his parents was approaching, and he was looking forward to company.

On the first day of their visit his father, a religious man, announced that the flat was 'haunted' and went about performing a blessing which he believed would lighten the atmosphere. I asked him to elaborate, and he explained that his father was known for possessing psychic abilities and had been asked on occasion to perform 'clearances' in the town where he lived. When he arrived he immediately sensed that something was wrong and talking with his son related what he was seeing. According to his father there were female spirits present in the flat, who had been killed many years ago when a building collapsed. Wasif was unable to say when this was meant to have happened, but he was told they did not want me to leave, which must have been terrifying. He went on to say: 'I asked my dad to perform the blessing, which he did, and afterwards was convinced the atmosphere in the flat felt better. I was also glad of the company after all that had happened. Sometime later I decided to put the flat back up for sale and soon after someone bought the property. I was glad it sold especially after my experience.'

Having lived in the exact same street myself, I was aware of the property in question and so had a brief look in the library for some clues. What little information there was showed the aftermath of the WW2 bombing raids which destroyed numerous buildings on the street. These however appeared to have been at the opposite end. Perhaps there was still some connection. Incidentally, my wife had a strange experience herself on the very same street some 25 years ago. She described how she woke abruptly at around 1am in morning and was drawn to the window by an unusual sound. The clatter of an approaching horse and cart could be heard distinctly which passed the flat, heading towards Victoria Road, yet the street was completely empty. A cup of tea and some serious pondering did not provide any closure.

Mention 'The Manser' to any Torry resident and they will instantly recognise the name as referring to Mansefield Brae. A precipitous slope sweeping up from the harbour through Victoria Road towards Mansefield Road, it is a stiff climb. The following was told to me by Una McDougall who recounted an interesting tale around 35 years ago whilst living at 43 Mansefield Road. She explained. 'I was looking out of my window as I could not sleep. It was still dark. I think it would have been about three in the morning to be precise. As I was looking over the back gardens, I saw two pretty, young women, in what I can only describe as floaty dresses. They had bare feet and were holding hands and dancing round and round the back garden. They looked happy. I momentarily looked away and when I looked back, they were gone. I still remember it to this day and like telling folk as the sight made me feel happy.' She never saw them again.

Moving on towards the Bay of Nigg we arrive at the ancient and ruinous church of St. Fitticks. The church was abandoned in 1829, although the graveyard continued to be used until the 20th century. Prey to body snatchers due to its remote location the remains of the watch-house can still be seen today and is well worth a visit, as is the surrounding churchyard. Inside, visitors can see last resting place of those drowned in the sinking of the 'Oscar' near the ruinous walls of the Church. Although just a shell today it is an atmospheric location, where one can still see the 'lepers keek.' This small window located on the side of the church, generously afforded a view of proceedings for those afflicted with leprosy, without alarming healthier members of the congregation. Unsurprisingly the churchyard is also allegedly haunted and is the location of our next tale. It was told to me some years ago by local resident Erin.

She recalls: 'I was walking past the graveyard around 12 years ago. It was at night, and I was with my parents. As I looked over towards the church, I saw what looked like a ghostly figure of a woman standing outside the gates (of the church) and she looked like she was crying. I turned to tell my parents but when I looked back, she was gone. To me she looked like a woman from the Victorian era. She had a bonnet on her head and was wearing a long gown. It looked as if she was crying as she had a hanky in her hand which was held to her face.'

Again at St. Fitticks, I was recently given a description of an event which took place in 1983. The witness, John, described the following during our phone call, which took place one foggy night while undertaking a vigil. I have used his description as it was given.

'The churchyard was well known among locals and one of the rumours was that it was supposed to be haunted by a green lady. Whether that was true or not, we had no idea but me and my pal had decided to debunk it. We sat there for hours, smoked some fags, and had some cans of lager. It was foggy, but I did see a figure crossing by the dyke, though I could not really make it out. Anyway, about ten minutes later and with the fog now totally clear I saw the same figure appear at the exact same spot. Even after all these years I can describe what I saw. It was the figure of an old man, and he was floating not walking next to the dyke. He was out of place and should not have been there. We ran for it and my friend ended up getting hurt after he ran into a gravestone.'

I do love a good churchyard it has to be said. There's something quite peaceful about them. Unsurprisingly, at least in fiction, they are regarded are something of a home from home for ghosts, and perhaps that's why people are drawn to them. Statistically speaking though they are regarded as one of the least likely places to see a spectre, at least by spiritualists. Why should this be? My question was soon answered while attending a lecture on life after death, no not Brexit, but the survival of the human soul. At the Q&A, an eager attendee took the onus by asking why cemeteries were considered, the least likely place to have a ghostly experience.

The answer, unsurprisingly, given the speakers credentials, was that if paradise awaited you why bother lingering in such gloomy surroundings. I could see his point.

Moving on we reach Victoria Road, the main thoroughfare in Torry. An elegant street it still retains its period charm and I know it well, being a former resident. Our old home near Mansfield Brae was typical of a late Victorian three-flatted tenement and although we had a few puzzling events take place in our property including a television switching itself on, and a figure being observed standing at the foot of the bed, it was our upstairs neighbour Suzanne who drew the short straw this time. When we met, she recounted what happened, not long after we had moved out: 'One night I was lying in bed when a motion detector went off. I was instantly awoken and must admit feeling unnerved by the sound of footsteps which were now walking back and forth in the next room. I lay there unsure of what to do, having initially thought I had been broken into. The footsteps which I might add were very loud continued for a while before stopping. I eventually investigated and found everything as before. I was perplexed and although I had felt the odd presence in the flat at times, I had never felt nervous about being there as the flat has a good energy.'

I asked if she had any further experiences and she confirmed there had been. It involved a large antique mirror which she indicated was behind me. She continued: 'As you can see the mirror is pretty big and heavy, and so if it fell off the wall you would assume the glass would smash and it would cause damage to the objects on the fireplace.' I agreed and so she continued, 'I went out for the day some time ago and when I left everything was as normal, on my return the mirror had been taken off the wall and was now perfectly balanced on the two candlesticks you see behind you. This would only have been possible if it had been carefully lifted off the hook and placed there. Had the hook given way it would have left a hole in the plaster and the weight of a falling mirror would undoubtedly have smashed the contents of the mantel into a hundred pieces. Suzanne finished off by saying: 'Unless my cats were able to perform this feat then I can only think it must have been moved by paranormal means. I did feel a little rattled for a while but thankfully this has not been repeated.' Having lived there for 10 years myself I can conclude it was an interesting building in which all three residents, myself included experienced things. I miss that flat.

Moving along Victoria Road, home-owner Kerry explained to me that her daughter then aged three, was in the habit of 'seeing people,' a notion her parents were slightly dubious about. They took her slightly more seriously when the youngster spotted what appeared to be a 'man in a uniform' in the front bedroom. He was described as wearing 'something like a postman's uniform with a hat, he wore a moustache and appeared to have something wrong with his hand.' Kerry was unable to establish what the 'something wrong' was but on hearing the description had felt 'freaked out.' I would imagine that from then, she listened to her daughter more closely. I was told however that the figure had not been seen since.

Our next stop is at the edge of town at the Torry Battery to be precise, where unusual occurrences have been reported for years. In this instance the protagonists unwittingly entered a time slip whose definition is described as an alleged paranormal incident in which a person or group travel through time witnessing scenes from the past. Though there have been many reported cases of individuals witnessing incidents from the past there has generally been no interaction between the two. However, there are exceptions as in the case of the 'Ghosts of Versailles 1901. The story involved two respected academics Anne Elizabeth Moberly and Eleanor Frances Jourdain the Principal and Vice Principal of St. Hugh's College in Oxford who believed they had been caught up in a time slip which transported them back to the time of the French revolution.

On August 10th, 1901, both women visited the Palace of Versailles and were strolling in the grounds when they became aware of a feeling of oppressive gloom. They encountered and interacted with people being described as wearing old fashion clothing as well as sighting someone who was thought to be Marie Antoinette. Critics of the story claimed that it was more likely to have been friends of the French poet Robert De Montesquiou who were known to dress up in period costume and give parties for charity. Others argued that this could not be the case as the story was not revealed till after the death of Ms. Jourdain in 1924 therefore ruling out a publicity stunt. It was also noted that admitting to being involved in an incident of this nature would have been tantamount to professional suicide for the pair. Ms. Moberly's account was rich in detail describing how an extraordinary depression came over her. The surrounding gardens then began to look unnatural with trees appearing flat and lifeless and that the air became intensely still. This otherworldly feeling has been recorded, accompanying other alleged times slips in which sound is either muted or ceases completely.

Other examples involve the witnessing of full-scale conflicts, marching armies, agricultural scenes from a different age and in a widely publicised case from 1979 the disappearance of a hotel. This tale involved two English married couples who came across an old-fashioned hotel while driving through France en route to Spain. They stayed the night and decided later to stop over at the same hotel on the return leg of their journey but had to change plans when they were unable to find the hotel. The photographs taken during their initial stay were also found to be missing. This was made more perplexing as the images were in the middle of the roll of film. Of course, one can only hope that the bill vanished also. Theories vary as to whether those experiencing time slips can take an active part in the event. In the case of the Versailles ghost story, it would appear so while the holidaymakers went one step further and ate dinner and breakfast during their 'visit.' In other reported incidents the witness is usually a passive observer of the event which tends to last for only a few minutes. The following two incidents occurred much closer to home as mentioned, at the Torry Point Battery. These are two of my favourite stories and in one instance the unwitting subjects literally wandered into a scene from the past.

With its unparalleled views of Aberdeen Bay, the Battery was built between 1859 and 1861 as a defence against possible attack from France, though ultimately it never saw action. Its defences included 200lb Armstrong guns capable of 'dropping a ball from Torry as far as Newburgh.' Despite the fearsome weaponry the Battery was mainly used as a training ground for soldiers. It served this purpose until the end of the Great War when a desperate housing shortage helped shape its destiny of the next twenty years. With many troops returning home to poverty and no chance of housing it provided temporary respite. The building's usage changed with the onset of World War Two and the now manned defences saw action during subsequent enemy raids. At the end of the conflict Britain once again faced a stark housing shortage and it was not long before homeless families began squatting at the site. The City Council realising the magnitude of the problem formalised a plan to allow families to take up residency in an array of huts and outbuildings where despite basic amenities there was a great sense of community. This situation lasted until 1953 when the last occupants moved out, but had they?

I met with Connie who told me the following which involved her mother. In the late 1960s her mother Sandra, and her friends witnessed events at both the Torry Battery and the Duthie Park which were very frightening. Her mother takes up the story.

'It was in the summer of 1968 at approximately 10pm. There were four of us on two motorbikes and we decided to stop at the Battery for a ciggie. We drove in the gate and parked beside two cellars. We were standing next to the bikes and chatted for about 15 minutes when two girls entered the gate in front of us. We all saw them and in fact I said to them jokingly, to watch out for the ghosts. They both turned and stared directly at me for what seemed like ages, it was a cold stare that went right through me. They never said a word and turned and walked away from us to the back of the Battery. We all started talking about their strange behaviour as the girls disappeared over a large mound. One of the guys who had been to the Battery before wondered where they were going as there was no way out that way. Anyhow we decided to follow them as it was beginning to get dark, and we were very puzzled. We looked over the mounds and in the old buildings which were ruined but we could not find them. We decided to get on our bikes behind the Battery which in those days was walled and had barbed wire round it, but there was still no sign. We suddenly felt uneasy, and so decided to go to the Duthie Park. When we got there the guys parked their bikes in the shelter and chained their front wheels together and we went to the duck pond where we sat chatting and having a ciggie. It was around 11pm. We had only been there a matter of minutes when we heard the motorbikes revving. My boyfriend Hughie immediately recognised his bikes engine, and so we all ran back towards the shelter. When we got there both bikes were lying on their side. The chain connecting them had been snapped and all the wheels were spinning. Everyone was frightened including the guys. They had their keys in their pockets, so we got the bikes and took off. A few weeks later while discussing the matter two different people told us that after WW2, two young girls had been found murdered on a mattress in one of the cellars at the Battery.' Sandra finished off by saying: 'All of us believed the incident was paranormal and never went back.'

I was indebted to Sandra for recounting her experience which is among one my favourites but could find no evidence of a murder taking place.

Our next tale took place in 1995 and as is often the case came to light through a series of coincidences. In January 2008 I was taking photographs of an old building and got chatting to the site manager Ian. He related to me an incident that happened to some of his friends in the 1990s at the Torry Battery, involving numerous apparitions. At the time we were unable to complete the interview, so I returned a little while later and as we sat in the bothy, I began by asking him to recount the story. He began to speak in greater detail about the incident and on finding out that I was a serious researcher admitted that he had also been present that night but had been reticent to say so for fear of ridicule. I assured him that I was taking his story seriously and mentioned as an example Sandra's story, without mentioning her name. The only other worker in the bothy immediately spoke up and asked if the ladies name was Sandra. I confirmed it was and it transpired she was his closest friend's grandmother. After I had picked my jaw up, he told me he was aware of the 'motor bike incident' having heard the story first-hand before. Ian then began to describe his experience and I have been given permission to repeat it in full.

'It was in the summer of 1995, and I was an apprentice at the time. We used to meet down at the breakwater near the mouth of the harbour and stay out playing football and having parties. On this night there were three of us heading towards the breakwater, myself and my two mates, Kevin Porter and Alan Black. It was a perfect night in the height of summer, no breeze and still hot. It was starting to turn dark and as we were running late someone suggested cutting through the Battery. We were walking through the Battery when out of the corner of my eye I noticed Alan looking at something. We were stopped in our tracks by the sight of a group of people wearing old-fashioned clothing, like out of the television programme 'Foyles War.' There were women wearing long dresses, just standing there, and a soldier standing nearby wearing army greens and a cap. There were others wearing flat caps. We were rooted to the spot and though I suppose it only lasted seconds, time seemed to stand still. It was surreal and though not exactly frightening. The air was perfectly calm, and I felt at peace. The strangest thing was that there were also children playing, and one wee boy wearing what looked like plus fours and of Asian appearance was running along with a hoop which he was directing with a stick. Like an old-fashioned toy. The only noise I could hear was the sound of the hoop rattling on the ground and the stick hitting it. We looked at each other and bolted across the Battery over the other side and ran all the way to where our mates were. When we arrived, we were breathless, and my friends looked pale. We told the rest of them what had happened, and they laughed and thought we were winding them up. After some persuasion they agreed to come back with us and so we did. Between us running to our mates and returning must have only taken around ten minutes but when we got there the place was deserted. There was no sign of life not even a crisp packet on the ground, silence. My mates continued to dispute what we saw claiming that it must have been someone making a film. They did not believe us, but we knew it wasn't a film set as there were no cars or vans about, nowhere for anyone to go. There is no way they could have cleared the place out in the ten minutes it took us to return. The experience has stuck with me and felt more surreal and peaceful than frightening, though we were alarmed to an extent.'

It goes without saying that both military personnel and civilians used the battery in the past, so the descriptions provided are very accurate. Perhaps what was witnessed will never again be repeated, maybe it was the right combination of time and the elements that opened this window to the past. If that is the case, I suggest that Ian was very lucky indeed.

Miscellaneous Ghosts

I am always happy to hear of peoples' experiences and over the years have accrued a fair few. It can be a slow process collecting tales and many months may go by before anything new appears. Some I am sent are given freely, while others, more reticent, ask that they remain unpublished. Perhaps they are uncomfortable due to religious believes or maybe fear acknowledging the unknown. Either way that is their prerogative and so I have adopted a glass half-full approach. I hope one day I can share these with a wider audience but for now I have included a small selection of those I am obliged to share. Some beg further research, others exist in isolation, but irrespective of that the contributors have my thanks.

The first contributor Mrs. H. Philips, described the following which took place in a large Victorian property in Cults: 'Strange things began to happen as soon as we moved in. My mother who stayed with us at the time was wakened on occasion by her bedroom door opening which at night was always closed. This would usually be accompanied by a very strong smell of tobacco smoke. One afternoon it was very dark and overcast. My daughter who at the time was almost three had gone down to the basement, appearing again minutes later only to announce she had seen a little old lady on the stair landing. My girl was very matter of fact about things and not at all imaginative. She said the lady had smiled at her and was wearing what she described as a brown dress. I mentioned his later to my next-door neighbour who told me our house had been occupied for years by an elderly doctor and his sister. His study happened to be where my mothers' bedroom was, and he habitually smoked a pipe. As regards what my daughter saw, there were apparently two maids in the house who always wore brown.'

Moving on to Bridge of Don, where the following again involved a small child. The contributor explained: 'My son his wife and my grandson were visiting at the time. My grandson was only seventeen months old but very clever for his age and was a good communicator. He seemed quite advanced for his age. One day he was in the big hallway speaking away to himself and looked like he was shadow boxing near the wall. When I asked him what he was doing, he said he was fighting with the man in the wall. We thought this strange and so when the opportunity arose, we asked our neighbour about the history of the building. I was told that the family who lived there before, had a son then aged nineteen who had died of an overdose. She told us he was very fond of kids and used to have play fights with them if any came round. The neighbour then gave my daughter a photo of the lad who in turn showed it my grandson. She asked if he knew who the man in the photograph was. To everyone's surprise he said, man in the wall! This however was the only time he appeared.

Tillydrone is featured next in this classic paranormal encounter told to me by Pauline Booth. As a dog owner she habitually took her Border Collie for early morning walks near the old Grandholm Bridge. Her route which took her past the 'Eventide' home came out at the river which lay to the left, flowing silently like a black ribbon, towards the sea. Her dog ran ahead as usual, but on arriving at the footbridge it appeared reticent to cross. She was then forced to lift him and carried him across but on the other side he wriggled free, bolting into a nearby field. Paula, perplexed by his behaviour but knowing she would catch up with him, walked on but now observed a figure hurrying towards her. As she got nearer, Paula noticed it was an elderly lady who was walking very briskly. The woman who did not look up or acknowledge her kept up a furious pace. Seen at close quarters, she was described as wearing a blue Gaberdine coat and a headsquare, carrying a brown handbag over her arm.

Paula told me: 'I thought it was a bit weird for someone so elderly to be out at that time of the morning, especially on her own, but when I glanced back, she had vanished.' Soon after she made enquiries with her neighbours and other long-term residents. They knew who the woman was recognising her description immediately. Paula was then shocked to hear that Mrs. M (name omitted) and her son had tragically passed within months of each other in the vicinity of the footbridge. A few years later I had the story verified by a friend of the family who said, 'that is exactly what happened.'

Our next stop is in Summerhill at Summerfield House where in 1976, Anne a patient in the former maternity hospital had an unforgettable encounter. She described to me that on wakening she saw the profile of a nun bent over a crib who then removed a baby. The nun then headed towards the door where they both vanished. A fellow patient woke to the sound of her cries and rang for help and within seconds a nurse appeared. She told me it took some time for her to regain her composure and only then she was able to explain what happened. The ward sister then arrived and offered her a cigarette, who was described as having the knowing look of someone who had heard a similar story before. Anne stated afterwards that although not afraid, she was mostly alarmed by the fact she thought someone was taking away a baby. I found out afterwards that opposite the hospital lay a children's home and locals used to tease children by saying, the nuns would get them if they did not behave.

Moving on we encounter another time slip, this time in the Cattofield area. A local resident, Heather, informed me that at one time some years back she had been plagued by frantic knocking at her front door and on investigating found no one there. The knocking apparently followed no set pattern and would stop suddenly, perhaps for months, before starting up again. It was always frantic which made her assume it was kids playing a practical joke. She described being completely exasperated with the situation and would wait at the window hoping to catch the culprit, but the strategy proved unsuccessful. At other times she would fly outside within seconds only to find the street deserted. The knocking however became more sporadic over time until it eventually stopped, and would no doubt have remained a mystery but for a random conversation with an elderly neighbour now in her eighties who had stayed on the same street for most of her life. She recounted in their conversation how during a particularly destructive bombing raid the Cattofield area was badly bombed. That night many people lost their lives including a local ARP warden who he had been banging on the door of the house Heather now resided in, trying to alert the occupiers, when a bomb struck. The resulting explosion killed him instantly. She told me afterwards that she found this revelation quite a surprise, but thankful that phenomena had ceased.

Hospitals have long been a stomping ground for spirit activity and the reason goes without saying. I was told recently two such tales the first involving a nurse, the other a patient. The first took place in ward 4 or latterly the Balgownie ward of the Old Royal Cornhill Hospital in Aberdeen. The hospital opened in the late eighteenth century and was known uncharitably as the Aberdeen Lunatic Hospital. It was described to me as having a reputation amongst staff and being a spooky place. Particularly oppressive were the corridors running between wards one and four and six and seven, where staff did not tend to linger. Retired nurse, Eileen worked there for many years and was aware of the feelings associated with that area. She takes up the story: It was around eight in the morning, and I was with a patient in the lower corridor washroom and toilet area. I was there to assist my patient with washing and dressing. There was most definitely no one else present. The vacant/engaged sign on the nearest toilet door started going from vacant to engage at an alarming rate. I pulled the door open and there was no one there. We left the area with great speed, and I felt very frightened and shaky.'

Eileen was thankful that the phenomena was never repeated though she was still uncomfortable in certain areas of the building, convinced she had experienced poltergeist activity. Since I first heard this story, the areas mentioned have now been demolished, as has a good portion of the original structure, while the remaining buildings have been turned into flats. I wish the new tenants all the best.

Speaking of nurses, Leadside Road is our next destination where student nurse, Linda, resided in 1991. This historic road, now a shadow of its former self, contains a huddle of tenements near the top end, and it is in one of those our story takes place. Sharing with three others, it was less than salubrious but the rent was cheap and the location central. Having only just moved in she was woken in the early morning by a crushing weight on her body. She lay awake petrified hardly daring to breath, feeling the weight of the body lying partially on top of her. After what seemed an age the feeling dissipated and getting dressed, she left the room. Her flatmates were naturally sceptical and were convinced she had been asleep at the time and suffering some type of sleep paralysis, but she remained convinced otherwise. To compound her feelings of unease she found herself returning from work on occasion to discover her bags scattered around the room and personal effects moved despite having locked the room on leaving. The atmosphere in the house, described as being heavy, only added to her unhappiness, not helped by an irate and seemingly irrational downstairs neighbours who continually complained. Dreading coming home and exhausted after a long shift she would be accosted on the stairs with the latest complaint. The most common of these were demands to stop thumping on the floor while walking. She refuted the claims, stating no one had been in, which was true, but they refused to believe her, complaining their light fittings had been seen to sway back and forth regularly as someone walked from above. Linda assured them that it had not been her but would question her flatmates only to find that at the time of the complaint everyone had been at work. The last straw came around two months later when her flatmate woke to find his stereo had been tampered with and rendered useless, the wires being severed. They of course suspected the downstairs neighbour but questioned how he could have gained access. It would have been impossible. Then who was responsible? The question was doomed to remained unanswered as soon after Linda announced her departure, closely followed by the rest. It was a horrible flat with a depressing atmosphere. Perhaps it was caused by the state of mind of some of the residents, perhaps it might have been the malicious neighbours. At the end of the day Linda was much happier in her new abode, as were the others. How do I know this? I was one of her flatmates.

Carrying down from Leadside Road we reach Rosemount Viaduct and then Aberdeen Central Library. One of my favourite buildings where I have spent many happy hours looking through the local history archive. Well, each to their own. I have also been blessed to have worked there on occasion and have used the old boardroom as my base. The room contains a beautifully carved fireplace, some very nice paintings and an old bureau desk. After I had finished working one day I asked if the building was haunted? I had of course heard that it was but wanted to hear it from, 'source'. The librarian, not at all taken aback, described an incident that involved her colleague which I enjoyed hearing. It took place during the day when her colleague was struggling to open said bureau. She was taken by surprise by the sudden appearance of an older gentleman wearing old-fashioned clothing. He stood for some moments before vanishing, and only then she found the bureau had opened. I asked how she had reacted and was told that she had felt no fear but rather a sense of calm. Later when describing the man, a colleague produced a photograph from which she was able to identify him. He was found to be G.M Fraser city librarian and author who died in 1939. I found the story more sweet than scary however people claim there are more negative energies also, though never having undergone any investigation myself I will merely repeat what has been recorded.

Areas described as being prone to phenomena include the West side of the building and the children's library. It goes without saying that the public only ever get to see part of the structure which is truly massive, therefore there are many dark nooks and crannies to explore. Strange noises have been reported by lone workers frequently as have sightings of shadow figures, but who they are remains a mystery. Strange bright lights have also been noted in different areas of the building, particularly in the basement. If you remember the library ghost scene at the beginning of 'Ghostbusters,' you will have an idea of how this area looks. According to a recent report I discovered, one member of staff working alone became aware of a bright ball of light which moved towards him rapidly. He jumped to the side to avoid it, describing how at the point of contact a charge of energy went through him. He was by all accounts left feeling euphoric. The library is a building I would like to explore more fully as the stories are at the very least persistent. Why should it be haunted is something I cannot answer. It has no tragic history that I know off, but I have been told by three different sources that a murder by poisoning took place in a building which previously stood on the site. At present I cannot very this or even if it has any bearing on events. Heading round the back past Woolmanhill, the iconic red brick of a derelict textile mill looms. This is 'Richards,' workplace of countless Aberdonians and allegedly haunted. I have heard rumours about this building for years including accounts by a night watchman who witnessed a dark figure loitering in one of the bays. But for now, here is a different account which if nothing else, proves that management were at least willing to listen to staff no matter how outlandish the complaint.

The mill consists of a large sprawl of both Georgian and Victorian buildings which are of great architectural merit. In recent years they have been prone to acts of vandalism while their future remains uncertain. I never visited the mill while open but was told by a former employee that on more than one occasion the figure of a small, pipe-smoking man in a cloth cap was seen by employees.

I randomly mentioned this to a friend in passing which proved fortuitous as he told me the following: 'Some time ago I was taking photographs of the building with a friend when a passer-by asked what we were doing. I explained it was a project we were working on and as he seemed interested, we stopped for a chat. It turned out he was an ex-employee of the mill and began to tell us a little of its history. It was fascinating to listen to. He mentioned during our conversation that the building was meant to be haunted. I then asked him if he could give me some the details. According to him, it turned out that there was one room in the building that female workers had predominantly worked in. This room had more than just a weird atmosphere and they lobbied the management to get that manufacturing process moved to another area because of this, which they ended up doing. He said that many of his colleagues had seen the figure of a woman in old fashioned clothing in this area and they had been scared to work there. The management figured it would be more productive to move the workforce to another part of the building because of this, so they must have either believed the story or perhaps had seen something themselves. He was not able to expand on this and carried on with his walk.'

I did a little urban exploration soon after attempting to find the room, which I did. There was something unsettling being alone in the vastness of the complex and I found myself constantly stopping and listening for any unusual sounds. Eventually I reached the spot and after a brief foray, left before my imagination ran wild.

Moving on we reach Trinity Quay House, once home to a shipbrokers and post office, now offices. The following incident involved staff from Momentum, an employment agency, who rented the attic floor. I met our protagonists, George and Sandra when I was tutoring their student group so got to know the building well. During the course I naturally mentioned my interests and was told of two incidents of note. George explained:

'Upon walking into the office, I became aware of music being played which I had not heard before leaving earlier. I then checked the various computers in the office, but they were also switched off. The sound of a radio being played happened on several occasions despite there being none on and no one else in the building.' I asked at this point if there had been further incidents and Sandra told me that one day, she went into the building out of hours to pick something up and as she left saw a figure standing by her. This is what she told me: 'I started walking down the stairs when I glanced to one side and saw a dark figure which I took to be a man standing motionless. I ran down the stairs, all four flights and then right out of the door. I got a real scare on that occasion. The atmosphere in the building was not very nice at times and felt that there was a presence in the office, which made me unhappy when working alone.'

Further along the quayside lies the Customs House or Old Customs House to be precise. This historic building has been written about on many occasions in the past the most notable being that of an incident involving a security guard who in the 1950s saw the figure of a female leaning over him. Coincidentally, a friend of mine, Fiona, worked there as a customs officer many years later and she told me that it was rumoured among staff to be haunted. The most prolific activity and apparently the most common was the sound of hammering on the front door, sounding as if someone was desperate to gain entry. I was told that staff initially thought it was someone playing a prank or the work of a passing drunk however when the hammering began people would fly to the window in haste and lean out only to find the street to be empty.

A short walk and we reach Shiprow one of the city's oldest thoroughfares and on it, Aberdeen Maritime Museum. The museum consists of two historic buildings including Provost Ross's House. Built in 1593 by Andrew Jamieson, it became the residence of Provost John Ross. During the 19th century the house like our old friend Provost Skene's House, was divided into tenements but by 1950 it was in a state of near dereliction before being rescued by National Trust for Scotland. The museum was originally housed in Provost Ross's House, before its expansion and rebirth in 1997. The most noteworthy incident to date involves an attendant making his rounds early one morning. As he reached the shipping gallery, he witnessed the figure of an elderly lady clad in black ascending the staircase in front of him. He was slightly taken aback as on reaching the top step, she vanished. I have also been told that in recent months the sound of typing has been heard by witnesses in the downstairs office despite no one being there.

Heading up Market Street we arrive at the Rox hotel or the Metro as it was known to an older generation. I was given the following accounts by former employee Sandra who was happy to discuss her time there. The phenomena, varied, and was witnessed by both staff and guests and I have detailed a selection of the most memorable incidents. Having a bit of a reputation, as far as ghosts are concerned it was described as haunted and typically there were certain areas people avoided. Just like our old friend The Travelodge this was also the third floor. Cleaners were known not to linger too long in the area, because of what they might bump into, including the spirit of a nun. Why should a nun be seen there? I am afraid I cannot answer but she had reportedly been seen on different occasions, including one time when she was described as floating rather than walking. A terrifying thought indeed, particularly after the current crop of 'Nun' movies we have been subjected to. Other spirits include a middle-aged man and a poltergeist type entity. Diane bore witness to the former when collecting ice and recalled: 'I was standing at the ice machine and felt someone standing behind me. when I turned around there was a man aged about fifty with grey hair and he half smiled at me before fading away. I later described him to colleagues who thought he may have been a former handyman who was employed when it was the Bon Accord Hotel. Another incident I remember occurred in the 90s, when there was an event with male strippers at the hotel. I was approached in the morning by one of the strippers' wives who said her husband had been rudely awakened by something sitting on the edge of the bed but on looking saw no one. She went on to say that while he was in the shower, his room key, which he placed on the opposite side of the room had been moved. Also, the chest of drawers had been opened when they had all been shut. No one else had been in the room of course and the door had been locked, so he asked for another room. I explained to his wife that I knew an offshore worker had passed away in that room some time back, but not to worry as he loved playing tricks on people.'

I am not sure how she took that, hopefully with good grace. The hotel of course has undergone many changes and was once home to the Mechanics Institute where it housed among other things Aberdeen's first library. This might explain the appearance of a nun. Now renovated perhaps those ghostly residents have now moved on and in the case of the stripper, well I suppose it was ironic that someone should put the 'willies up him!' for a change.

One last story on our whistle-stop tour of haunted locations. All of them warrant further investigation, though some like our next story may prove more difficult than others as the building no longer exists. The location which older Aberdonians will no doubt remember was the tenements of Baltic Place, situated near St. Clements Church. The following encounter took place around 1965 and involved Jan Brooks late husband, Billy, who was in his mid-teens at the time. She kindly passed on this story which he had told her on occasion, and it is suitable spooky. What caused it to happen is open to question, perhaps some wandering negative entity or maybe something much older, connected to the area. Jan explained: 'Billy told me that every time he was on a particular part of the stair the hair on the back of his neck would rise up and the family pet, a Bearded Collie, would always start to growl. This one night he was going down the stairs when 'something,' picked him up and bodily threw him down to the next landing. It was a terrifying experience though never repeated. The building was later demolished I believe.'

She could not elaborate on the aftermath of the event, but I suspect the family would have been very wary for some time after. I wonder if other people experienced something similar in those buildings, maybe one day I will find out.

The Aberdeen Sack Murder

Most Aberdonians will recognise the following description. It relates to one of the most shocking crimes ever committed in the city and around 10 years ago I was told a ghost story potentially relating to it. Spooky as it was, the link could perhaps be described as tenuous. What I found however, would prove without question the authenticity of the report.

On April 25th, 1934, Aberdonians woke to horrific news of a young girls' body being found in the back lobby of 61 Urquhart Road. The girl Helen Priestly had gone missing the previous day and despite a frantic search nothing had been found until then. There was no trace on the night before but in the cold light of day, there it lay covered by a sack. Suspicion immediately fell on the men in the block who were quickly rounded up and questioned, due to what was described as an 'outrage.' But all was not what it seemed and slowly the truth emerged as the perpetrator was found to be the Priestly's downstairs neighbour Jeannie Donald. Having refused to participate in the initial search suspicions were already aroused. It was also common knowledge that Mrs Donald harboured a grudge against the family. Quick of temper, she had taken a dislike to her neighbours' child viewing her as competition to her own daughter, whom she doted on. The young victim had further fuelled the situation by giving Mrs. Donald the nick name 'Coconut.'

The subsequent forensic evidence was damning and even though she was reticent to give any indication of the motive, it appeared she had grabbed the young girl on her return from the shop in a fit of rage and shook her violently. A rare medical condition meant the child was prone to faint during moments of stress and it is assumed this was the case when grabbed. Assuming she had died Jeannie desperately tried to cover her tracks by faking a sexual assault but when the child awoke suddenly Jeannie chose to silence her. Afterwards the mood in the city was ugly, prompting the trial to take place in Edinburgh where it took the jury just 18 minutes to reach their verdict. Found guilty and sentenced to death by hanging she was given a reprieve, and the sentence commuted to life imprisonment, though ultimately served just 10 years. She never once gave any reason for her actions, a secret she carried to the grave dying in 1976. History has proven its one of the most notorious murders ever to take place in the city. It was also one of the first to use extensive forensic techniques. We now move forward around twenty years or so and a young Jim Thomson fresh out of school was now working at the King Street bus depot. I interviewed him at length about his experiences some years ago and this fascinating extract is in his own words.

'It was early 1954 and I was working as a parcel boy with Aberdeen Corporation Transport. I was sent to deliver a parcel to a tenement in Roslin Place, but I cannot remember the number. It was to be delivered to a flat on the first floor and on the way up the stairs I noticed a young girl sitting on the steps, she was aged 10 or 11. She was wearing an old-fashioned looking print dress and didn't speak to me, instead she gave me a funny look before moving to the side to let me pass. I climbed to the first floor and knocked on the door. As I waited, I glanced back down but could see no sign of the girl. She had just disappeared. She could not have left the house, or I would have noticed as I could sense her in my peripheral vision. It left me thinking, had I really seen her? The hairs on the back of my neck were standing up and I was scared! I went back immediately. The chap I was working with then asked how I had got on. I explained what had happened and he looked thoughtful for a bit. He then told me that many years ago a girl had gone missing in Urquhart Road and her body was found some months later stuffed under a sink in Roslin Place. Could I have seen the ghost of this poor murdered girl? I am now 74 and have thought about this for many years.'

Local people acquainted with the facts of the case, realise of course that she was not discovered in Roslin Place, so his theory was unlikely, but was it?

Historic crime is always grimly fascinating and the subject of the infamous 'sack murder' again surfaced, around three years ago. It was during a local history project and the group consisting of six participants were astonished to hear that committee member Sheila had first-hand knowledge of events. For the next five minutes you could have heard a pin drop as we listened intently. It transpired her mother had been good friends with Mrs. Priestly. Sheila of course had been party to numerous conversations pertaining to the feud, though usually from the other side of the door and so had knowledge of the events. On the day of the murder, Jeannie, who was always finding things to complain about had seized Helen on her return from the shop, after the child allegedly scraped her door with a coin. The rest as they say is history. Sheila went on to say that not long after Mrs. Priestly arrived looking upset. Her mother welcomed her in, before hustling Sheila out of the room, who then stood in the lobby 'lugging' in. Barely heard snatches of conversation could be heard but one thing stuck in her mind to this day. She recalls: 'I heard them talking about the situation and as you can imagine Helens' mum was desperate to move. The strange thing was you would expect them to want to get as far away as possible but instead they just moved a few streets away, it was Roslin Place. I could never understand that.' It was a stunning revelation. Another example of coincidence? I contacted Jim recently passing on this new information and told him that likely, Helen had been visiting her new home.

COUNTRY STRIFE: ABERDEENSHIRE HAUNTINGS

Crathie

Moving away from the city we take a foray into the wilds of Aberdeenshire where the following incident took place in the summer of 2005 at Crathie near Ballater. The party of eight, accommodated in two large tents had travelled from nearby Aberdeen for the weekend. The area itself is incredibly beautiful and there were several geographic points of interest in the vicinity. These included nearby Gallows Hill and Craig Nam Ban: the women's or witches hill which lay brooding in the distance.

The group spent the first day exploring and walked to the nearby peak known locally as the witches' hill. This hill, according to records, was the site of the last witch to be burned in Scotland. As the day wore by, they returned to camp to prepare their evening meal and light the fire. After dinner, the group were relaxing round the fire when both Sandra and Carol decided to go outside to look around. It was such a beautiful clear night that the sky was alive with stars and the pair stood and gazed in awe. It was around ten in the evening and as they shone torches into the night sky a movement in nearby caught their eye. Sandra, sensing this movement brought her torch to bear and shone it directly into the field illuminating a moving figure.

She related the following: 'I saw a figure dressed in a monk's garment with a hood pulled far over his head, I saw no face and his hands were crossed and hidden in the sleeves of the garment'. She drew Carol's attention to the figure and they both watched in silence. The figure was described as 'gliding and hovering above the ground with a green shimmery area where he went'. The monk remained visible for ten to fifteen seconds and so they followed him at a distance through the field before he vanished. I was told that they shone their torches on the figure the whole time and could see him very clearly despite it being dark out with the circle of the beam. He did not interact or show any signs of being aware of their presence.

Shaking and with the hairs on their neck standing on end they returned to the tent where they recounted their experience to a wide-eyed audience. Babbling excitedly some then ran outside hoping to see the figure while those less brave remained huddled within their sleeping bags. The figure of course had long gone.

In the morning they inspected the field which being expansive and completely flat afforded no hiding place or dip in which someone could have hidden. In the cold light of day, they wondered if they should broach the subject with the owners. There was still a nagging suspicion that it might have been an elaborate practical joke, played for the benefit of unsuspecting customers. This theory was quickly quashed when the owners, completely unaware of what had transpired, pointed out that similar figures had been seen over the years in the same vicinity. It came as no surprise to Carol when the owner pointed out that nearby lay the ruined foundations of a very ancient chapel. No prizes for guessing who lived there.

Braemar

Moving further inland from Ballater lies Braemar and on its' outskirts Morrone Lodge. At the time of writing, an outdoor pursuit centre, it is now likely a private residence. The lodge existing for many years as a hostel for visiting community groups and team building events until recently before being sold by Aberdeenshire Council. I was given the following account by Annie McIntosh who along with other community workers stayed at the lodge a few years back. It is also worth mentioning, that she knew little of the building's reputation at the time and only subsequently found out others had experienced the same unsettling phenomena.

Part of a group of eight hailing from Aberdeen, they arrived amid the banter and excitement of the weekend ahead. After dumping their rucksacks in the dormitories, they gathered in the communal living room where everything appeared normal, before exploring the building. After being assigned tasks, the group split up with some going outside while the rest remained indoors. Annie who had remained inside began to feel an uneasy sensation, nothing particularly tangible but the feeling of wanting to leave became very strong. However, she put the feelings of unease down to the new environment.

She described to me that there was tangible atmosphere in her dormitory and so feeling uncomfortable decided to stay up as late as possible. She eventually became too tired and reluctantly decided to retire for the night. Some of the group however remained downstairs planning their activities. She promptly fell asleep despite her misgivings, waking later to find the room pitch black and the sound of movement from the bed above. She recalled: 'I felt that there was someone moving in the bed above me and there were noises of a duvet folding, I sat tight but was terrified.' In the morning all was quiet and she checked to see if anyone had decided to swap beds during the night which they hadn't. Fortunately, the following night passed without further incident. Back home, she casually mentioned the incident to her colleague Christine knowing she had visited previously and was not surprised by the response.

Christine said: 'I awakened to find a figure standing at the foot of the bed. He was, what I can only describe as a doctor figure. He was tall with a large moustache and wearing a dark jacket.' As word got around other visitors from the community network began to tell similar stories. Some were certain they had seen shadowy figures in the dorms while others claimed they had been pushed down into their beds and held there. An obviously distressing experience.

On a more sinister note, I was later told about a youth group consisting of 'hard nuts' between the age of 17-19 who ended up terrified after holding a séance, subsequently feeling an evil presence in the living room. Soon afterwards I tried to find out what the original purpose of the building was, and it was very revealing. Records though a little thin on the ground mentioned that in the early 1900s it was used as an isolation hospital or as it was more accurately described a 'fever hospital.'

The Gelder Bothy

Relatively near lies our next stop, the Gelder Bothy, Gelder stable or Gelder Shiel Stable. The name may vary but it is synonymous among walkers as a place of disquiet and mystery. Set high on a wind-swept plateau en route to Lochnagar it is not the most accessible of places, and yet for the walker, is the only shelter for miles around, and much welcomed. Set in the Balmoral estate the Gelder Bothy was originally the royal stables for Queen Victoria when staying in the adjacent lodge and in the late 1870s was much used by the Royal Family. Rarely written about its reputation is well known among walkers who have borne witness to strange and frightening experiences.

I first became aware of the Gelder when in conversation with my colleague Thane. He and his two companions had spent the day walking in the area and were tired when they arrived at the bothy. Upon entering they discovered that there were four wooden cot beds in the room, two on one side with the same opposite. The single room also had a table and some benches in it but very little else in the way of furniture and of course no electricity.

After catching up on the day's events it made sense to have an early night and soon after they settled for the night.

Unaware of how long he had slept, he suddenly found himself awake, terrified as he heard a loud groaning coming from the centre of the room. He described how he was too scared to shout out to his friends who were sleeping on the other side of the room and instead lay rigid with fear. The groaning sound went on for what seemed for around 20 minutes before it stopped abruptly, leading to a restless nights' sleep. In the morning he asked his friends if they had heard anything themselves the previous night. One had and agreed it sounded like it had been inside the room rather than out with. But what was it? The question continued to prey on their mind so when they returned home, they felt obliged to contact their friends' wife to ask if he made strange noises in his sleep. The answer was no.

My research uncovered further reports concerning faces being seen at the window, and mysterious noises keeping visitors awake so to find out more I asked around. I was pleased to receive a prompt reply from another climber who wrote: 'A mutual friend of ours, Mike, who is unfortunately now dead, once told me, that he and two pals spent a night in the Gelder in Winter (this was in the days before the bunks were installed and had only planks nailed onto the rafters with a ladder for access.) He said that they were awakened by continuous hammering on the door and could not understand why the person didn't just enter as the latch was on the outside of the door. When Mike climbed down the ladder to open the door, the noise stopped. He opened the door to find no one there. But the strange thing about this was that a lot of snow had fallen that evening and yet there were no footprints on the doorstep. I knew Mike very well and he was not the type to make up stuff like that'.

Afterwards I spoke to Thane about my findings and was interested to learn there was a rumour that someone had died in a storm near the Gelder; though no one was quite sure when this had taken place. Needing verification, I contacted another seasoned climber, his reply arrived later the same day, containing a startling revelation. It read: 'It is certainly true. A walker coming down from Lochnagar in very bad weather tried to enter the Gelder stable, but found it was locked. He did in fact die on the doorstep. I think it was around 1948. Apparently when the King George V1 heard about it he told the Balmoral estate factor that the stable should always remain unlocked. Thereafter the stable was used at weekends by climbers and then became known as the Gelder Bothy. I have also been fascinated by the tales associated with the place and have made a point of staying there alone on several occasions out of curiosity, but had no strange experiences, but there are some people who claim they have.'

I was very grateful for his contribution but felt saddened that someone had lost their life in that lonely spot. A passing such as this, in my opinion is likely to leave strong emotions in the air. One can only hope that his spirit has moved on and the recording that replays under certain conditions is only that.

Aden Country Park: Mintlaw

Heading back towards the coast and travelling Northwards, the hills of the Cairngorms are now replaced by the farming land of the north-east. On the main route to Fraserburgh you pass the village of Mintlaw and in it sits Aden Country Park. Next to its entrance sits a blue metallic storage depot built in 2002 which is home to Aberdeenshire Councils Museum collection. The storage facility is an innocuous looking building and like many modern buildings of its kind seems at odds with the pleasant green of its surroundings. Once inside the building, a labyrinth of corridors awaits, with both workshops and storerooms running off them. Given the modernity of the surroundings you would find it hard to believe that the building had been exorcised, but it was.

From around 2005 onwards it has been recorded that strange things began to happen within the facility. Strange enough to warrant the depot manager seeking help from the church to perform a clearance and blessing. The first indications of activity were when staff noticed the atmosphere in certain parts of the building was oppressive and heavy. The two upper floor stores were the worst offenders and staff disliked working there. Objects were moved, and in some cases vanished much to their annoyance and spectral figures were often seen.

I was put in touch with the manager of the depot who agreed to let me visit and have a look around. When I arrived on a cold and bright morning, the first thing I noticed was the fact that the surroundings were mundane and not at all the kind of place that typifies a haunted house. I remained focused and was taken along to the storage area where I was shown into one of the main storerooms. It was still quite empty, the museum collection yet to find a home there, but an uneasy sensation came over me particularly at one end of the room where some large storage cabinets stood.

While there I had the opportunity to speak to three members of staff who provided me with some very interesting anecdotes. The first took place in the Autumn of 2006 when John, who worked opposite the staff room, was taken by surprise as two almighty crashes sounded behind him. Fearing something had happened to a colleague he 'leapt up' and went straight to the staff room only to find the door was closed and the lights were out. On switching on the light, he was surprised to see the wall clock had been knocked from its hook and was sitting upright against the opposite wall, the number twelve showing on its face. Even more perplexing was the fact that all the papers on the notice board were scattered on the other side of the room while the pins were still in the board. He then left the room and returned to his workspace where he waited for his co-workers. Later I was told that no one else in the building had heard anything.

A few days later his colleague Ray asked him into his office as he wanted to show him something. Inside, sitting on the floor, was a neat pile of crumpled paper lying in a perfect circle. The bin had been upended and the paper formed like a sandcastle when you lift off the bucket. When finding out the door had been locked all night his colleague remarked, 'the poltergeist has struck again then.' When pressed to elaborate Ray explained that there had been paranormal activity in the building for some time which they were at a loss to explain, becoming so bad their line manager had the building exorcised. The current manager acknowledged this though was reluctant to comment further. Despite the blessing staff remain reluctant to work upstairs with one cleaner refusing to go there due to seeing 'grey people.'

I returned home and filed away the accounts hearing nothing more until October 2007, when I was surprised to be contacted by employee Joan. Since my last visit there had been more incidents, and she described the following:

'I was coming out of the store and facing down the corridor when I saw a small dark male figure through the glass panels of the fire doors. I kept walking towards him, but he moved away and appeared to go down the stairs, so I followed and went through the door only to find the stairs empty.'

It was not till later that she realised she may have possibly seen a ghost though at the time did not feel particularly afraid. A few weeks later staff began to complain that the lift was playing up and being vital to their work an engineer was called. He stayed for some time but found no fault and was perplexed as to why the lift kept ascending to the top floor. Despite numerous tests nothing untoward was found and he commented that the lift appeared to be sensing someone that was not there. It was the only explanation he could offer. He knew nothing of the stories attached to the store and left after the lift appeared to be functioning.

Last but certainly not least I was passed on a series of notes from a long-time cleaner, Lorraine, who having worked there for many years had witnessed much of the activity. She was known to keep a record of her experiences and frequently mentioned the sighting of a man who wore a uniform not dissimilar to that of the Royal Air Force. She described herself as mediumistic and said she did not get the best feeling from him. She also mentioned in some detail that the first indication of his presence was the sudden manifestation of unexplained odours. These include the smell of 'rotten neeps,' which indicated to her someone unpleasant or 'nae good' was in the vicinity, while at other times she sensed the odour of perfume or tobacco. For some reason the spirit was attracted to the upper floors, possibly as it was used for storing objects, and would play tricks on her by constantly switching off her vacuum cleaner. This prompted her to shout, 'if you want peace just let me get on with it and I will be out of your way!' The question of why there is so much activity present remains unanswered though it has been speculated that perhaps the entities are attached to the objects they knew in life. The depot holding a vast collection of artefacts, would appear to be a magnet of sorts if that is the case.

Around fourteen years ago a friend ended up being based in the depot as part of a project I was involved with. It proved to be opportune as I was able to spend some time there, conducting interviews. During one of my visits, my friend confided in me stating that she had also seen the small dark figure recently. She went on to say the sighting had made her very anxious and so had mentioned it to Lorraine. The cleaner looked thoughtful and then stated that there was something stored in the building that had a very negative energy and was at least partially responsible for some of the phenomena.

My friend asked what it was and was surprised to learn it was mummified remains which are held in a sealed storage unit. Lorraine went on to say that when she walks by it, she picks up on a very unpleasant vibe. This did not make my friend feel any better. Since then, my friend has moved on to pastures new as have I and it has been quite some years since I visited last. I did however speak recently to a colleague Pauline who has worked there in more recent times. I was pleased to be told that the stories still circulate.

Fraserburgh: Kinnaird Head

Heading northwards from Aden Park lies Fraserburgh once one of the busiest fishing ports in the region and nearby stands Kinnaird Head lighthouse. It is noted as being the first lighthouse built on mainland Scotland and is now home to the Museum of Scottish Lighthouses. The lighthouse was purchased from the Fraser family in 1787 being converted from a sixteenth castle keep and is an iconic structure. Robert Stevenson, a name synonymous with Scottish Lighthouse design then improved the building in 1824 by building a tower within the existing keep. This construction, originally used as living quarters, houses the largest type of lighthouse lens that was ever made, while outside sits the keepers' cottages, the last built in 1902. Popular with tourists, the museum and cottages now hold a vast collection of Scottish lighthouse artefacts.

Kinnaird Head also has many stories and legends attached to it particularly that of a phantom piper and the alleged haunting of the nearby Wine Tower. The Wine Tower remains something of a mystery, though cited as being built around 1570 by Sir Alexander Fraser its original purpose remains a point of debate. The tower stands around 50 yards from the museum on the edge of an outcrop of rock, built directly above a 30m long cave, known as 'Selches Hole.' The entrance to this building, now locked is on the second floor with entry being gained by a ladder, leading to a second-floor vaulted chamber, containing heraldic motifs associated with the Fraser family.

There is a legend surrounding the Wine Tower and it concerns Sir Alexander Frasers' daughter Isobel who incurred the wrath of her father by having a dalliance with a piper of lowly stock. The enraged father forbade the union locking Isobel in her room. The piper was then taken to 'Selches Hole' and chained up inside, after which Fraser intended to dissuade him from continuing the romance. In the morning with Isobel at his side, Fraser approached the cave but unbeknownst to him the cave had flooded leaving the unfortunate piper dead. In despair Isobel fled from the terrible scene and climbing the Wine Tower threw herself to her death below. And so, on stormy nights the sound of piping has reportedly been heard coming from the cave. A great story, though like many of its kind with its theme of doomed romance and tragedy, it appears somewhat fanciful in the cold light of day.

Not so fanciful though are the sightings of both men and women in old fashioned clothing, spotted in and around the lighthouse in recent times. Incidents of this nature are relatively commonplace, or so I was told. I was delighted soon after to be offered the chance of a tour. My colleague Jane was to be my guide and with great anticipation we set off.

Our first stop was a former keepers' cottages where she had previously experienced something unusual in the kitchen, and on entering we were stopped in our tracks by the 'atmosphere' that greeted us. It was apparent that there was someone there, a female we thought, who was surprised to see us. Our hair began to rise as we put out our hands and felt the energy moving around us. We were completely taken aback by the intensity of the experience though we agreed it was not at all unpleasant. We continued our tour though nothing further occurred and so we headed over to the lighthouse where we had the good fortune to meet a former keeper.

During our conversation he told me of incidents connected to the building and described the following.

'Several years ago one of our guides was taking a party on a tour of the lighthouse. On reaching the top and while in the middle of his talk, he noticed one woman turn and leave the group. Slightly perplexed he continued and on completing the tour ascended the stairs where he found the woman was waiting for him. Once the visitors had dispersed, she apologised for leaving so abruptly and hoped he did not think her rude. She went on to explain that while he was talking, she noticed a woman standing directly behind him wearing a dark shawl who was looking at her. The tour guide completely understood though was taken aback by the revelation, noting that her description matched that of a fisherwoman.'

Afterwards I asked him about the cottage where I had felt a presence and though he had not felt anything himself in that building a former employee and resident had. He stated that the employee and particularly his wife had often complained about the atmosphere in one of the back bedrooms. He went on to say that she had mentioned that she hated being in the kitchen, on many occasions. His personal theory was that objects hold memories and ties for people as much as building's and perhaps the various energies find it hard to disconnect from them.

Port Elphinstone Inverurie

Moving south towards Aberdeen lies Inverurie and within it, Port Elphinstone, where the following was provided by Jan and Ingrid.

'I have had only one paranormal experience I can recall, and it took place in the bedroom I shared with my younger brother in the family home. There was an old cabinet in the room and at night it would be the last thing I saw before sleeping. It was a strange piece of furniture, dark oak I suspect, with a flat bottom section and two doors that inclined sharply which were of glass. One sweltering summer night I woke to see a small boy sitting on the incline of the cabinet. I remember thinking how strange it was as it would have been impossible to sit there, it being glass. Why wasn't he sliding off? I thought. He appeared to be in silent mirth, with sparkling eyes. He made no noise but by the light of the moon he seemed to be made of shades of brown and grey, unnaturally so. His eyes were very white, and he unnerved me, so much so that I was afraid to move or call out. He never moved but just sat there. The next thing I remember, was being comforted by mother and I assume I had eventually cried out.'

In hindsight, and as an adult, Jan questioned if it was real or just a dream but settled on the former. He never saw the boy again who he described as 'faun-like.' The cabinet surplus to requirement, ended its days in their garage.

Cove

Cove, a traditional Northeast fishing village situated on the outskirts of Aberdeen is our next destination and the location a relatively new building situated on Loirston Road. Used at the time as supported accommodation for adults with learning difficulties and run by Partnership it is now renamed Inspire. It was used for this purpose for around eighteen years before closing towards the end of 2010.

I was given the following account by Steve who worked there for eight years before leaving in 2006. Neighbours of the property stated that prior to Partnership purchasing the building the previous owner had been a lone male who was believed to have died in the property though this was never verified. From the outset staff members experienced frequent and strange incidents which defied rational explanation. These incidents appeared to be most prolific in and around the staff room apparently a very small room and in the long L-shaped corridor central to the house. One of the most common occurrences was the sound of footsteps running along the corridor. I was told they would always stop at either the sleep-in room or the living room. They were always, short fast steps, usually heard at night. Were the steps those of a child? Steve recalled:

'I worked there for many years and one of my duties would include sleeping over. On this occasion I was in the little staff bedroom. It was at the end of my shift, and I was helping a female colleague with some computer work. The door to the room was shut but not fully as it had not clicked. At this point I should explain that the residents were all in bed and everything was quiet. Night shifts could be peaceful but sometimes emergencies could happen such as people falling over or getting up for a variety of reasons so you could never fully relax. I remember that we made a cup of tea and were engrossed in writing a report. We were talking about the content of the report and the wording when we both suffered an involuntary shudder at the same time. My colleague looked round before letting out a bit of a scream as the door previously closed was now fully open. We initially thought our minds were playing tricks, but we did have a sense of trepidation. We waited for a little while, but nothing further happened and so after a time returned our attention to the report. I then jumped as my colleague let out another scream and when I looked behind me the door was again fully open. It had obviously opened silently as we never heard a sound. We closed the door for a third time and despite our growing alarm tried to concentrate on the report. We did everything to keep our mind off the door, we looked outside, continuing to talk and eventually forgot about it. Again, an icy cold shiver brought us back to reality but this time the door was only fractionally open. Feeling brave, I assume as there were two of us, I suggested we conduct a little experiment. We figured that something was trying to get our attention and so putting out the lights we asked aloud if anyone wanted to communicate and if so, could they please open the door. Nothing happened and the room was deathly still. We then asked if there was anything we could do to help. But again, there was no response until we looked away and only then did the door opened slightly. We closed it again and all was quiet for the next five minutes, until a sudden bang made us jump. We were feeling scared but realised that whatever was causing this would only communicate if that's what you would call it once our backs were turned. Twice more we asked out and both times it opened but only when we were not looking directly at it and not focusing on it. It also did not seem to respond to any questions which of course was difficult to ascertain as its only means of communication was the odd thump and the door being opened to different degrees. We naturally analysed what had happened and wondered if it could be the child ghost that folk had mentioned due to its responses. I might add we were also not thinking about anything creepy before it started up so I could not put it down to imagination.'

It goes without saying that the sleepover shift is not hugely popular for those needing to catch up on their beauty sleep and for those poor souls on the rota it was a long night. Having to be constantly alert in case of emergencies was bad enough but now staff complained of bad feelings within the staffroom. There was also the sensation of someone staring at them from the edge of the bed as they rested to contend with, which Steve elaborated on:

'One member of staff awoke in the sleep-room and saw the sheet at the foot of the bed flapping. She described it as if someone was flapping it up and down, which sent them cowering to the top of the bed. Also, a member of our relief pool awoke from a nightmarish dream in which she had dropped a doll. She found herself suddenly awake and sitting up pinned against the back wall for about five seconds. She said that she felt there was a malevolent force in the room and somehow it was connected to the doll. Such was her state of fear over this she vowed never to sleep in the room again.

Of course, things did not always happen at night, even during the day things would happen. Again, they would usually take place when someone was alone and the most commonplace, were very loud bangs. They were described as sounding like furniture falling over and of course had to be investigated, however when they got there everything would be in order. An equally loud bang would then sound from the room that had just been vacated resulting in a quick backtrack, again finding nothing. Frustrated, they concluded that whatever it was liked to play tricks, so perhaps it was the spirit of a child after all?

I thanked Steve for the interview which I found fascinating. He told me that there had apparently been an older building there at one point according to a local but did not have any details as to who had lived or indeed died there. Now the property is in new hands, and I can only hope that their tenure will be more peaceful.

Oldmeldrum

Moving deeper into the shire we arrive at the village of Oldmeldrum, and it is here we look at our final two stories. Doreen Kemp, a resident of the village, wrote to me some time ago relating her experiences at home in 'Meadows Vale.' This is what I was told: 'Since moving in we have been plagued by numerous incidents which are more frequent in the early morning. The houses are all new-builds but I was told that in the area witches were burned here in the past, though I cannot verify this. In the beginning we found that things like ornaments would be moved while other household items would disappear. It was very frustrating rather than frightening. Strangely, when it happened recently, it did us a favour. During the night three ornaments had been removed from their stands were found next morning placed next to each other in front of the fire. We had a bit of a jump of course but when we went to pick them up, we discovered that nearby there was evidence of a leak in the back boiler. Perhaps someone had wanted to draw our attention to this. Other incidents of note have included our bed covers being pulled off the bed. This we found very frightening One night they were pulled down the bed, we then pulled them back up, but whatever it had pulled them back down again. It happened quite frequently, though I did not mind what appeared to be communication from family members. There have been quite a few examples of this including the night when my husbands' uncle died. I should mention that he was fond of a drop of whisky. Anyway, as we sat talking, we heard a strange noise coming from the wall unit in the living room. It lasted for around about a minute before stopping. We then went to investigate and on opening the door we found a whiskey bottle on its side and a tumbler sitting next to it, which contained the bottle cap. My husbands' Auntie was there at the time and could not believe what she was seeing. Then when my uncle died, the clock in my spare room was placed on its side five times in a row despite being righted each time. I can accept phenomena like this, if its' from family members as I know they wish us no harm, but other incidents that have left me very afraid. For example, around 11.30 one night my husband woke, convinced he heard someone walking about. We both lay there listening. Initially it sounded like it was coming from outside the house, so I got up and looked out the window. There was nothing there but on turning, I noticed that there was someone standing in the gloom at the side of the bed. It gave me a real fright. The figure which was female then walked around the bed with her hand trailing on the covers, she then walked towards the wall and went straight through it. I will never forget that.'

Our last stop in Aberdeenshire is the Meldrum House Hotel a grand mansion built round a medieval tower on the outskirts of the village of Oldmeldrum. Its history can be traced back to the 13th century when the original tower house first appeared. The property owned by Philip de Fedarg was thought to have been a Knight Templar. In 1628 further additions to the property included a stable block and the central tower which still exists today. The house was then considerably extended in both the 17th and 18th centuries by prominent Scottish families before the creation of a formal garden. Again, the house was remodelled with the removal of the turreted pavilion leaving the L-shaped building of today and like most country houses it allegedly has its own resident ghost.

The ghost thought to be that of former 'lady of the house' Isabella Douglas has been known to make infrequent appearances particularly during thunderstorms. She has been given the rather unimaginative moniker of the 'White Lady' due to the light gown she wears and joins the ranks of her other illustrious namesakes. Described as being kind to children and 'looking after them,' there have been a few well documented examples. The same cannot be said for male visitors who have reportedly been scratched on the chest and back whilst in bed. The most well documented story we know of came from a guest who in 1985 received a cold kiss on the cheek from the White Lady during a thunderstorm.

Other incidents include that of housekeepers having had their apron strings pulled while cleaning and kitchen staff having been jostled by an invisible entity. Intrigued, I contacted the hotel soon after but unfortunately was unable to secure a visit due to a major refurbishment. I was however given permission to contact staff in pursuit of the truth and soon received some interesting letters, from employees, past and present. The phenomena they witnessed suggested the 'white lady' was more than just a legend with statements mentioning, unusual sounds, cold spots, and the reflection of a woman seen in a mirror, the latter taking place in room three which is regarded as the 'haunted room.' It is there, I was told, that guests have witnessed a woman standing behind them while looking in the mirror.

Browsing through my emails a more recent example of her activities was given to me by the hotel's receptionist in which she described an incident involving a chef. I was told that it occurred after his shift when due to the late hour he had stayed over at the hotel. He was given the 'haunted room' to sleep in, which I would have questioned, and on wakening in the morning, discovered unaccountable marks on his legs. The receptionist said that to all intents and purposes they looked like burns, though they could find no discernible reason for their sudden appearance. The chef by all accounts slept well and had felt nothing, and although it cannot exactly be considered proof of survival after death, it possibly made him question his sleeping arrangements.

My favourite story however I have reserved till last which was given to me by my colleague Annie Scott. In conversation she mentioned that a good friend of hers, Nina, had been employed at the hotel but had been unable to continue working there due to seeing the 'White Lady.' The sighting had left her very afraid. She had worked on the reception for some time and during her time there were quiet periods when the building could be near empty. Here is her story.

When Nina first started work at the hotel the subject of the alleged haunting was of course mentioned but she paid little heed to it. Nothing at first seemed untoward, however she became increasingly aware of the sound of banging doors when there was no one around. The noises occurred around the kitchen area and often happened at night which was mildly disconcerting however it was a more tangible experience that caused her to leave. One afternoon, while taking a short break, she found herself standing at the windows overlooking the garden. The windows afforded a clear view of the mist covered grounds and from her vantage point she was able to see across the lawn. A thick fog billowed and though dense, she could still see quite clearly. Suddenly a piece of fog detached itself from the rest and began to move across the lawn towards the place where she stood. As it approached, she was shocked to see that the strange shape was unmistakably that of a female figure though it faded away as it neared the house much to her relief. This incident was the final straw for Nina. I was told by her friend that not long afterwards she left her job at the hotel.

Conclusion

Meldrum House is full of fascinating stories, and I particularly enjoyed reading about Nina's experience. It contained all the elements of a classic ghost story right down to the rolling mist, which I would have loved to have seen. You might think that is a strange statement to make and I can appreciate why, as most people spend their lives trying to avoid such situations. And who can blame them when we are bombarded with the notion that ghosts are out to get us. One has only to look at how the ghost or spirit is portrayed in fiction, be it film or the written word, to see why. Or in another example how 'ghost hunters,' operate, seeking drama and confrontation, rather than contemplation. The latter of course will inevitably include a little stone throwing. Scary ghosts like a terrifying rollercoaster are big business after all and the demand for thrills may be at the cost of something deeper. It is in my opinion the fear of the unknown that scares us, rather than the ghost which is merely emblematic of the bigger question. Is there something after this, and if so, what? Of course, my question hardly matters to a non-believer, as you will unlikely be reading this in the first place. On that note I remember a recent article in the Edinburgh Evening News, when the question of belief in ghosts and the afterlife was posed. As I had suspected a good proportion of women did, or at least were open minded about the possibility, while the majority of the blokey blokes as expected did not. They appeared to be affronted by the very notion, and could not countenance the idea, spluttering indignantly between mouthfuls of pie. I felt a little sorry for them. One chap claimed (and you could sense his anger) that life only ended in one place, a box. Fact. I wondered afterwards if he worked as a life coach. This however got me thinking (again) about the big question, would we end up in a box, like a forgotten packet of digestives at the back of the cupboard or like living in a Stewart Milne home? The thought made me a little sad, but I digress. Perhaps I was being a little gloomy, but I often ponder on things and one of my latest ponders, had me thinking about my own experiences and of the buildings I visited. I thought about those that are now derelict or surplus to requirement and asked myself these questions. Do the ghosts wonder where everyone has gone in such places? And if they cannot find anyone to scare, do they get bored? Seriously though, I do. For example, my mind continually dwells on Victoria Road School, and I often wonder what the 'ghosts' therein are up to? Is Lizzie still there? Is she lonely? Does she wring her hands in despair, over the state of the building? What does she remember from her day? Is she sad because the happy sounds of the children are gone? I suppose what I am trying to convey is that I hope the ghosts in this book are just recordings from the past or at worse are occasional visitors, who somewhere, have a warmer fireside to sit by.

Index

A

Aberdeen Art Gallery, 73, 82
Aberdeen Maritime Museum, 253
Aberdeen Sack Murder, 257
Aden Country Park, 270

B

Beechwood School, 91
Boddam, 220
British Home Stores, 6, 169

C

Captain Beaton, 109, 110, 111, 119
Castle Street, 46, 47
Castlegate, 45
Castlehill Barracks, 58, 59, 60
Cattofield, 246

Commerce Street, 53, 56, 59
Constitution Street, 80, 82
Crathie, 262
Crombie Johnston Halls, 188
Cults, 205, 210, 243

E

Elliot O' Donnell, 151

F

First Bus, 109

G

Gelder Bothy, 267, 269
Gibberie Wallie, 223
Gordon Barracks, 196

H

Hazlehead Academy, 95, 98
His Majesty's Theatre, 26, 35, 36

K

Kaimhill school, 90
Kincorth, 74, 75, 157, 158, 159, 163
Krakatoa, 13, 14

L

Leadside Road, 248, 249
Lemon Tree, 39, 191, 192
Littlewoods, 18, 175, 177

M

Marchburn Crescent, 218
Marischal College, 191, 225, 226
Marischal Court, 61, 64
Meldrum House Hotel, 286
monks, 18, 73, 74, 77, 83, 84, 157
Morrone Lodge, 264

N

Nazareth House, 164, 165

Nelson Street, 77, 78, 81
New Market, 6, 10, 18, 169
North Silver Street, 105

R

Religious Figures, 73
Rosemount Community Centre, 142
Roslin Place, 258, 259, 260
Rox hotel, 254

S

Springhill Road, 204
St. Katherines, 39
Strange but True, 212
Summerfield House, 245
Sunnybank Community Centre, 146

T

Tivoli Theatre, 35, 37
Tolbooth, 48, 121, 124, 169
Torry, 99, 101, 104, 230, 232, 235, 236, 238, 239, 240
Tunnels, 18, 177

U

Union Street, 7, 20, 123, 167, 168, 170, 171, 174, 175, 177, 178

V

Victoria Court, 50

Victoria Road School, 99, 100, 104, 291
View Terrace, 153, 155

Further Reading

- Adams, Norman, Haunted Neuk: Ghosts of Aberdeen and Beyond (Tolbooth Books, Banchory 1994)

- Adams, Norman, Hangman's Brae: True Crime and Punishment in Aberdeen and the North-East (Black and White Publishing, Edinburgh 2005)

- Holden, Geoff, Haunted Aberdeen & District (The History Press 2010)

- Moss, Peter, Ghosts over Britain (Elm Tree Books, London 1977)

- Whitaker Terence, Scotland's Ghosts, and Apparitions (Robert Hale 1991)